D0351988

SKELMERSDALE

FICTION RESERVE STOCK L 60

Outside In
Stories to Grow Up With

Edited by
Niall MacMonagle

NIALL MacMONAGLE is a teacher, critic and broadcaster. He also edited *Real Cool, Poems to Grow Up With*.

First published in 1995 by
Marino Books
An imprint of Mercier Press
16 Hume Street Dublin 2

Trade enquiries to Mercier Press
PO Box 5, 5 French Church Street, Cork

A Marino Original

Introduction © Niall MacMonagle 1995
The acknowledgements' page is an extension of this
copyright notice

ISBN 1 86023 026 1

10 9 8 7 6 5 4 3 2 1

A CIP record for this title is available from the British
Library

Cover photo and design by Niamh Sharkey
Set by Richard Parfrey in Garamond Narrow (120% wide)
10/14
Printed in Ireland by ColourBooks, Baldoyle Industrial
Estate, Dublin 13

For Sharon, Caroline, Hannah, Rourke, Lorca and Catherine
— 'no enemy but time'

CONTENTS

RIGHT HERE, OUT THERE

Go on, tell us! These words, so often heard, capture the impulse, the desire and the pleasure of storytelling. The life we live, added up, becomes our most important story, a long story, but there are hundreds of stories heard and told along the way that become part of this larger one. And we can never hear too many of them. There are even stories about stories. I can't remember where I came across this one or who told it but the story itself has never left me. A group of men incarcerated in a prisoner-of-war camp willingly sacrificed a small piece of the already tiny portion of their daily bread and gave it to one of their group each evening in return for something as important as food: they gave it to the storyteller and the stories he told them fed their hearts and minds and imaginations.

What he gave them was otherness: other places, other worlds, an experience held and shaped and complete. It is something different and separate from the higgledy-piggledy commotion of our own lives. We are on a bus or a beach, we are waiting for the rain to stop, we are in bed, and we are in none of these places: we are in Vietnam, in New Jersey, in a country town, in a Dublin suburb; in a place called loneliness, happiness, ignorance or disappointment as the case may be. When we listen to a story, we are both here and there. Joseph O'Connor puts it this way: 'Readers want to know what it is like to be someone else for a moment, so that they know in some profound sense what it is like to be themselves.'

Modern life is noisy and fast. It is also more challenging and complex and the short story is particularly suited to lives lived at fast forward. In forty minutes you can enter into the shaped experience of the story, but an experience so open-ended that the story stays with you for much longer. The stories in this book look at familiar and unfamiliar worlds such as school, growing up, home, journeys, long ago, adults, violence . . . but they will also take you outside yourself, take you elsewhere, delivering you back with something gained along the way.

This is why reading has been called a 'living through' experience. To read is to be free. It is to live many lives, to become within one self many selves. Those who fall in love with reading early on in life discover something that will never let them down. It brings a freedom which involves, in Iris Murdoch's words, the freedom of 'knowing and understanding and respecting things quite other than ourselves'.

> Whoever you are, no matter how lonely,
> the world offers itself to your imagination,

says the American poet Mary Oliver. Life isn't always a bag of laughs. We do end up lonely, bored, directionless some days, but the world does offer itself to our imaginations every morning and it offers us stories from outside ourselves that can bring alive in our minds and imaginations worlds within. Outside in.

When Doris Lessing imagines what our vision of the world would be like without storytellers, she imagines that it would be like 'the dark side of the moon, or the sea floors where fishes still unknown to science live'. But of course it doesn't have to be like that: 'literature makes us all kin, because every tale is a report from people whose differences are only variations on the theme of our humanity.'

Niall MacMonagle

American spelling has been retained in the American stories.

LAST OF THE MOHICANS

JOSEPH O'CONNOR

It was about three years since I'd seen him. And here he was, sweating behind the burger bar in Euston Station, a vision in polyester and fluorescent light. Jesus Christ, so Marion was right that time. Eddie Virago, selling double cheeseburgers for a living. I spluttered his name as he smiled in puzzled recognition over the counter. My God, Eddie Virago. In the pub he kept saying it was great to see me. Really wild, he said. I should have let him know I was coming to London. This was just unreal.

Eddie was the kind of guy I tried to hang around with in college. Suave, cynical, dressed like a Sunday supplement. He'd arrive deliberately late for lectures and swan into Theatre L, permanent pout on his lips. He sat beside me one day in the first week and asked me for a light. Then he asked me for a cigarette. From then on we were friends. After pre-revolutionary France we'd sit on the middle floor of the canteen sipping coffee and avoiding Alice, the tea-trolley lady.

'Where did you get that tray?' she'd whine, 'No trays upstairs.' And Eddie would interrupt his monologue on the role of German Expressionism in the development of *film noir* to remove his feet from the perilous path of her brush. 'Alice's Restaurant,' he called it. I didn't know what he was talking about but I laughed anyway.

He was pretty smart, our Eddie. He was a good-looking bastard too. I never realised it at first, but gradually I noticed all the girls in the class wanted to get to know me. Should have known it wasn't me they were interested in.

'Who's your friend?' they'd simper, giggling like crazy.

The rugby girls really liked him. You know the type. The ones who sit in the corridors calculating the cost of the lecturers' suits. All school scarves, dinner dances, summers in New York without a visa – more exciting that way. Eddie hated them all. He resisted every coy advance, every uncomfortable, botched flirtation. They were bloody convent schoolgirls. All talk and no action. He said there was just one thing they needed and they weren't going to get it from him.

Professor Gough liked making risqué jokes about the nocturnal activities of Napoleon and everyone in the class was shocked. Everyone except Eddie. He'd laugh out loud and drag on his cigarette and laugh again while everyone blushed and stared at him. He said that was the trouble with Ireland. He said we were all hung up about sex. It was unhealthy. It was no wonder the mental homes were brimming over.

Eddie had lost his virginity at the age of fourteen, in a thatched cottage in Kerry. Next morning, he'd shaved with a real razor and he'd felt like a real man. As the sun dawned on his manhood he had flung his scabby old electric into the Atlantic. Then himself and his nineteen-year-old deflowerer ('deflorist', he called her) had strolled down the beach talking about poetry. She'd written to him from France a few times, but he'd never answered. It didn't do to get too involved. Western civilisation was hung up on possession, Eddie said. People had to live their own lives and get away from guilt trips.

We were close, Eddie and me. I bought him drinks and cigarettes, and he let me stay in his place when I got kicked out that time. His parents gave him the money to live in a flat in Donnybrook. He called them his 'old dears'. I went back home after a while but I never forgot my two weeks on the southside with Eddie. We stayed up late looking at films and listening to The Doors and The Jesus and Mary Chain and talking about sex. Eddie liked to talk about sex a lot. He said I didn't know what was ahead of me. He was amazed that I hadn't done it. Absolutely amazed. He envied me actually, because if he had it all to do over again the first time was definitely the best. But that was Catholic Ireland. We were all repressed, and we had to escape. James Joyce was right. Snot green sea, what a line. It wasn't the same in India, he said. Sex was divine to them. They had their priorities right.

Eddie went away that summer, to Germany, and he came back with a gaggle of new friends. They were all in Trinity, and they'd worked in the same gherkin factory as him. They were big into drugs and funny haircuts and Ford Fiestas. Eddie had the back and sides of his head shaved and he let his fringe grow down over his eyes and he dyed it. Alice the tea-trolley lady would cackle at him in the canteen.

'Would you look?' she'd scoff. 'The last of the Mohicans.'

Everyone laughed but Eddie didn't care. He didn't even blush. He rubbed glue and toothpaste into his quiff to make it stand up, and even in the middle of the most crowded room you could always tell where Eddie was. His orange hair bobbed on a sea of short back and sides.

He went to parties in his new friends' houses, and they all slept with each other. No strings attached. No questions asked. He brought me to one of them once, in a big house in Dalkey. Lots of glass everywhere, that's all I remember. Lots of glass. And paintings on the walls, by Louis le Brocquy and that other guy who's always painting his penis. You know the one. That was where I met Marion. She was in the kitchen, searching the fridge while two philosophy students groped each other under the table. She didn't like these parties much. We sat in the garden eating cheese sandwiches and drinking beer. Eddie stumbled out and asked me if I wanted a joint. I said no, I wasn't in the mood. Marion got up to leave with some bloke in a purple shirt who was muttering about deconstruction. Eddie said he wouldn't know the meaning of the word.

We bumped into her again at a gig in The Underground one

Sunday night. It turned out the deconstructionist was her brother and he was in the band. When she asked me what I thought, I said they were pretty interesting. She thought they were terrible. I bought her a drink and she asked me back to her place in Rathmines. In the jacks I whispered to Eddie that I didn't want him tagging along. He said he got the picture. Standing on the corner of Stephen's Green he winked at us and said, 'Goodnight young lovers, and if you can't be good, be careful.'

It wasn't at all like Eddie said it would be. Afterwards I laughed when she asked me had it been my first time. Was she kidding? I'd lost it in a cottage in Kerry when I was fourteen. She smiled and said yes, she'd only been kidding. All night long I tossed and turned in her single bed, listening to the police cars outside. I couldn't wait to tell Eddie about it.

We went for breakfast in Bewleys the next morning. Me and Marion, I mean. She looked different without make-up. I felt embarrassed as she walked around the flat in tights and underwear. It was months later that I admitted I'd been lying about my sexual experience. She laughed and said she'd known all along. She said I paid far too much attention to Eddie. That was our first row. She said that for someone who wasn't hung up he sure talked a lot of bullshit about it.

At first Eddie was alright about Marion and me. I told him we had done it and he clapped me on the back and asked me how it was. I said I knew what he'd been talking about. It'd been unreal. That was the only word for it. He nodded wisely and asked me something about positions. I said I had to go to a lecture.

But as I started spending more and more time with Marion he got more sarcastic. He started asking me how was the little woman, and what was it like to be happily married. He got a big kick out of it and it made me squirm. He'd introduce me to another one of the endless friends.

'This is Johnny,' he'd say, 'he's strictly monogamous.'

We still went for coffee after lectures, but I felt more and more alone in the company of Eddie and his disciples. Marion took me to anti-amendment meetings and Eddie said we were wasting our time. He said it didn't make any difference. Irish people took their direction straight from the Catholic Church. He told me we hadn't a hope.

'Abortion?' he said, 'Jesus Christ, we're not even ready for contraception.'

I tried to tell him it wasn't just about abortion, but he scoffed and said he'd heard it all before.

Eddie dropped out a few months before our finals. He left a note on my locker door saying he'd had enough. He was going to London to get into film. Writing mainly, but he hoped to direct, of course, in the end. London was where the action was. He was sick and tired of this place anyway. It was nothing. A glorified tax haven for rich tourists and popstars. A cultural backwater that time forgot. He said no one who ever did anything stayed in Ireland. You had to get out to be recognised.

I was sad to see him go, specially because he couldn't even tell me to my face. But in a way it was a relief. Me and Eddie, we'd grown far apart. It wasn't that I didn't like him exactly. I just knew that secretly we embarrassed the hell out of each other. So I screwed his note into a ball and went off to the library. And as I sat staring out the window at the lake and the concrete, I tried my best to forget all about him.

Marion broke if off with me the week before the exams started. She said no hard feelings but she reckoned we'd run our course. I congratulated her on her timing. We were walking through Stephen's Green and the children were bursting balloons and hiding behind the statues. She said she just didn't know where we were going any more. I said I didn't know about her, but I was going to Madigan's. She said that was the kind of thing Eddie would have said, and I felt really good about that. She kissed me on the cheek, said sorry and sloped off down Grafton Street. I felt the way you do when the phone's just been slammed down on you. I thought if one of those Hare Krishnas comes near me I'll kick his bloody head in.

I got a letter from Eddie once. Just once. He said he was getting on fine, but it was taking a while to meet the right people. Still, he was glad he'd escaped 'the stifling provincialism' and he regretted nothing. He was having a wild time and there was so much to do in London. Party City. And the women! Talk about easy. I never got around to answering him. Well, I was still pretty upset about Marion for a while, and then there was all that hassle at home. I told them I'd be only too happy to get out and look for a job if there were any jobs to look for. My father said that was fine talk, and that the trouble with me was that they'd been too bloody soft on me. He'd obviously wasted his time, subsidising my idleness up in that bloody place that was supposedly a university.

Eventually it all got too much. I moved in with Alias, into an upstairs flat on Leeson Street. My mother used to cry when I went home to do my washing on Sunday afternoons. Alias was a painter. I met him at one of Eddie's parties. The walls of the flat were plastered with paintings of naked bodies, muscles rippling, nipples like champagne corks. He said it didn't matter that they didn't look like the models. Hadn't I ever heard of imagination? I said yeah, I'd heard of it.

He was putting his portfolio together for an exhibition and living on the dole. He told everyone he had an Arts Council grant. He was alright, but he didn't have the depth of Eddie and he was a bit of a slob. He piled up his dirty clothes on the middle of his bedroom floor and he kept his empty wine bottles in the wardrobe. And the bathroom. And the kitchen. I got a job eventually, selling rubbish bags over the phone. There are thirty-seven different sizes of domestic and industrial plastic refuse sack. I bet you didn't know that! I had to ring up factories and offices and ask them if they wanted to re-order. They never seemed to want to. I wondered what they did with all their rubbish.

'Shredders,' said Mr Smart. 'The shredders will be my undoing.'

It was always hard to get the right person on the line. Mr Smart said not to fool around with secretaries, go straight for the decision-makers. They always seemed to be tied up though. The pay was nearly all commission too, so I never had much cash to spare. The day I handed in my notice Mr Smart said he was disappointed in me. He thought I would have had a bit more tenacity. I told him to shag off. I said sixty-five pence basic per hour didn't buy much in the way of tenacity.

'Or courtesy either,' he said, tearing up my reference.

That afternoon I ran into Marion on O'Connell Bridge. We went for coffee and had a bit of a laugh. I told her about chucking the job and she said I was dead right. She told me a secret. It wasn't confirmed yet, but fingers crossed. She was going off to Ethiopia. She was sick of just talking. She wanted to do something about the world. If Bob Geldof could do it, why couldn't she? I said it all sounded great, and maybe I'd do the same. Then she asked me all about Alias and the new flat and we talked about the old days. It seemed so long ago. I had almost forgotten what she looked like. She said her friend Mo had just written a postcard from London. She'd seen a guy who looked just like Eddie Virago working in a burger joint in Euston Station. Except he had a short back and sides now. I laughed out loud. Eddie selling hamburgers for a living? Someone of his talent? That would be the day. She said it was nice to get postcards, all the same. She showed it to me. It had a guy on it with a huge red mohican haircut. Mo said she'd bought that one because it reminded her of how Eddie used to look in the old days. She said she'd always fancied him. Marion said she'd send me a card from Ethiopia, if they had them. She never did.

In the pub Eddie and I didn't have much to say, except that it was great to see each other. When I told him the postcard story he said it all went to prove you couldn't trust anyone, and he sipped meaningfully at his pint. After closing time we got the Tube up to the West End, to a disco Eddie knew in Soho. Drunks lolled around the platforms, singing and crying. The club was a tiny place with sweat running down the walls. Eddie asked the black bouncer if Eugene was in tonight.

'Who?' said the bouncer.

'You know Eugene, the manager,' Eddie said.

The bouncer shrugged and said, 'Not tonight, man. I dunno no Eugene.'

I paid Eddie in, because it wasn't his pay day till Thursday. He was really sorry about that.

Downstairs he had to lean across the table, shaking the drinks, to shout in my ear. The writing was going alright. Of course, it was all contacts, all a closed shop, but he was still trying. In fact, he'd just finished a script and although he wasn't free to reveal the details he didn't mind telling me there was quite a bit of interest in it. He only hoped it wasn't too adventurous. Thatcher had the BBC by the short and curlies, he said. They wouldn't take any risks at all. And Channel Four wasn't the same since Isaacs left. Bloody shame that, man of his creative flair.

He'd made lots of friends though, in the business. I'd probably meet them later. They only went out clubbing late at night. Nocturnal animals, he said. It was more cool to do that. They were great people, though. Really wild. Honestly, from Neil Jordan downwards the business was wonderful. Oh sure, he'd met Jordan. He'd crashed at Eddie's place one night after a particularly wild party. Really decent bloke. There was a good scene in London, too. No, he didn't listen to any of the old bands any more. He was all into Acid House. He said that was this year's thing. Forget The

16

Clash. Guitar groups were out. The word was Acid. I said I hadn't heard any and what was it like? He said you couldn't describe it really. It wasn't the kind of music you could put into words.

I did meet one of his friends later on in the night. He saw her standing across the dance floor and beckoned her over. She mustn't have seen him. So he said he'd be back in a second and weaved through the gyrating bodies to where she was. They chatted for a few minutes, and then she came over and sat down. Shirley was a model. From Dublin too. Well, trying to make it as a model. She knew Bono really well. He was a great bloke, she said, really dead on. She'd known him and Ali for absolute yonks, and success hadn't changed them at all. 'Course she hadn't seen them since Wembley last year. Backstage. They were working on the new album apparently. She'd heard the rough mixes and it was a total scorcher. This friend of hers played them to her. A really good friend of hers, actually, who went out with your man from The Hot House Flowers. The one with the hair. She kept forgetting his name. She said she was no good at all for Irish names. She really regretted it, actually, specially since she moved over here, but she couldn't speak a word of Irish. She let us buy her a drink each. I paid for Eddie's. Then she had to run. Early start tomorrow, had to be in the studio by eight-thirty.

'Ciao,' she said, when she went. 'Ciao Eddie.'

It was after four when they kicked us out. The streets of Soho were jostling with minicabs and hot-dog sellers. A crowd filtered out of Ronnie Scott's, just around the corner. Sleek black women in furs and lace. Tall men in sharp suits. Eddie apologised for his friends not showing up. He said if he'd known I was coming he would have arranged a really wild session. Next time. He knew this really happening hip-hop club up in Camden Town, totally wild, but in a very cool kind of way.

In the coffee bar in Leicester Square he was quiet. The old career hadn't been going exactly to plan. He was getting there

17

alright. But much slower than he thought. Still, that was the business. Things got a bit lonely, he said. He got so frustrated, so down. It was hard being an exile. He didn't want to be pretentious or anything, but he knew how Sam Beckett must have felt. If he didn't believe in himself as much as he did, he didn't know how he could go on. He would have invited me back to his place, only a few people were crashing there, so there just wasn't the room. But next time. Honest. It was a big place, but still, it was always full. People were always just dropping in unannounced.

'You know how it is,' he laughed.

I ordered two more cappuccinos.

'I have measured out my life in coffee spoons,' he said, and he sipped painfully. He always drank Nicaraguan, actually, at home. Very into the cause. I said I knew nothing about it. He started to tell me all the facts but I said I really had to go. My aunt would be worried sick about me. If I didn't get home soon she'd call the police or something. He nodded and said fair enough. He had to split as well.

We stood in the rain on Charing Cross Road while he scribbled his address on a soggy beermat. He told me it was good to see me again. I told him I nearly didn't recognise him with the new haircut. Oh that, he'd had to get rid of that, for work. Anyway, punk was dead. It was all history now.

'You should come over here for good,' he said, 'it's a great city.'

I shook his hand and said I'd think about it. He told me not to let the opportunity pass me by.

The taxi driver asked me where I wanted to go. He loved Ireland. The wife was half Irish and they'd been over a few times now. Lovely country. Terrible what was going on over there, though. He said they were bloody savages. Bloody cowboys and Indians. No offence, but he just couldn't understand it. I said I couldn't either. In his opinion it was all to do with religion.

By the time we got to Greenwich the sun was painting the sky over the river. He said he hoped I enjoyed the rest of my holiday. I hadn't any money left to give him a tip.

VICTORY OVER JAPAN

ELLEN GILCHRIST

When I was in the third grade I knew a boy who had to have fourteen shots in the stomach as the result of a squirrel bite. Every day at two o'clock they would come to get him. A hush would fall on the room. We would all look down at our desks while he left the room between Mr Harmon and his mother. Mr Harmon was the principal. That's how important Billy Monday's tragedy was.

Mr Harmon came along in case Billy threw a fit. Every day we waited to see if he would throw a fit but he never did. He just put his books away and left the room with his head hanging down on his chest and Mr Harmon and his mother guiding him along between them like a boat.

'Would you go with them like that?' I asked Letitia at recess. Letitia was my best friend. Usually we played girls chase the boys at recess or pushed each other on the swings or hung upside down on the monkey bars so Joe Franke and Bobby Saxacorn could see our underpants but Billy's shots had even taken the fun out of recess. Now we sat around on the fire escape and talked about rabies instead.

'Why don't they put him to sleep first?' Letitia said. 'I'd make them put me to sleep.'

'They can't,' I said. 'They can't put you to sleep unless they operate.'

'My father could,' she said. 'He owns the hospital. He could put me to sleep.' She was always saying things like that but I let her be my best friend anyway.

'They couldn't give them to me,' I said. 'I'd run away to Florida and be a beachcomber.'

'Then you'd get rabies,' Letitia said. 'You'd be foaming at the mouth.'

'I'd take a chance. You don't always get it.' We moved closer together, caught up in the horror of it. I was thinking about the Livingstons' bulldog. I'd had some close calls with it lately.

'It was a pet,' Letitia said. 'His brother was keeping it for a pet.'

It was noon recess. Billy Monday was sitting on a bench by the swings. Just sitting there. Not talking to anybody. Waiting for two o'clock, a small washed-out-looking boy that nobody paid any attention to until he got bit. He never talked to anybody. He could hardly even read. When Mrs Jansma asked him to read his head would fall all the way over to the side of his neck. Then he would read a few sentences with her having to tell him half the words. No one would ever have picked him out to be the center of a rabies tragedy. He was more the type to fall in a well or get sucked down the drain at the swimming pool.

Fourteen days. Fourteen shots. It was spring when it happened and the schoolroom windows were open all day long and every afternoon after Billy left we had milk from little waxy cartons and Mrs Jansma would read us chapters from a wonderful book about some children in England that had a bed that took them places at night. There we were, eating graham crackers and listening to stories while Billy was strapped to the table in Doctor Finley's office waiting for his shot.

'I can't stand to think about it,' Letitia said. 'It makes me so sick I could puke.'

'I'm going over there and talk to him right now,' I said. 'I'm going to interview him for the paper.' I had been the only one in the third grade to get anything in the Horace Mann paper. I got in with a story about how Mr Harmon was shell-shocked in the

21

First World War. I was on the lookout for another story that good.

I got up, smoothed down my skirt, walked over to the bench where Billy was sitting and held out a vial of cinnamon toothpicks. 'You want one,' I said. 'Go ahead. She won't care.' It was against the rules to bring cinnamon toothpicks to Horace Mann. They were afraid someone would swallow one.

'I don't think so,' he said. 'I don't need any.'

'Go on,' I said. 'They're really good. They've been soaking all week.'

'I don't want any,' he said.

'You want me to push you on the swings?'

'I don't know,' he said. 'I don't think so.'

'If it was my brother's squirrel, I'd kill it,' I said. 'I'd cut its head off.'

'It got away,' he said. 'It's gone.'

'What's it like when they give them to you?' I said. 'Does it hurt very much?'

'I don't know,' he said. 'I don't look.' His head was starting to slip down onto his chest. He was rolling up like a ball.

'I know how to hypnotise people,' I said. 'You want me to hypnotise you so you can't feel it?'

'I don't know,' he said. He had pulled his legs up on the bench. Now his chin was so far down into his chest I could barely hear him talk. Part of me wanted to give him a shove and see if he would roll. I touched him on the shoulder instead. I could feel his little bones beneath his shirt. I could smell his washed-out rusty smell. His head went all the way down under his knees. Over his shoulder I saw Mrs Jansma headed our way.

'Rhoda,' she called out. 'I need you to clean off the blackboards before we go back in. Will you be a sweet girl and do that for me?'

'I wasn't doing anything but talking to him,' I said. She was beside us now and had gathered him into her wide sleeves. He was starting to cry, making little strangled noises like a goat.

'Well, my goodness, that was nice of you to try to cheer Billy up. Now go see about those blackboards for me, will you?'

I went on in and cleaned off the blackboards and beat the erasers together out the window, watching the chalk dust settle into the bricks. Down below I could see Mrs Jansma still holding on to Billy. He was hanging on to her like a spider but it looked like he had quit crying.

That afternoon a lady from the PTA came to talk to us about the paper drive. 'One more time,' she was saying. 'We've licked the Krauts. Now all we have left is the Japs. Who's going to help?' she shouted.

'I am,' I shouted back. I was the first one on my feet.

'Who do you want for a partner?' she said.

'Billy Monday,' I said, pointing at him. He looked up at me as though I had asked him to swim the English Channel, then his head slid down on the desk.

'All right,' Mrs Jansma said. 'Rhoda Manning and Billy Monday. Team number one. To cover Washington and Sycamore from Calvin Boulevard to Conner Street. Who else?'

'Bobby and me,' Joe Franke called out. He was wearing his coonskin cap, even though it was as hot as summer. How I loved him! 'We want downtown,' he shouted. 'We want Dirkson Street to the river.'

'Done,' Mrs Jansma said. JoEllen Scaggs was writing it all down on the blackboard. By the time Billy's mother and Mr Harmon came to get him the paper drive was all arranged.

'See you tomorrow,' I called out as Billy left the room. 'Don't forget. Don't be late.'

When I got home that afternoon I told my mother I had volunteered to let Billy be my partner. She was so proud of me she made me some cookies even though I was supposed to be on a diet. I took the cookies and a pillow and climbed up into my treehouse to read a book. I was getting to be more like my mother every day. My mother was a saint. She fed hoboes and played the organ at early communion even if she was sick and gave away her ration stamps to anyone that needed them. She had only one pair of new shoes the whole war.

I was getting more like her every day. I was the only one in the third grade that would have picked Billy Monday to help with a paper drive. He probably couldn't even pick up a stack of papers. He probably couldn't even help pull the wagon.

I bet this is the happiest day of her life, I was thinking. I was lying in my treehouse watching her. She was sitting on the back steps putting liquid hose on her legs. She was waiting for the Episcopal minister to come by for a drink. He'd been coming by a lot since my daddy was overseas. That was just like my mother. To be best friends with a minister.

'She picked out a boy that's been sick to help her on the paper drive,' I heard her tell him later. 'I think it helped a lot to get her to lose weight. It was smart of you to see that was the problem.'

'There isn't anything I wouldn't do for you, Ariane,' he said. 'You say the word and I'll be here to do it.'

I got a few more cookies and went back up into the treehouse to finish my book. I could read all kinds of books. I could read Book-of-the-Month Club books. The one I was reading now was called *Cakes and Ale*. It wasn't coming along too well.

I settled down with my back against the tree, turning the pages, looking for the good parts. Inside the house my mother was bragging on me. Above my head a golden sun beat down out of a blue sky. All around the silver maple leaves moved in the breeze. I went back to my book. 'She put her arms around my neck and pressed her lips against mine. I forgot my wrath. I only thought of her beauty and her enveloping kindness.

' "You must take me as I am, you know," she whispered.

' "All right," I said.'

Saturday was not going to be a good day for a paper drive. The sky was gray and overcast. By the time we lined up on the Horace Mann playground with our wagons a light rain was falling.

'Our boys are fighting in rain and snow and whatever the heavens send,' Mr Harmon was saying. He was standing on the bleachers wearing an old baseball shirt and a cap. I had never seen him in anything but his gray suit. He looked more shell-shocked than ever in his cap.

'They're working over there. We're working over here. The Germans are defeated. Only the Japs left to go. There're canvas tarps from Gentilly's Hardware, so take one to cover your papers. All right now. One grade at a time. And remember, Mrs Winchester's third grade is still ahead by seventy-eight pounds. So you're going to have to go some to beat that. Get to your stations now. Get ready, get set, go. Everybody working together ...'

Billy and I started off. I was pulling the wagon, he was walking along beside me. I had meant to wait awhile before I started interviewing him but I started right in.

'Are you going to have to leave to go get it?' I said.

'Go get what?'

'You know. Your shot.'

'I got it this morning. I already had it.'

'Where do they put it in?'

'I don't know,' he said. 'I don't look.'

'Well, you can feel it, can't you?' I said. 'Like, do they stick it in your navel or what?'

'It's higher than that.'

'How long does it take? To get it.'

'I don't know,' he said. 'Till they get through.'

'Well, at least you aren't going to get rabies. At least you won't be foaming at the mouth. I guess you're glad about that.' I had stopped in front of a house and was looking up the path to the door. We had come to the end of Sycamore, where our territory began.

'Are you going to be the one to ask them?' he said.

'Sure,' I said. 'You want to come to the door with me?'

'I'll wait,' he said. 'I'll just wait.'

We filled the wagon by the second block. We took that load back to the school and started out again. On the second trip we hit an attic with bundles of the *Kansas City Star* tied up with string. It took us all afternoon to haul that. Mrs Jansma said she'd never seen anyone as lucky on a paper drive as Billy and I. Our whole class was having a good day. It looked like we might beat everybody, even the sixth grade.

'Let's go out one more time,' Mrs Jansma said. 'One more trip before dark. Be sure and hit all the houses you missed.'

Billy and I started back down Sycamore. It was growing dark. I untied my Brownie Scout sweater from around my waist and put it on and pulled the sleeves down over my wrists. 'Let's try that brick housse on the corner,' I said. 'They might be home by now.' It was an old house set back on a high lawn. It looked like a house where old people lived. I had noticed old people were the ones who saved things. 'Come on,' I said. 'You go to the door with me. I'm tired of doing it by myself.'

He came along behind me and we walked up to the door and rang the bell. No one answered for a long time although I could hear footsteps and saw someone pass by a window. I rang the bell again.

A man came to the door. A thin man about my father's age.

'We're collecting papers for Horace Mann School,' I said. 'For the war effort.'

'You got any papers we can have?' Billy said. It was the first time he had spoken to anyone but me all day. 'For the war,' he added.

'There're some things in the basement if you want to go down there and get them,' the man said. He turned a light on in the hall and we followed him into a high-ceilinged foyer with a set of winding stairs going up to another floor. It smelled musty, like my grandmother's house in Clarksville. Billy was right beside me, sticking as close as a burr. We followed the man through the kitchen and down a flight of stairs to the basement.

'You can have whatever you find down here,' he said. 'There're papers and magazines in that corner. Take whatever you can carry.'

There was a large stack of magazines. Magazines were the best thing you could find. They weighed three times as much as newspapers.

'Come on,' I said to Billy. 'Let's fill the wagon. This will put us over the top for sure.' I picked up a bundle and started up the stairs. I went in and out several times carrying as many as I could at a time. On the third trip Billy met me at the foot of the stairs. 'Rhoda,' he said. 'Come here. Come look at this.'

He took me to an old table in a corner of the basement. It was a walnut table with grapes carved on the side and feet like lion's feet. He laid one of the magazines down on the table and opened it. It was a photograph of a naked little girl, a girl smaller than I was. He turned the page. Two naked boys were standing together with their legs twined. He kept turning the pages. It was all the same. Naked children on every page. I had never seen a naked boy. Much less a photograph of one. Billy looked up at me. He turned another page. Five naked little girls were grouped together around a fountain.

'Let's get out of here,' I said. 'Come on. I'm getting out of here.' I headed for the stairs with him right behind me. We didn't even close the basement door. We didn't even stop to say thank you.

The magazines we had collected were in bundles. About a block from the house we stopped on a corner, breathless from running. 'Let's see if there're any more,' I said. We tore open a bundle. The first magazine had pictures of naked grown people on every page.

'What are we going to do?' he said.

'We're going to throw them away,' I answered, and started throwing them into the nandina bushes by the Hancock's vacant lot. We threw them into the nandina bushes and into the ditch that runs into Mills Creek. We threw the last ones into a culvert and then we took our wagon and got on out of there. At the corner of Sycamore and Wesley we went our separate ways.

'Well, at least you'll have something to think about tomorrow when you get your shot,' I said.

'I guess so,' he replied.

'Look here, Billy. I don't want you to tell anyone about those magazines. You understand?'

'I won't.' His head was going down again.

'I mean it, Billy.'

He raised his head and looked at me as if he had just remembered something he was thinking about. 'I won't,' he said. 'Are you really going to write about me in the paper?'

'Of course I am. I said I was, didn't I?' I'm going to do it tonight.'

I walked on home. Past the corner where the Scout hikes met. Down the alley where I found the card shuffler and the Japanese fan. Past the yard where the violets grew. I was thinking about the boys with their legs twined. They looked like earthworms, all naked like that. They looked like something might fly down and eat them. It made me sick to think about it and I stopped by Mrs Alford's and picked a few iris to take home to my mother.

Billy finished getting his shots. And I wrote the article and of course they put it on page one. BE ON THE LOOKOUT FOR MAD SQUIRREL, the headline read. By Rhoda Katherine Manning. Grade 3.

> We didn't even know it was mean, the person it bit said. That person is in the third grade at our school. His name is William Monday. On April 23 he had his last shot. Mrs Jansma's class had a cake and gave him a pencil set. Billy Monday is all right now and things are back to normal.
>
> I think it should be against the law to keep dangerous pets or dogs where they can get out and get people. If you see a dog or squirrel acting funny go in the house and stay there.

I never did get around to telling my mother about those magazines. I kept meaning to but there never seemed to be anywhere to start. One day in August I tried to tell her. I had been to the swimming pool and I thought I saw the man from the brick house drive by in a car. I was pretty sure it was him. As he turned the corner he looked at me. *He looked right at my face.* I stood very still, my heart pounding inside my chest, my hands as cold and wet as a frog, the smell of swimming pool chlorine rising from my skin. What if he found out where I lived? What if he followed me home and killed me to keep me from telling on him? I was terrified. At any moment the car might return. He might grab me and put me in the car and take me off and kill me. I threw my bathing suit and towel down on the sidewalk and started running. I ran down Linden Street and turned into the alley behind Calvin Boulevard, running as fast as I could. I ran down the alley and into my yard and up my steps and into my house looking for my mother to tell her about it.

She was in the living room, with Father Kenniman and Mr and Mrs DuVal. They lived across the street and had a gold star in their window. Warrene, our cook, was there. And Connie Barksdale, our cousin who was visiting from the Delta. Her husband had been killed on Corregidor and she would come up and stay with my mother whenever she couldn't take it anymore. They were all in the living room gathered around the radio.

'Momma,' I said. 'I saw this man that gave me some magazines . . .'

'Be quiet, Rhoda,' she said. 'We're listening to the news. Something's happened. We think maybe we've won the war.' There were tears in her eyes. She gave me a little hug, then turned back to the radio. It was a wonderful radio with a magic eye that glowed in the dark. At night when we had blackouts Dudley and I would get into bed with my mother and we would listen to it together, the magic eye glowing in the dark like an emerald.

Now the radio was bringing important news to Seymour, Indiana. Strange, confused, hush-hush news that said we had a bomb bigger than any bomb ever made and we had already dropped it on Japan and half of Japan was sinking into the sea. Now the Japs had to surrender. Now they couldn't come to Indiana and stick bamboo up our fingernails. Now it would all be over and my father would come home.

The grown people kept on listening to the radio, getting up every now and then to get drinks or fix each other sandwiches. Dudley was sitting beside my mother in a white shirt acting like he was twenty years old. He always did that when company came. No one was paying any attention to me.

Finally I went upstairs and lay down on the bed to think things over. My father was coming home. I didn't know how to feel about that. He was always yelling at someone when he was home. He was always yelling at my mother to make me mind.

'What do you mean, you can't catch her,' I could hear him

yelling. 'Hit her with a broom. Hit her with a table. Hit her with a chair. But, for God's sake, Ariane, don't let her talk to you that way.'

Well, maybe it would take a while for him to get home. First they had to finish off Japan. First they had to sink the other half into the sea. I curled up in my soft old eiderdown comforter. I was feeling great. We had dropped the biggest bomb in the world on Japan and there were plenty more where that one came from.

I fell asleep in the hot sweaty silkiness of the comforter. I was dreaming I was at the wheel of an airplane carrying the bomb to Japan. Hit 'em, I was yelling. Hit 'em with a mountain. Hit 'em with a table. Hit 'em with a chair. Off we go into the wild blue yonder, climbing high into the sky. I dropped one on the brick house where the bad man lived, then took off for Japan. Down we dive, spouting a flame from under. Off with one hell of a roar. We live in flame. Buckle down in flame. For nothing can stop the Army Air Corps. Hit 'em with a table, I was yelling. Hit 'em with a broom. Hit 'em with a bomb. Hit 'em with a chair.

COME IN — I'VE HANGED MYSELF

MARY O'DONNELL

The social worker had described him as fairly typical of his age group. 'You know the sort of thing I mean,' he drawled casually over the phone, 'a bit mixed-up, needs somebody patient to take an interest.' And Lorna, eager to appear cooperative and parental, had replied, 'I know, I can imagine,' when she could do neither. Missing his parents. Father in England. Mother in a psychiatric ward. She made a point of not tidying the house on the day of his arrival. An air of spit-and-polish would inhibit him, she thought. He'd want to relax, feel at home, as if he belonged. No point in creating a formal sanctuary, a sacramental atmosphere. Feeling slightly apprehensive she left the previous day's papers tossed on the floor of the sitting room and decided not to arrange fresh flowers in a vase in place of wilting carnations.

When they opened the hall door, the social worker was hearty. He grinned, pulling on his beard as he introduced his charge. 'And this bod here is our Martin!' he enthused with a flourish of the hand. 'Go on shake hands with Lorna and Luke like a good man,' he intoned encouragingly. They shook hands. Lorna heard herself respond brightly, cheerfully, to the mumbled greeting. Her head, unexpectedly alarmed and unsettled, whirred with attentiveness. He was pathetically ugly. It had nothing to do with dress or build. He wore black and grey, the current A-bomb garb of despair and redundancy: black trousers which ended mid-calf, a grey shirt under a black tunic. A chain belt hung round his narrow hips. He was much what they'd expected. 'Come on in,' Luke beckoned, sounding hospitable and easy-going. Fatherly. 'The fire's just on — it'll only take a wee minute to warm up.'

They chatted, the first awkward moments mitigated by mugs

of coffee. Mugs, not cups. Deliberately chosen for the occasion. One part of her responded superficially. Another wrestled with uncertain feelings. The boy looked around aimlessly. He could only be described as unfortunate looking: his hair was wiry and short, neither brown nor blonde but pale and neutral. His face was ravaged with acne, the skin waxy, the cheeks and chin pocked with volcanic swellings, angry pimples, and the scars of half-healed eruptions. His jaw showing the primitive angularity of a young male. Here and there, wisps of hair sprouted. His eyes were pale blue, ringed with a pig-like pinkness.

They'd painted the walls of his room a plain buff, in case he wanted to put up posters. He shuffled from one foot to the other, sheepish and tongue-tied.

'D'you think you'll be OK here, Martin?' she asked.

'Yeh.'

'If there's anything you need you'll let us know, won't you?'

'Where's the jacks?'

'Oh of course, nearly forgot,' Luke half-apologised. 'This way.' The chain belt clanked all the way across the landing.

All young people liked chips. Burgers and chips, Luke had suggested. So Lorna chopped onions, minced round steak, added herbs and bound the lot with egg in big juicy mounds.

The chips were home-made. They sat down together, feeling awkward.

'Are you hungry, Martin?' she asked, certain of culinary success.

'Yeh.'

'Oh — you can wash your hands at the sink before you begin, if you want,' Luke interjected. They'd agreed on this in advance. No direct requests yet. Certainly no orders. You achieved more by example.

'I washed them half an hour ago.'

'Fine. Fine,' Lorna said quickly, her look meeting Luke's. She handed the boy a plate. He eyed it uncertainly.

'I don't eat chips.'

'Oh?' she queried, surprised. Waiting for him to say more. He didn't. Began to pick at the burger.

'I don't like pepper in things.'

'Oh well, we'll get you something else then.' She made to remove the plate. He stopped her.

'It's all right. I'll eat it this time.' He sounded almost aggressive with his deep and half-broken croak.

'Are you sure? It's no trouble.' She laughed uneasily. She was uncharacteristically nervous. He poked at the burger, cut it finally and ate a mouthful, looking straight ahead. This had to be what a blind date was like. No inkling of what was in the other person's head. No clue to their wants. And natural parents could imagine things. Could trace things, mistakenly or not, to genetics. But this was *tabula rasa*. He lifted his fork solemnly. 'I'll eat this today. The chips make me skin worse. I like them. But that's why I don't eat them.'

It was as if a light had gone on. She found herself admiring his blithe reference to his skin, to the distorted plumage of his face. He had declared his cards, in a manner of speaking. Or some of them. Had told them something about the sort of person he was. She was flooded with curiosity. All things in time. The rest of the meal passed easily. She and Luke tried to tell him about their friends and their friends' children. Their relatives and the Sunday visit in a few weeks time.

He liked toad-in-the-hole, he told Lorna suddenly, one Friday. 'And shepherd's pie. Me Ma used to make things like that when she was feelin' up to it,' he remarked.

'I'll do shepherd's pie tomorrow,' she said, delighted at this reference to his mother. Things were shaping up.

'No. Do whatever ya were goin' to do,' he said hastily, in a wavering baritone voice. Of course, she thought. How stupid. How insensitive not to realise that to cook a favourite meal would perhaps make him lonely.

She knocked on his door that night. To say good-night, even though they'd already done that. 'Yeh,' he called expressionlessly. She pushed the door. He lay on the bed, arms behind his head, staring at the ceiling. The radio was on. They'd get him a better one, with headphones. And tapes perhaps. He liked AC/DC and Cindy Lauper. 'Good-night,' she mouthed, unwilling to disturb him. Unwilling also, perhaps, to deal with the uneasiness he aroused in her each time they attempted communication. It was apparently simpler for Luke. No complications. A bland directness. Mutual. Devoid of complexities. What could they really say about what went on behind that face? That pock-marked face. Sometimes, it seemed as if he wasn't really with them. Like a strange bird, an alien creature moulding itself to an existence where everything was cruelly unfamiliar, where the other denizens were made of paper. Hollow where he was full. Useless at meeting his wants. Or perhaps *they* were the aliens.

He grew sullen. More truculent in manner. Determined seemingly to thwart their efforts. He despised routine. The night before the Sunday visitors arrived, he stayed awake, listening to music. That did not disturb them. More the notion of a wakeful and slightly hostile presence stalking around downstairs. The next morning, Lorna asked him if he did that often.

'What?' he muttered blankly, staring into space.

'Stay up all night.'

'Yeh.'

She would be patient. This was the sort of thing you got.

'Can't you sleep then?' she continued casually, pretending to be more interested in the cookery book she held in her hand.

The boy was silent. Just when she'd decided that he was going to be perverse, he stirred.

'I can think better.'

'Oh. I see.'

35

Don't tell me we're going to have four months of nocturnal philosophising, she thought. In the summer too. He should be out and about during the day, getting some air. Still. Fairly typical behaviour, when you thought about it. Attention. He probably did lots of things for attention. They'd have to ignore the exhibitionism. Make him feel important in other ways. Build up his self-esteem. Life makes you what you are.

Later that morning, she tried to involve him in the dinner preparations. But he dawdled uninterestedly, arms folded. Watching her. She had to admit that he was tiresome. The old understanding between herself and Luke vanished in his presence, so bent were they on pleasing him. Nothing pleased him. He was a gigantic puzzle, brooding and mysterious, who foiled their anxious attempts to find the missing piece — some anodyne to a mutual and mounting chagrin. Her patience was dwindling steadily. He'd been with them two weeks.

'Right Martin,' she announced briskly, trying a new approach, 'you can set the table — you'll find cutlery in that drawer and the crockery's here beside you.' She smiled matter-of-factly. He didn't smile back. Just looked. Instantly seeing through her facile adult psychology. But he went to the drawer and got out the cutlery.

Dinner was a disaster. The vegetables were passed around while Luke sliced the lamb. The boy stared at his plate, pale-eyed. Somebody — Luke's father, she thought — started grumbling about unemployment. It was an easy topic, the sort of thing about which everybody could rave, feel hard done by. They bantered agreeably for a few minutes over the clink of plates and cutlery. 'What do you think, Martin?' Luke's mother asked gently.

'About what?' he muttered, not looking at her.

'Well,' she hesitated,' about unemployment and that, all those young people like yourself who'll be leaving school in a few years and no jobs for them — what do you think's going to happen?' He put down his knife and fork as if about to make a statement of policy.

'I don't know and I don't give a damn,' he spat.

There was a brief, uneasy silence. Lorna cut in.

'Right, you don't give a damn. Very original, Martin,' she smiled.

'I'm not tryin' to be *original*,' he scowled, mimicking her.

Her face flared. 'More lamb please,' Luke's father said, clearing his throat.

'The streets are going to run red.' They all looked up startled by the sudden announcement made five minutes later.

'What you were askin',' he gestured at Luke's mother with his knife.

'It's going to be a blood-bath in ten years.' He helped himself to another piece of meat.

'However do you mean?' Luke's mother asked quizzically.

'Don't have to explain, streets are goin' to run red — I don't have to justify that to anybody,' he growled, head swaggering in the glow of their acute attention. Somebody — Luke more than likely — sighed.

They talked in low voices as they did the dishes.

'A lot of it's for attention,' Luke reasoned. 'If we ignore it he'll stop eventually.' Lorna disagreed.

'We have ignored it and there's no change,' she fumed.

'He's still acting as if he were doing us a favour by being here — it's as if we're idiots — can you imagine him when he goes back to school?' She paused to pull the plug, and dried her hands angrily. 'Carrying on about us: how we behave, imitating us!'

When they went into the sitting-room, he was rolling his own cigarettes. As if he were alone. She watched him, fascinated. Totally self-engrossed. Oblivious to their presence as he fiddled with the flimsy paper, his shoulders hunched, head and neck protruding forwards. Sixteen. She reminded herself of their obvious advantages. And his disadvantages. Insecurity, fear, immaturity, no experience of a loving home. And an appalling appearance. Pity was the last thing he needed. She felt so little affinity with him. Because he gave nothing. Went through the motions of being cooperative. If he enjoyed anything, he never said. Presumably he'd never been shown how to express pleasure. Maybe there'd been none to express in the first place. No. It was up to her and Luke to make the effort. Go farther than half-way. Beyond the median line of compromise. Possibly nobody had ever gone beyond what was necessary on his account.

'Don't flick ash on to the carpet, love — there's an ashtray beside you.' He glared at her. The family left early. They departed quietly. Luke's mother would probably phone the following day.

No doubt he saw them as set in their ways, committing over and over the mortal sin of middle-class adulthood. Dinosaurs with pea-brains, who knew nothing about pain, loneliness, anguish, who were eternally sure of themselves. Yet his own behaviour was so familiar. Predictable. The very thing he objected to continuously. *Come In — I've Hanged Myself*, proclaimed a sign on his door. Another, on the bedroom wall, read: *Life Is Like A Shit Sandwich*. Everything about him was an indication of internal furies, an unsubtle display of nihilism and youthful ennui.

It came to a head the next day. Luke had gone shopping, unable to persuade the boy to accompany him.

'That's wimin's stuff,' he announced to Lorna.

'In this house it's everybody's stuff,' she replied firmly. 'You can go next week, Martin — we all take turns here.'

He rolled his eyes heavenwards, curled his pale lips down defiantly, helped himself to one of her cigarettes.

'Are you out of pocket-money already?' she asked. He lit up, contemplating the smoke. 'Nope,' he muttered.

'What would you have done if I'd said you couldn't have one?'

'I'd have taken it anyway.'

The little shite. He knew how to rise her.

'Look,' she began reasonably, 'we've tried to make life pleasant for you but all you do is throw everything back at us . . . as if . . . as if . . .'

'I don't owe you anything,' he shouted, hammering the table with his fist. A hint of violence that made her stomach curdle. She studied him carefully, lighting a cigarette herself. Distant and assessing. He was hateful-looking when he was angry. He returned her gaze, challengingly.

'Martin, the one thing you do owe us,' she began softly, determined not to raise her voice, 'is consideration.' She gesticulated with the lit cigarette. 'And that means making an effort — some attempt at playing your part — and none of this 'I-don't-give-a-damn' nonsense. We only want you to feel at home . . .'

Suddenly he rose, pushing the chair back noisily, stubbing the cigarette so roughly that it broke in two.

'Nobody could be at home in this . . . *Kip*!' he bellowed. He might as well have hit her.

'Well, if that's how you feel Martin you've only to say the word; we don't want to hold you against your will if you're not happy; if you can do better elsewhere . . . ' Echoes of her own mother, years ago, when faced with mutiny. Her voice was even, controlled, in spite of the hurt. To her surprise, his face flooded pinkly.

'You don't really want me here at all,' he croaked. Her face dropped.

'Ya couldn't have yer own kids so ya got me on trial, like y'can hand me back when me time's up, forget all about me.'

He paused momentarily, like a hurricane building up to its peak of destruction, the veins on his neck bulging.

'I don't want to be stuck with a pair of cranks who couldn't have their own; you're batty, that's what you are, with your books and music,' he goaded effectively. Despising. Determined to stab where it hurt most.

'Anybody that listens to operas, ah – whatever ya call it — has to be up the creek. A header. That's what you are,' he hissed maliciously, pointing at her.

There had to be some redemption. Something positive had to come out of this. A reason she could connect with, some moment of salvation that would heal them both. She would ignore most of it. She would. She would. She tried to control the nervous tremor in her voice. But she could not let him see her reduced. Perceptive boy. She'd call his bluff. 'You're right, Martin,' she tried to sound blasé, unshockable. 'We couldn't have our own kids. And you're right again. You are second-best. In fact, come to think of it, you're third-best, because we couldn't adopt either.' He shrank visibly. But she couldn't stop. Knew she was hitting back. Meeting him with even greater maliciousness, And she didn't want to stop. 'That's if you go around measuring things. We don't. It's nothing to do with third-best. You're you. You're nearly grown up. You're not a child even if you behave like one. We thought we'd like to have somebody like you live with us. We have lots of space. It could be handy for a fellow...and we're not trying to be your parents.' Her voice jerked. He started to shriek at her. 'But y'are, y'are!'

The perversity of it dawned. The real want. But, by then, she could not relent. 'Look honey, I wouldn't want to be your Ma for all the tea in China. Don't delude yourself,' her voice hard.

Luke came in then. Looked expectantly from one to the other, sensing an airing of emotion on the normally neutral domestic channels. 'I hate you, *bitch*!', he roared, kicking the chair as he made for his room. Crying. She was crying too.

It was fifteen minutes before she could say anything comprehensible. It poured down her face. They couldn't get this right either. Came across to the boy as a pair of stuffed shirts. Tied up in reproductive tensions and what they had transmitted to him as 'culture'. Antiques who knew nothing about anything that mattered. Who would soon be extinct. Acting Mr and Mrs Bountiful and *understanding*. In reality, they understood nothing. They had nothing. He'd stripped them, bared the hoarded pain of years, the mask she wore to conceal it. Like some wild thing tearing at flesh. And she was no better. Had kicked back every bit as hungry. As defiant. Had reaffirmed the image of self-loathing and repulsion which he harboured towards himself.

Unforgivable.

They decided not to disturb him when he didn't appear for tea. Let him cool off. She began to think of the sign on the door. Supposing? Would he realise they cared? Before they went to bed, she knocked on his door. Silence. She tried again. A rustling sound. Then silence. She knocked a third time.

'It's open,' rasped a half-fledged voice.

He didn't look at her. Lying on the bed, smoking, the air curling grey-blue. Flat out, locked up in himself, impenetrable as a piece of steel. Wrap the tender part up. Bury it like a broken bone. Let it fester.

'Martin?' Silence. He exhaled.

'I'm sorry. Just called in to say . . . that I really didn't mean . . . never let the sun set on your anger . . .' She was incoherent. Touched his shoulder. He flinched.

'There's food in the fridge . . . if you're hungry . . .' She left quietly.

Went to bed, doomed and impotent. They were a right pair. Clueless. And the boy hated her. Clearly. The venom he packed. The blind energy of something unexploded, which could shred their civilised masks to ribbons, expose the raw nerve of need. Headers. That's what he'd called them. Called *her*.

She wanted to crawl away. Anywhere. To find peace. Somewhere safe. Where the effort of doing the right thing wouldn't always backfire in her face like a badly-primed pistol. A place of reason and salvation. Some people had it easy. She drifted towards sleep. So easy. All fell into place. Two point five: average family.

YOU SHOULD HAVE SEEN THE MESS

MURIEL SPARK

I am now more than glad that I did not pass into the grammar school five years ago, although it was a disappointment at the time. I was always good at English, but not so good at the other subjects!!

I am glad that I went to the secondary modern school, because it was only constructed the year before. Therefore, it was much more hygienic than the grammar school. The secondary modern was light and airy, and the walls were painted with a bright, washable gloss. One day, I was sent over to the grammar school, with a note for one of the teachers, and you should have seen the mess! The corridors were dusty, and I saw dust on the window ledges, which were chipped. I saw into one of the classrooms. It was very untidy in there.

I am also glad that I did not go to the grammar school, because of what it does to one's habits. This may appear to be a strange remark, at first sight. It is a good thing to have an education behind you, and I do not believe in ignorance, but I have had certain experiences, with educated people, since going out into the world.

I am seventeen years of age, and left school two years ago last month. I had my A certificate for typing, so got my first job, as a junior, in a solicitor's office. Mum was pleased at this, and Dad said it was a first-class start, as it was an old-established firm. I must say that when I went for the interview, I was surprised at the windows, and the stairs up to the offices were also far from clean. There was a little waiting-room, where some of the elements were missing from the gas fire, and the carpet on the floor was worn. However, Mr Heygate's office, into which I was shown for the interview, was better. The furniture was old, but it was polished, and there was a good carpet, I will say that. The glass of the bookcase was very clean.

I was to start on the Monday, so along I went. They took me to the general office, where there were two senior shorthand-typists, and a clerk, Mr Gresham, who was far from smart in appearance. You should have seen the mess!! There was no floor covering whatsoever, and so dusty everywhere. There were shelves all round the room, with old box files on them. The box files were falling to pieces, and all the old papers inside them were crumpled. The worst shock of all was the tea-cups. It was my duty to make tea, mornings and afternoons. Miss Bewlay showed me where everything was kept. It was kept in an old orange box, and the cups were all cracked. There were not enough saucers to go round, etc. I will not go into the facilities, but they were also far from hygienic. After three days, I told Mum, and she was upset, most of all about the cracked cups. We never keep a cracked cup, but throw it out, because those cracks can harbour germs. So Mum gave me my own cup to take to the office.

Then at the end of the week, when I got my salary, Mr Heygate said, 'Well, Lorna, what are you going to do with your first pay?' I did not like him saying this, and I nearly passed a comment, but I said, 'I don't know.' He said, 'What do you do in the evenings, Lorna? Do you watch Telly?' I did take this as an insult, because we call it TV, and his remark made me out to be uneducated. I just stood, and did not answer, and he looked surprised. Next day, Saturday, I told Mum and Dad about the facilities, and we decided I should not go back to that job. Also, the desks in the general office were rickety. Dad was indignant, because Mr Heygate's concern was flourishing, and he had letters after his name.

Everyone admires our flat, because Mum keeps it spotless, and Dad keeps doing things to it. He had done it up all over, and got permission from the Council to remodernise the kitchen. I well recall the Health Visitor remarking to Mum, 'You could eat off the floor, Mrs Merrifield.' It is true that you could eat your lunch off Mum's floors, and any hour of the day or night you will find every corner spick and span.

Next, I was sent by the agency to a publisher's for an interview, because of being good at English. One look was enough!! My next interview was a success, and I am still at Low's Chemical Co. It is a modern block, with a quarter of an hour rest period, morning and afternoon. Mr Marwood is very smart in appearance. He is well spoken, although he has not got a university education behind him. There is special lighting over the desks, and the typewriters are the latest models.

So I am happy at Low's. But I have met other people, of an educated type, in the past year, and it has opened my eyes. It so happened that I had to go to the doctor's house, to fetch a prescription for my young brother, Trevor, when the epidemic was on. I rang the bell, and Mrs Darby came to the door. She was small, with fair hair, but too long, and a green maternity dress. But she was very nice to me. I had to wait in their living-room, and you should have seen the state it was in! There were broken toys on the carpet, and the ash trays were full up. There were contemporary pictures on the walls, but the furniture was not contemporary, but old-fashioned, with covers which were past standing up to another wash, I should say. To cut a long story short, Dr Darby and Mrs Darby have always been very kind to me, and they meant everything for the best. Dr Darby is also short and fair, and they have three children, a girl and a boy, and now a baby boy.

When I went that day for the prescription, Dr Darby said to me, 'You look pale, Lorna. It's the London atmosphere. Come on a picnic with us, in the car, on Saturday.' After that I went with the Darbys more and more. I liked them, but I did not like the mess, and it was a surprise. But I also kept in with them for the opportunity of meeting people, and Mum and Dad were pleased that I had made nice friends. So I did not say anything about the cracked lino, and the paintwork all chipped. The children's clothes were very shabby for a doctor, and she changed them out of their school clothes when they came home from school, into those worn-out garments. Mum always kept us spotless to go out to play, and I do not like to say it, but those Darby children frequently looked like the Leary family, which the Council evicted from our block, as they were far from houseproud.

One day, when I was there, Mavis (as I called Mrs Darby by then) put her head out of the window, and shouted to the boy, 'John, stop peeing over the cabbages at once. Pee on the lawn.' I did not know which way to look. Mum would never say a word like that from the window, and I know for a fact that Trevor would never pass water outside, not even bathing in the sea.

I went there usually at the week-ends, but sometimes on week-days, after supper. They had an idea to make a match for me with a chemist's assistant, whom they had taken up too. He was an orphan, and I do not say there was anything wrong with that. But he was not accustomed to those little extras that I was. He was a good-looking boy, I will say that. So I went once to a dance, and twice to films with him. To look at, he was quite clean in appearance. But there was only hot water at the week-end at his place, and he said that a bath once a week was sufficient. Jim (as I called Dr Darby by then) said it was sufficient also, and surprised me. He did not have much money, and I do not hold that against him. But there was no hurry for me, and I could wait for a man in a better position, so that I would not miss those little extras. So he started going out with a girl from the coffee bar, and did not come to the Darbys very much then.

There were plenty of boys at the office, but I will say this for the Darbys, they had lots of friends coming and going, and they had interesting conversation, although sometimes it gave me a surprise, and I did not know where to look. And sometimes they had people who were very down and out, although there is no need to be. But most of the guests were different, so it made a comparison with the boys at the office, who were not so educated in their conversation.

Now it was near the time for Mavis to have her baby, and I was to come in at the week-end, to keep an eye on the children, while the help had her day off. Mavis did not go away to have her baby, but would have it at home, in their double bed, as they did not have twin beds, although he was a doctor. A girl I knew, in our block, was engaged, but was let down, and even she had her baby in the labour ward. I was sure the bedroom was not hygienic for having a baby, but I did not mention it.

One day, after the baby boy came along, they took me in the car to the country, to see Jim's mother. The baby was put in a carry-cot at the back of the car. He began to cry, and without a word of a lie, Jim said to him over his shoulder, 'Oh shut your gob, you little bastard.' I did not know what to do, and Mavis was smoking a cigarette. Dad would not dream of saying such a thing to Trevor or I. When we arrived at Jim's mother's place, Jim said, 'It's a fourteenth-century cottage, Lorna.' I could well believe it. It was very cracked and old, and it made one wonder how Jim could let his old mother live in this tumble-down cottage, as he was so good to everyone else. So Mavis knocked at the door, and the old lady came. There was not much anyone could do to the inside. Mavis said, 'Isn't it charming, Lorna?' If that was a joke, it was going too far. I said to the old Mrs Darby, 'Are you going to be re-housed?' but she did not understand this, and I explained how you have to apply to the Council, and keep at them. But it was funny that the Council had not done something already, when they go round condemning. Then old Mrs Darby said, 'My dear, I shall be re-housed in the Grave.' I did not know where to look.

There was a carpet hanging on the wall, which I think was

there to hid a damp spot. She had a good TV set, I will say that. But some of the walls were bare brick, and the facilities were outside, through the garden. The furniture was far from new.

One Saturday afternoon, as I happened to go to the Darbys, they were just going off to a film and they took me too. It was the Curzon, and afterwards we went to a flat in Curzon Street. It was a very clean block, I will say that, and there were good carpets at the entrance. The couple there had contemporary furniture, and they also spoke about music. It was a nice place, but there was no Welfare Centre to the flats, where people could go for social intercourse, advice, and guidance. But they were well-spoken, and I met Willy Morley, who was an artist. Willy sat beside me, and we had a drink. He was young, dark, with a dark shirt, so one could not see right away if he was clean. Soon after this, Jim said to me, 'Willy wants to paint you, Lorna. But you'd better ask your Mum.' Mum said it was all right if he was a friend of the Darbys.

I can honestly say that Willy's place was the most unhygienic place I have seen in my life. He said I had an unusual type of beauty, which he must capture. This was when we came back to his place from the restaurant. The light was very dim, but I could see the bed had not been made, and the sheets were far from clean. He said he must paint me, but I told Mavis I did not like to go back there. 'Don't you like Willy?' she asked. I could not deny that I liked Willy, in a way. There was something about him, I will say that. Mavis said, 'I hope he hasn't been making a pass at you, Lorna.' I said he had not done so, which was almost true, because he did not attempt to go to the full extent. It was always unhygienic when I went to Willy's place, and I told him so once, but he said, ' Lorna, you are a joy.' He had a nice way, and he took me out in his car, which was a good one, but dirty inside, like his place. Jim said one day, 'He has pots of money, Lorna,' and Mavis said, 'You might make a man of him, as he is keen on you.' They always said Willy came from a good family.

But I saw that one could not do anything with him. He would not change his shirt very often, or get clothes, but he went round like a tramp, lending people money, as I have seen with my own eyes. His place was in a terrible mess, with the empty bottles, and laundry in the corner. He gave me several gifts over the period, which I took as he would have only given them away, but he never tried to go to the full extent. He never painted my portrait, as he was painting fruit on a table all that time, and they said his pictures were marvellous, and thought Willy and I were getting married.

One night, when I went home, I was upset as usual, after Willy's place. Mum and Dad had gone to bed, and I looked round our kitchen which is done in primrose and white. Then I went into the living-room, where Dad has done one wall in a patterned paper, deep rose and white, and the other walls pale rose, with white woodwork. The suite is new, and Mum keeps everything beautiful. So it came to me, all of a sudden, what a fool I was, going with Willy. I agree to equality, but as to me marrying Willy, as I said to Mavis, when I recall his place, and the good carpet gone greasy, not to mention the paint oozing out of the tubes, I think it would break my heart to sink so low.

ABSENT CHILDREN

JOHN MacKENNA

I

There was weather that year like no weather I ever remember. From Good Friday on there wasn't a drop of rain and you could count the clouds on the fingers of one hand. Right into the late part of September it stayed clear and hot.

I was working as a painter, a house painter. There was no shortage of work but the weather was the problem. I couldn't spend eight hours a day, five days a week, in the sun. But everyone wanted their house to look immaculate in the good weather. Every white had to be sparkling and every door had to be bright. People go mad at times like that. They expect it's going to last, they think the future is going to be full of sunny days and everything is always going to be as it is at that moment. That's the major problem with the human race — unbounded, groundless optimism.

Still, I wasn't about to turn down work. Even if no one else realised it, I saw the dark days of November when I'd sit looking out at rain and know there wouldn't be another stir of work until the following April.

But I wasn't going to fry for the sake of the money. So I devised a system. I'd get up at four, start at five, work till ten and knock off for the day. Then I'd come back in the evening at six and work till nine. Paint early and paint late was the philosophy. People are impressed when the painter has a philosophy. They reckon they're getting something extra for the money.

I was on a run at the time. I'd got five houses on one road. Once the first emerged shining white from four days' work the others began to fall like albino dominoes. It suited me. I didn't have to lug the ladders somewhere new every couple of days and I could buy the paint in bulk and leave it in the yards. Plus, there was the prospect of two or three weeks of watching Mrs Turner. Life wasn't always so kind.

The Turners lived in the second house on the road. I knew that because two days into the first house the bloke who lived there came up on the garage roof and sat there looking down the street at this woman weeding her garden. She was dressed, more or less, in shorts and a bikini top. I'd already seen her myself but this bloke gave me a step-by-step account of how incredible her body was.

When I'd finished work that morning I called to the rest of the houses to see if anyone else wanted work done while I was in the area. That was when the rest of the orders came in. I called to Turner's as well.

A small boy, five or six years old, opened the front door and then went off to find her.

She arrived wearing the same top and another pair of shorts. The bloke in the first house had been conservative in his enthusiasm. I asked her whether she wanted any painting done. She did but she thought her brother was coming to do it for her but would I call back on Wednesday and she could tell me for sure.

Apart from her figure, the most attractive thing about her was her hair. She had a shock of wild brown hair that seemed to explode like an almond firework around her head. When she moved this dance of colour moved in the sun, framing her tanned face and her mouth. In concentrating on her figure, the bloke in the first house had missed what her attractiveness was all about. But who was I to tell him?

I thought about her from the moment I woke on Wednesday morning. I thought about her as I cycled across the Square at five o'clock in the morning. I thought about her as I eyed the blistering paint on the shop fronts, thinking there might be work there after the winter frost got into the cracks. I thought about her as I watched the dust swirl behind my bicycle coming up the road.

In the silence of the morning I pedalled slowly past her house. A tricycle lay on its side on the front lawn. The grass was untrimmed, the side gate left open, the few flowers in the flower bed had given up.

From the top of the ladder, on a street like this, you could always match the garden to the house. The tidy gardens with well-kept flowers and neat tool sheds belonged with the houses I got to work on. The gardens full of blocks and uncut grass belonged with the peeling walls that were left half-painted or never touched at all.

That morning I looked down the line of houses and I knew by the half-finished wall in Turner's back garden that I'd get no work. Her brother would come and paint parts of the house and lose interest and not be seen again for six or seven months.

When I finished at ten, I called to her door. This time she answered herself and asked me to come in, offered me coffee. I sat with her in the kitchen. Straight away she told me her brother was coming to do the job but she'd be interested in buying the paint from me because I'd know how much was needed and I'd be sure to give her something that would last.

I told her that was no problem.

She asked me about myself and I told her as much as I'd want anyone to know. And I told her I thought her hair was smashing.

She laughed.

Well, at least it's my hair you noticed, she said.

It's really nice, I said.

Men tend to comment on other things, she said.

I nodded.

Two days later her brother arrived down to me and I gave him the paint.

Some days I'd see her and she'd wave at me. Other days I didn't see her at all. The following Monday her brother started work, scraping the walls. He did a good job. I stopped to tell him so. Every morning, over the next couple of days, I'd check how he was doing. He was a slow worker but methodical.

Mrs Turner would come and stand in the garden watching him, sometimes. I'd see her from the top of my ladder. I never seemed to see her husband come or go. His car would be there in the morning and again when I'd come back at six but I never saw him.

The following Monday I started on a house across from Turner's. Her brother had obviously worked through the weekend. The ladder was left against the front of the house. About a quarter of the wall had been painted. Three cans of paint sat at the foot of the ladder and a rag was tied loosely around the top rung. I reckoned he should finish the job that day. But he didn't. He didn't come at all and there was no sign of life about the place. Nor the next day nor the next.

On the Thursday, I saw her little boy out cycling his tricycle on the path but still the work stayed undone.

That kind of thing annoyed me. The least he could have done was to start with the front wall and leave the back undone. It was stupid.

When I saw how bloody awful it looked on the Friday morning I was even more pissed off. It wasn't Michelangelo breaking out in me, it was just so pathetic to leave a house looking that way. Why didn't her husband get off his arse and do it?

Still, I thought, I'd leave it to the Monday, see if anyone stirred and if not I'd call on the pretext of seeing what was happening. There might be a half-day's work in finishing it. It wasn't the money but I knew I'd enjoy the view from the ladder if she came out now and then.

Cycling into the street, on the Monday morning, I was praying that the job was still undone. It was. The ladder sat there, the rag still hanging in the early light, the tins untouched.

I worked until ten and then went over. The hall door was open so I tapped on it and called into the hallway. She came from the kitchen. It seemed to take her a moment to realise who I was. I put it down to the sun behind me. Then she smiled but her mouth dropped in a crooked sag that made her look stupid.

I just wondered how the work was going, I said.

She asked me to come in.

I just thought you might like the job finished off, I said. I could run it off in a couple of hours.

Would you? she said.

Of course, I said, if your brother doesn't mind.

He won't be back, she said. His little boy was killed.

Oh, I said.

It came out without my knowing and I could think of nothing else to say.

He cycled his bike out under a lorry, she said. He was ten. Just cycled it out of his gate under a lorry.

I'm sorry to hear that, I said.

And when we went over, the day it happened, she said, his wife was just back from the hospital and she was out on the street, on her knees, washing the tar where he fell. The neighbours had already done it and, anyway, they said there was very little blood. But she was out there with a brush and a basin of water, scrubbing and scrubbing. And the same the morning of the funeral, before we left for the church, she was out scrubbing the roadway. And every day since, my brother said, every day she's out there.

She stopped talking and we both sat there in the sunlit kitchen. She looked different to me. Not that she didn't look as well but this thing threw a different light on her. Hearing this little intimacy had done it. A week earlier I would have treasured any intimacy from her but now that I had heard one it had killed everything.

Whatever everything was. Nothing but my imagination. But that was killed, too. I noticed that the twist of her mouth made her look even more stupid and I was angry with myself because I couldn't put my finger on how I felt.

Why should tragedy make this woman seem stupid? There was no logic in what I felt. Was it because it impinged on my fantasy about her? I couldn't explain anything to myself. I only knew that everything had changed in my point of view. That little boy's death and his distraught mother had made this woman look sadly stupid. That had to say something about me. But I couldn't figure what.

I finished her house that morning. I worked on into the midday heat and got it finished. I laid the ladder and the cans at the side of the house and left without saying anything.

I was back at half past four the following morning and I'd finished the last of my houses by nine.

I brought up the van and put the ladders, brushes, paints and covers away. I was gone by ten, before her door was even opened. I never really thought of her again. I thought of me and her, me and the way I'd changed in looking at her and what perplexed, perplexes, most is the fact that I cannot define what happened. That frightens me. I changed inside in that moment in my way of seeing her and for no good reason other than her grief. That must say something, something terrifying, about me but the worst part is that I don't know what.

II

People think because we collect shite that we are shite. They never seem to realise how much we see into their little lives. What they shite, what they drink, what they puke, what they eat. It all ends up in the bins, doesn't it? And we see them for what they really are. You are what you throw in your bin, isn't that it? Bloody sure it is. So don't come the heavy with us. We see it all, friends, and then some.

I mean, some people throw everything out, good as new. Others throw nothing out. You can see stuff building up in their garages, in their yards and gardens, flowing out through gateways but still they hang on to the last little bit.

I mean, you see it all. Like a few weeks back I was doing the early round, right in the middle of that frigging heatwave and I was not, I mean bloody not, prepared for pissing about. But still, even in a circumstance like that you try to be a little bit, you know, discerning, you try not to fuck things up completely. Not totally. I mean, you get guys working with you who do fuck things up and automatically, without really trying, it just comes as natural to them as shit to a pig. But I try not to be like that. I meet weirdos, very strange, I mean very, very strange, people but I try to take most people as I find them. Never assume, that's what I say. Never assume, never presume. Take things as you see them. Fair's fair. I mean, that is the way to tread, isn't it?

Anyway, this morning, whatever morning, we were out doing the early run and one of the blokes is a street ahead, lining up the bins for us on one side, speeds things up instead of criss-crossing all over the place. There is a method, you know, to everything. Collecting shit has its own method, believe me.

Anyway, we swing into the road and he's walking past us, on his way to the next one, and he says to me — I just saw a fuckin' lunatic woman out scrubbing the street.

What? I said.

Scrubbing the road with a brush, there, he says, pointing to a damp patch on the road outside one of the houses.

Maybe she's Islamic, I said, throwing the head towards Mecca.

Fuckin' header, he says, throwin' the head towards the nuthouse.

We walked down the road he had just come off. The damp patch was outside a house like any other but so what? I've seen people manicuring their lawns with scissors at six o'clock on frosty mornings. There's no accounting for taste.

My clever comrade had thrown a bicycle on top of the two bins outside this house, a child's bicycle. Now, sometimes it's hard to tell shite from possessions, I know, but there are places where you draw the line and a kid's bike with one handlebar bent is not our kind of thing. I threw it back onto the lawn of the house and hoisted the first bin into the feeder bay. I turned back to get the second bin and a woman came running from the door of the house.

Take it, for Christ's sake take it, she was shouting.

Take the bicycle, take it.

She was screaming.

Okay, I said, I'll take it. I thought it was there by mistake.

Take it, she said again.

But she wasn't screaming now. The words came out in short bursts of breath.

I'll take it, I said. No big deal.

I shoved the second bin up onto the feeder and then left it back on the path. I lifted the bike and hung it on the feeder bar. There was no way I was throwing a perfectly good bike into the feeder. Anyway, she didn't even notice. She had gone back up her path and was closing the front door by the time I got to the next house.

Like I say, there's no accounting for taste. If someone wants to get rid of a good TV, a good sofa, a good bike, I'm happy to oblige. I have a shed full of stuff and people come and look at it and, eventually, it all moves.

I straightened the handle on the bike. There's a bloke coming to see it this evening. He wants a good second-hand bike for his young fellow.

I have just the job, I told him.

That's the way it goes, swings and roundabouts. I mean, that's the way it goes, isn't it?

III

There are times, when you come face to face with raw emotion, when you don't know what to say, so you say little or nothing. And there are other times when you're drawn into saying something that surprises you, leaves you in awe at your own daring.

It was like that with me. I was sitting in the yard of the house with the boy's mother. I knew her, knew her well. We'd met through all kinds of committees and things but we weren't on any kind of intimate level, we'd never had an intimate conversation in all our years. But I was sitting there with her, in the yard, two or three days after he'd been buried.

I was away when the accident happened, on a course, so when I got back and heard about it I called up to sympathise. I wasn't looking forward to it, I can tell you. But you have to get these things done. Anyway, we sat there, drinking tea, under a sunshade. The heat was just amazing. I had never experienced anything like it. I kept thinking about how difficult it must have been for the gravediggers with the ground so hard.

She was talking and talking about the little fellow and about how everytime she stepped out in the street she imagined there were flecks of his blood in the ruts of the tar.

And she stopped talking for a moment and then she said: You've no idea what it's like, have you?

I was about to say, no, I haven't, but something stopped me. I think I have, I said.

She looked at me. She hadn't expected me to say that.

I started telling her a story that I hadn't thought about for years, a story about four boys setting out one winter evening, it must have been in the end of January. Four ten-year-olds tramping out the road from Castledermot, the three miles to Mullaghcreelan Hill to sledge down the slopes in the frozen snow.

It must have been after four when we left the village. Each of us had something to slide on. A sack, two sacks, a wooden board, a car bonnet.

We were singing Christmas carols, well out of season — is anything more unseasonal than a carol in January? I asked this woman, sitting in the eighty-degree heat.

We weren't the only ones walking. There were dozens of people coming and going and no cars on the frozen, snow-locked roads between the village and the hill.

It was a blue-white evening with an almost complete moon hanging up over Ballyvass bog. Every tree in Mullaghcreelan wood was clear in its own space. I had never seen the trees so individually set before.

We traipsed up the path through the trees, following the shouts that guided us to where the procession of sledges shot down the incline and into the flattened furze bushes at the base of the hill.

The summit was a milling collection of hats, scarves, laughing figures whose faces were dark in the shadow of the moon.

We joined the queue and took our turns at screaming out into the chilled air and shooting helpessly into the frozen furze. It was worth the wait and worth the three-mile walk.

The stream of voices crying in helpless laughter went on and on and as one group disappeared home for tea another replaced it.

I don't remember exactly what I was doing when it happened, the accident. I may have been twenty yards away, on the other side of the hill, and then everything seemed to go silent and I turned and saw the adult figures disappearing awkwardly now, all their grace at sliding gone, over the edge of the hill. The children stood on the brow, staring down. I ran across to join them. A huddle of coats stood at the bottom of the slippery run, out beyond the furze, where the snow gave way to the darkness of the evergreens. Somewhere between them a figure lay on the whiteness.

She went out over the furze, someone whispered, as if what the figure had done was deserving of awe.

We stood there for seven, ten, minutes and then one of the men at the foot of the hill took off his heavy overcoat and draped it across the dark figure on the ground and we knew, without being told, that the girl was dead.

I remember her name. Miriam Thompson.

Another of the men came up the hill and took the car bonnet we had and brought it down and lifted the girl's body onto it. He and two other men began to carry it down through the trees.

The four of us followed, I think only because the bonnet was ours and we were determined not to lose it.

The men carried it down and hoisted it over the stepping stones onto the road.

No cars coming in this weather, one of them said and they set off walking for Castledermot.

We followed behind, gradually closing in on them.

At one point, coming through Hallahoise, one of them slipped and the coat slid from the girl's face. It was perfectly white in the moon and there was one slight bruise on her temple.

That couldn't have killed her, I said.

She broke her neck, one of the men said.

I didn't understand what that meant but I nodded anyway.

The longer we walked the colder it got, and the colder it got inside me. I began to shiver and I wished the men would walk faster. Coming in to Castledermot we met a group coming out. They already knew about the accident, though how I never knew. One of them was her father. Miriam Thompson's father. He took one corner of the bonnet, never lifted back the coat or anything, just took the corner, as if it had been left for him all those miles.

I was too numb to cry. I just let the procession drift away from me, ahead of me, and I turned at MacDonald's corner and walked home alone.

You still have no idea what it's like, the woman said.

I have, I have, I kept thinking. But I said nothing.

I'M RUNNING LATE

BRIDGET O'CONNOR

It started off like a normal Saturday really.

I told my mum if John rang or Andy or Eddie or Gary I wasn't in. My mum said, 'You're old enough to do your own dirty work.' I said, 'Well, I won't answer it.' My dad joined in, yelling up the stairs, 'So how many boyfriends has Lady Muck got *now*?' I said, 'In my day . . .'

He said, 'In my day, we only had one . . .'

I said, all shocked, '*You* had a boyfriend dad?'

Mum came in with the extension lead while I was diffusing my hair. 'What a surprise Tina, it's for you.' I gave her my look. I said 'Ooh . . . you-wouldn't-let-it-lie', I snatched the phone. I said, 'If that's you John Buckley you can piss right off,' but it wasn't John it was Sandy. Sandy, my mate.

She was crying. I heard her go, 'Oh Tina,' then she got taken over by a sob and the phone crashed down. What a drama queen. When I'd done my make-up and got a decent side parting I rang her back. I said, 'Oh no, really . . . did ja . . . no! . . . would you believe it . . . bloody right!' But I couldn't really listen as — with the curtains drawn and the lamp on the floor shining up into my mirror — my teeth looked really yellow. I went and drew back the curtains, switched off the light and what a relief, it was just a funny shadow. I picked up the phone again. Sandy was still bawling, '. . . it's not fair, I only did it once . . . and you know I can't stand needles . . . and oh God *hospitals* . . .' I said 'Eh?' I thought, oh-oh, silly cow's preggers. She was off again so I said, 'Look I'm running a bit late today Sandy but, Sandy, Sandy *listen* . . .' and I arranged to meet her in the arcade for a coffee and a proper chat-ette, cheer her up.

I had to go there anyway to get some new leggings for tonight.

When my dad dropped me off on the highstreet I was a couple of minutes early so I popped into Next (it's really gone down), and, when I was sure no one I know would see me, I dived into What She Wants and bought the leggings and a top that looks like silk but ain't.

By the time I get to the arcade I'm running a bit late and I see Sandy through the crowd by the telephone hoods looking well pissed off so I look like I've got the hump too so she won't say nothing. She's wearing pink Catwoman sunglasses, and a stone-washed fashion mistake. Trainers. I note them but I don't say nothing. Me, I wear black.

Sandy wants to 'talk' first, more like 'sob', but I go, 'Later love,' and pat her hand. 'Let's liven this place up a bit, God it is boring. Look how bored people are. Bored. BORING.' Sandy goes, 'Let's shop,' getting into it, and I go, 'Yeah, till we drop.' We go into Our Price first to have a look at their new boy (ugly), then The Accessory Shop. Sandy buys a pink bum-bag and a matching baseball cap and I buy a really *special* Mexican necklace and a pair of really delicate silver filigree earrings. At the counter it's obvious, the difference between us.

When we come out though we have a right laugh. We see this — nerd we went to school with, Ronnie Boyle, dressed up as the Security Guard in a big brown uniform, looking well dodgy. When he sees us his lips go, 'Oh no,' and all the colour drains from his spots. It was really funny right. He sort of side-stepped into these potted trees. Sandy goes, 'Ooh, isn't that, er, *Ronnie Boyle*' and I go, 'Nah,' studying my nails, 'it's a big lump of dogshit.' We follow him up and we follow him down the arcade and Sandy's calling out, 'Pin-head boily, boily boily pus-head.' And I'm going, 'Cor, hasn't he grown a nice bum Sandy. It's got *really* tight.' We march behind him like Nazis, Sieg-heiling and talking in loud voices about all the shops we're going to rob and all these bored people are well happy now and Ronnie Boyle is dead miserable and Sandy's going, 'Tina. If you forgot that Semtex again . . .' I almost wet my knickers. We let him off by the fountain going, 'See ya next week then, Ronnie.'

They're piping in some of Bananarama's Greatest and we sway to that for a while and dance about us as we have our fags. Then Sandy thinks she sees Sister Emelda, a nun from our old school, dressed up in a leather coat and silver leggings with dyed black, nylony hair, just like the hair on my old My Little Pony. There is a *bit* of a resemblance. The hair goes into Boots and we follow her, ducking and diving behind the counters, to see if she's going to buy any 'sanitary protection gals'. That's Sandy imitation. Sometimes Sandy's deadly boring but sometimes she's a right laugh.

We go into McDonald's. I get the coffee and some chips and Sandy takes off her sunglasses and her eyes are squinty and in slits. She goes, 'Oh Tina,' and her head is right down there on the table like it weighs a ton. I let her cry for a bit even though it's *deadly* embarrassing right and she's really showing me up. Every now and again I say, 'That's right, let it out love,' and pat her hand. I've smoked two more fags by the time she's decent. Down the next booth though, there's these three boys, leather jackets, and one of them thinks he's God's gift and starts imitating Sandy and the thing is, it's really funny, I mean he was a *really* good mimic, like Rory Bremner, but of course I can't laugh even though it's hurting my lips not to. While Sandy's recovering and putting on her make-up though I go right over and tell them to piss off out of it. The other two are nothing special but this Rory Bremner one, he's alright, so I look at him when I say it and the other two are going, 'Ooh-wa, ooh-wa,' really juvenile, and this Rory Bremner one looks me up and then looks me down and just says, really low, 'Open your coat,' and it was really embarrassing, I blushed.

When I got back to the table Sandy had her glasses back on

and it's odd when people wear dark glasses indoors because it's like they're blind and deaf. She was OK but a bit gulpy and her nose was a bit disgusting. She said this really stupid thing though. She said, 'It's funny to think I won't be around,' and I thought that was really just typical drama queen talk because she'd only have to be in a clinic for an afternoon. To take her mind off it I told her some things about the girls at work and more about this one girl, Patsy, who's got really long hair and knows it so she's always lifting it up like it's deadly heavy and oh-so luxurious and I tell her what Patsy was wearing *all* last week and that makes Sandy laugh. Then I tell her how this same girl, Patsy, and this other girl she's always going on about, 'my model friend', 'my friend the model' Murial, a right dog, when I went out with them last night and Murial saw her boyfriend in Cheers with this other girl. It was bloody funny. When I finish Sandy laughs but then the laugh turns into crying again, as I've obviously hit a nerve. I said, lying, 'Oh, come on Sandy, it won't hurt,' and these boys and the Rory Bremner one comes up and it's really funny right because this Rory one starts pretending he's a doctor and tries to take Sandy's pulse and he puts on this Swedish accent and the other two boys are being like robot nurses and I must admit it did really crack me up, though I did tell them to piss right off. Sandy gets up and tries to run to the loo but one of the boys trips her up, a bit, for a joke, and she sort of falls flat on her face and when she gets up one of the lenses from her Catwoman sunglasses is missing and she doesn't seem to know it so she looks really funny. She runs to the loo and when she's gone this Rory boy suddenly goes into The Fonz and starts calling me Babe and orders his mates to wait for him outside so they go outside and they're acting like bodyguards with their arms folded high up on their chests and he puts his arm round me and goes all Italian calling me Bella bella and I go, all thick, 'No, it's Tina tina actually.' So Sandy come back and I say, 'Excuse me kind sir,' but he won't let me out — for ages.

When I look up Sandy's just outside the door and these two boys are messing about a bit, pretending everything's in slow motion and pushing Sandy at each other and going, 'Whoops, whoop-sy,' and Sandy's ponytail is coming undone, she looks a right mess and she's blubbering again. One of them gets her from behind and holds her and the other one starts tickling her around the waist, a little bit rough. Anyway, this Rory boy starts lighting up all my fags and pretending like he can give them up any-time-he-wants, and he's got them in his nose and in his ears and a couple of girls on the next table are going, 'Look at that wanker,' but they start laughing as well. Some boys don't need much encouragement. Soon, right, he's on top of the table pretending to be Elvis Presley and singing into a ketchup bottle and it's really good and me and these two other girls pretend to be backing singers going, 'oo oo oo oo,' and swimming backwards. It was such a laugh. I mean really. Then me and these two girls pretend to be crazy fans and rush at his legs going, 'ELVIS, YOU'RE ALIVE!' Well, I'm going, 'ELVIS, YOU'RE ALIVE,' these two other girls, they're going, 'ELVIS, YOU'RE A WANKER,' but he loves it anyway and soon he's being Tom Jones with a fist down his knickers and a hungry Bob Geldof but the best one was his Jason Donovan on drugs. When the manager comes out with his staff I leg it.

There's no sign, typical, of Sandy and I'm running a bit late. Then I see quite a big crowd over by the fountain, quite a commotion. I think I hear Sandy's voice going, 'Help me, help me,' but I can't be sure as it's a bit noisy. I go to the loo, do my lips and scrunch my hair. The side parting looks really good, even though I say so myself. Then I go to the jewellers to see if they've got this new watch strap in. They ain't. When I get out of there I'm lighting up when Ronnie Boyle lurches past, pulling his portable phone out like it's a gun. When he sees me he stops dead and this big smirk stretches all his spots. I sort of *know* then. It'll be Sandy. Sandy, showing me up. He goes, and he's well pleased, 'Tina, wanna see something lovely? Over 'ere, by the fountain?' I give him the finger, pushing in the crowd, but even so when I saw what I saw, my jaw dropped.

She's only drowning in the fountain. The two leather jackets are in the fountain up to their knees in splashy water, with Sandy, my mate. They're playing to the crowd, lowering her head in and out like it's a yo-yo. Her shirt was right up round her neck, so it was bloody lucky she was wearing a body. I roll my eyes; it could only happen to Sandy. This little kid next to me is going, 'Daddy I *can't see*!' so the kid gets lifted up and the kid's going, 'I can see now, dunker dunker,' and everybody goes, 'Dunk Her Dunk Her,' and they're dunking Sandy in the water. She's soaking wet already. The funny thing is, Sandy isn't screaming or crying or struggling, nothing. When I see her face it's just — blank. Ronnie Boyle is standing on the rim of the fountain laughing, swinging the phone and his cap's right at the back of his head. His other hand conducts the crowd. Anyway, the boys do this yo-yo routine for a few minutes and everybody is chanting and I'm going, 'Hey, leave her alone,' but I can't really get heard. Then the two girls from McDonald's are next to me and one of them goes, 'Isn't that your mate?' and I say, 'Yeah,' and it was nerves really, but I laughed. The next thing I know they're in the fountain as well and I thought they were going to do something really funny right because they both bow to the crowd but then — one of them kicks this boy in the face, whips round and knees the other boy in the balls. The other girl sort of flicks her fingers under this other boy's chin and he collapses in the water. It was amazing. And they didn't seem to mind getting wet either. These two boys crawl over the rim of the fountain on to the floor and start crawling towards the arcade doors. It was all over in a second and except for fountain noise and Bananarama piping out and this little kid still singing, 'Dunker dunker,' it was deadly quiet. They carried Sandy out and her head and arms were lolling backwards. This big space was cleared for her. I sort of couldn't breathe. This picture comes into my mind of Sandy in the school playing-fields imitating Sister Emelda and another of Sandy in the dinner hall starting off a food fight. Before I know what I'm doing I'm screaming, 'SANDY SANDY WAKE UP,' and one of the girls yells to Ronnie Boyle, 'Hey, fuckwit, that better be an ambulance you're calling.' I'm on my knees by this time and I'm rubbing Sandy's hand. One of these girls pushes me out of the way and starts giving Sandy the kiss of life. I start blubbering. Me! I see me and Sandy in Debenham's trying on the wigs and both of us wetting our knickers. Then this other girl whacks me across the face and tells me to shut the fuck up and I shudder to a halt. Then, Sandy opens her eyes and looks straight at me, sort of through me, like she don't know me, turns her head and vomits up all this green water and bits of chips. The ambulance man and a woman come and they put Sandy in a chair, strap her down and carry her off. Then the woman ambulance driver comes back with red blankets and wraps them around these two girls. She puts her arms round them. Everybody is looking at me like *I* done something. Somehow I get out into the highstreet. At the ambulance the driver says to me, 'Are you coming?' and — it was nerves really. I looked at my watch. 'Oh,' I said, 'I *can't*, I'm running a bit late.'

When I got home I fell on my bed and cried and cried. Then I looked in the mirror: oh no, *centre* parting.

MIDWIFE TO THE FAIRIES

EILÍS NÍ DHUIBHNE

We were looking at the *Late Late*. It wasn't much good this night, there was a fellow from Russia, a film star or an actor or something — I'd never heard tell of him — and some young one from America who was after setting up a prostitute's hotel or call-in service or something. God, what Gay wants with that kind I don't know. All done up really snazzy, mind you, like a model or a television announcer or something. And she made a mint out of it, writing a book about her experiences if you don't mind. I do have to laugh!

I don't enjoy it as much of a Friday. It was much better of a Saturday. After the day's work and getting the bit of dinner ready for myself and Joe, sure I'm barely ready to sit down when it's on. It's not as relaxing like. I don't know, I do be all het up somehow on Fridays on account of it being such a busy day at the hospital and all, with all the cuts you really have to earn your keep there nowadays!

Saturday is busy too of course — we have to go into Bray and do the bit of shopping like, and do the bit of hoovering and washing. But it's not the same, I feel that bit more relaxed, I suppose it's on account of not being at work really. Not that I'd want to change that or anything. No way. Sixteen years of being at home was more than enough for me. That's not to say, of course, that I minded it at the time. I didn't go half-cracked the way some of them do, or let on to do. Mind you, I've no belief in that pre-menstrual tension and post-natal depression and what have you. I come across it often enough, I needn't tell you, or I used to, I should say, in the course of my duty. Now with the maternity unit gone of course all that's changed. It's an ill wind, as they say. I'll

67

say one thing for male patients, there's none of this depression carry-on with them. Of course they all think they're dying, oh dying, of sore toes and colds in the head and anything at all, but it's easier to put up with than the post-natals. I'm telling no lie.

Well, anyway, we were watching Gaybo and I was out in the kitchen wetting a cup of tea, which we like to have around ten or so of a Friday. Most nights we wait till it's nearer bedtime, but on Fridays I usually do have some little treat I get on the way home from work in The Hot Bread Shop there on the corner of Corbawn Lane, in the new shopping centre. Some little extra, a few Danish pastries or doughnuts, some little treat like that. For a change more than anything. This night I'd a few Napoleons — you know, them cream slices with icing on top.

I was only after taking out the plug when the bell went. Joe answered it of course and I could hear him talking to whoever it was and I wondered who it could be at that hour. All the stories you hear about burglars and people being murdered in their own homes . . . there was a woman over in Dalkey not six months ago, hacked to pieces at ten o'clock in the morning. God help her! . . . I do be worried. Naturally. Though I keep the chain on all the time and I think that's the most important thing. As long as you keep the chain across you're all right. Well, anyway, I could hear them talking and I didn't go out. And after a few minutes I could hear him taking the chain off and letting whoever it was in. And then Joe came in to me and he says:

'There's a fellow here looking for you, Mary. He says it's urgent.'

'What is it he wants? Sure I'm off duty now anyway, amn't I?'

I felt annoyed, I really did. The way people make use of you! You'd think there was no doctors or something. I'm supposed to be a nurse's aide, to work nine to five, Monday to Friday, except when I'm on nights. But do you think the crowd around here can get that into their heads? No way.

'I think you'd better have a word with him yourself, Mary. He says it's urgent like. He's in the hall.'

I knew of course. I knew before I seen him or heard what he had to say. And I took off my apron and ran my comb through my hair to be ready. I made up my own mind that I'd have to go out with him in the cold and the dark and miss the rest of the *Late Late*. But I didn't let on of course.

There was a handywoman in this part of the country and she used to be called out at all times of the day and night. But one night a knock came to her door. The woman got up at once and got ready to go out. There was a man standing at the door with a mare.

He was a young fellow with black hair, hardly more than eighteen or nineteen.

'Well,' says I, 'what's your trouble?'

'It's my wife,' he said, embarrassed like. He'd already told Joe, I don't know what he had to be embarrassed about. Usually you'd get used to a thing like that. But anyway he was, or let on to be.

'She's expecting. She says it's on the way.'

'And who might you be?'

'I'm her husband.'

'I see,' says I. And I did. I didn't come down in the last shower. And with all the carry-on that goes on around here you'd want to be thick or something not to get this particular message straight away. But I didn't want to be too sure of myself. Just in case. Because, after all, you can never be too sure of anything in this life. 'And why?' says I to him then. 'Why isn't she in hospital, where she should be?'

'There isn't time,' he said, as bold as brass. See what I mean about getting used to it?

'Well,' says I then, 'closing maternity wards won't stop them having babies.' I laughed, trying to be a bit friendly like. But he didn't see the joke. So, says I, 'And where do you and your wife live?'

'We live on this side of Annamoe,' he said, 'and if you're coming we'd better be going. It's on the way, she said.'

'I'll come,' I said. What else could I say? A call like that has to be answered. My mother did it before me and her mother before her, and they never let anyone down. And my mother said that her mother had never lost a child. Not one. Her corporate works of mercy, she called it. You get indulgence. And anyway I pitied him, he was only a young fellow and he was nice-looking, too, he had a country look to him. But of course I was under no obligation, none whatever, so I said, 'Not that I should come really. I'm off duty, you know, and anyway what you need is the doctor.'

'We'd rather have you,' he said.

'Well, just this time.'

'Let's go then!'

'Hold on a minute, I'll get the keys of the car from Joe.'

'Oh, sure I'll run you down and back, don't bother about your own car.'

'Thank you very much,' I said. 'But I'd rather take my own, if it's all the same to you. I'll follow on behind you.' You can't be too careful.

So I went out to start the car. But lo and behold, it wouldn't go! Don't ask me why, that car is nearly new. We got it last winter from Mike Byrne, my cousin that has the garage outside Greystones. There's less than thirty thousand miles on her and she was serviced only there a month before Christmas. But it must have been the cold or something. I tried, and he tried, and Joe, of course, tried, and none of us could get a budge out of her. So in the heel of the hunt I'd to go with him. Joe didn't want me to, and then he wanted to come himself, and your man . . . Sean O'Toole, he said his name was . . . said OK, OK, but come on quick. So I told Joe to get back inside to the fire and I went with him. He'd an old Cortina, a real old banger, a real farmer's car.

'Do not be afraid!' said the rider to her. 'I will bring you home to your own doorstep tomorrow morning!'
   She got up behind him on the mare.

Neither of us said a word the whole way down. The engine made an awful racket, you couldn't hear a thing, and anyway he was a quiet fellow with not a lot to say for himself. All I could see were headlights, and now and then a signpost: Enniskerry, Sallygap, Glendalough. And after we turned off the main road into the mountains, there were no headlights either, and no house-lights, nothing except the black night. Annamoe is at the back of beyonds, you'd never know you were only ten miles from Bray there, it's really very remote altogether. And their house was down a lane where there was absolutely nothing to be seen at all, not a house, not even a sheep. The house you could hardly see either, actually. It was kind of buried like at the side of the road, in a kind of hollow. You wouldn't know it was there at all until it was on top of you. Trees all around it too. He pulled up in front of a big five-bar gate and just gave an almighty honk on the horn, and I got a shock when the gate opened, just like that, the minute he honked. I never saw who did it. But looking back now I suppose it was one of the brothers. I suppose they were waiting for him like.

   It was a big place, comfortable enough, really, and he took me into the kitchen and introduced me to whoever was there. Polite enough. A big room it was, with an old black range and a huge big dresser, painted red and filled with all kinds of delph and crockery and stuff. Oh you name it! And about half a dozen people were sitting around the room, or maybe more than that. All watching the telly. The *Late Late* was still on and your one, the call-girl one, was still on. She was talking to a priest about unemployment. And they were glued to it, the whole lot of them, what looked like the mother and father and a whole family of big grown men and women. His family or hers I didn't bother my head asking. And they weren't giving out information for nothing either. It was a funny set up, I could see that as clear as daylight, such a big crowd of them, all living together. For all the world like in *Dallas*.

Well, there wasn't a lot of time to be lost. The mother offered me a cup of tea, I'll say that for her, and I said yes, I'd love one, and I was actually dying for a cup. I hadn't had a drop of tea since six o'clock and by this time it was after twelve. But I said I'd have a look at the patient first. So one of them, a sister I suppose it was, the youngest of them, she took me upstairs to the room where she was. The girl. Sarah. She was lying on the bed, on her own. No heat in the room, nothing.

After a while they came to a steep hill. A door opened in the side of the hill and they went in. They rode until they came to a big house and inside there were lots of people, eating and drinking. In a corner of the house they lay a woman in labour.

I didn't say a word, just put on the gloves and gave her the examination. She was the five fingers, nearly into the second stage, and she must have been feeling a good bit of pain but she didn't let on, not at all. Just lay there with her teeth gritted. She was a brave young one, I'll say that for her. The waters were gone and of course nobody had cleaned up the mess so I asked the other young one to do it, and to get a heater and a kettle of boiling water. I stayed with Sarah and the baby came just before one. A little girl. There was no trouble at all with the delivery and she seemed all right but small. I'd no way of weighing her, needless to say, but I'd be surprised if she was much more than five pounds.

'By rights she should be in an incubator,' I said to Sarah, who was sitting up smoking a cigarette, if you don't mind. She said nothing. What can you do? I washed the child . . . she was a nice little thing, God help her . . . I wrapped her in a blanket and put her in beside the mother. There was nowhere else for her. Not a cot, not even an old box. That's the way in these cases as often as not. Nobody wants to know.

I delivered the afterbirth and then I left. I couldn't wait to get back to my own bed. They'd brought me the cup of tea and all, but I didn't get time to drink it, being so busy and all. And afterwards the Missus, if that's what she was, wanted me to have a cup in the kitchen. But all I wanted then was to get out of the place. They were all so quiet and unfriendly like. Bar the mother. And even she wasn't going overboard, mind you. But the rest of them. All sitting like zombies looking at the late-night film. They gave me the creeps. I told them the child was too small, they'd have to do something about it, but they didn't let on they heard. The father, the ould fellow, that is to say, put a note in my hand . . . it was worth it from that point of view, I'll . . . admit . . . and said, 'Thank you.' Not a word from the rest of them. Glued to the telly, as if nothing was after happening. I wanted to scream at them, really. But what could I do? Anyway the young fellow, Sean, the father as he said himself, drove me home. And that was that.

Well and good. I didn't say a word about what was after happening to anyone, excepting of course to Joe. I don't talk, it's not right. People have a right to their privacy, I always say, and with my calling you've to be very careful. But to tell the truth they were on my mind. The little girl, the little baby. I knew in my heart and soul I shouldn't have left her out there, down there in the back of beyonds, near Annamoe. She was much too tiny, she needed care. And the mother, Sarah, was on my mind as well. Mind you, she seemed to be well able to look after herself, but still and all, they weren't the friendliest crowd of people I'd ever come across. They were not.

But that was that.

Until about a week later, didn't I get the shock of my life when I opened the evening paper and saw your one, Sarah, staring out at me. Her round baby face, big head of red hair. And there was a big story about the baby. Someone was after finding it dead in a shoebox, in a kind of rubbish dump they had at the back of the house. And she was arrested, in for questioning, her and maybe Sean O'Toole as well. I'm not sure. In for questioning. I could have dropped down dead there and then.

I told Joe.

'Keep your mouth shut, woman,' he said. 'You did your job and were paid for it. This is none of your business.'

And that was sound advice. But we can't always take sound advice. If we could the world would be a different place.

The thing dragged on. It was in the papers. It was on the telly. There was questioning, and more questioning, and trials and appeals and I don't know what. The whole country was in on it.

And it was on my conscience. It kept niggling at me all the time. I couldn't sleep, I got so I couldn't eat. I was all het up about it, in a terrible state really. Depressed, that's what I was, me who was never depressed before in my life. And I'm telling no lie when I say I was on my way to the doctor for a prescription for Valium when I realised there was only one thing to do. So instead of going down to the surgery, didn't I turn on my heel and walk over to the Garda barracks instead. I went in and I got talking to the sergeant straight away. Once I told them what it was about there was no delaying. And he was very interested in all I had to say, of course, and asked me if I'd be prepared to testify and I said of course I would. Which was the truth. I wouldn't want to but I would if I had to. Once I'd gone this far, of course I would.

Well, I walked out of that Garda station a new woman. It was a great load off my chest. It was like being to confession and getting absolution for a mortal sin. Not that I've ever committed a mortler, of course. But you know what I mean. I felt relieved.

Well and good.

Well. You'll never believe what happened to me next. I was just getting back to my car when a young fellow . . . I'd seen him somewhere before, I know that, but I couldn't place him. He might have been the fellow that came for me on the night, Sean, but he didn't look quite like him. I just couldn't place him at all . . . anyway, he was standing there, right in front of the car. And I said hello, just in case I really did know him, just in case it really was him. But he said nothing. He just looked behind him to see if anyone was coming, and when he saw that the coast was clear he just pulled out a big huge knife out of his breast pocket and pointed it at my stomach. He put the heart crossways in me. And then he says, in a real low voice, like a gangster in *Hill Street Blues* or something:

'Keep your mouth shut. Or else!'

And then he pushed a hundred pounds into my hand and he went off.

I was in bits. I could hardly drive myself home with the shock. I told Joe of course. But he didn't have a lot of sympathy for me.

'God Almighty, woman,' he said, 'what possessed you to go to the guards? You must be off your rocker. They'll be arresting you next!'

Well, I'd had my lesson. The guard called for me the next week but I said nothing. I said I knew nothing and I'd never heard tell of them all before, the family I mean. And there was nothing they could do, nothing. The sergeant hadn't taken a statement from me, and that was his mistake and my good luck I suppose, because I don't know what would have happened to me if I'd testified. I told a priest about the lie to the guards, in confession, to a Carmelite in Whitefriar Street, not to any priest I know. And he said God would understand. 'You did your best, and that's all God will ask of you. He does not ask of us that we put our own lives in danger.'

There was a fair one day at Baile an Droichid. And this woman used to make market socks and used to wash them and scour them and take them to the fair and get them sold. She used to make them up in dozen bunches and sell them at so much the dozen.

And as she walked over the bridge there was a great blast of wind. And who should it be but the people of the hill, the wee folk! And she looked among them and saw among them the same man who had taken her on the mare's back to see his wife.

'How are ye all? And how is the wife?' she said.

He stood and looked at her.

'Which eye do you see me with?' he asked.

'With the right eye,' she said.

Before he said another word he raised his stick and stuck it in her eye and knocked her eye out on the road.

'You'll never see me again as long as you live,' he said.

Sometimes I do think of the baby. She was a dawny little thing, there's no two ways about it. She might have had a chance, in intensive care. But who am I to judge?

PLACES TO LOOK FOR YOUR MIND

LORRIE MOORE

The sign said 'Welcome to America', in bold red letters. Underneath, in smaller blue, Millie had spelled out *John Spee*. Comma, *John Spee*. She held it up against her chest like a locket, something pressed against the heart for luck: a pledge of allegiance. She was waiting for a boy she didn't know, someone she'd never even seen a photograph of, an English acquaintance of her daughter Ariel's. Ariel was on a junior semester abroad, and the boy was the brother of one of her Warwickshire dorm-mates. He was an auto mechanic in Surrey, and because he'd so badly wanted to come to the States, Ariel had told him that if he needed a place, he could stay with her parents in New Jersey. She had written ahead to inform them. 'I told John Spee he could stay in Michael's old room, unless you are still using it as an "office". In which case he can stay in mine.'

Office in quotation marks. Millie had once hoped to start a business in that room, something to do with recycling and other environmental projects. She had hoped to be hired on a consultant basis, but every time she approached a business or community organisation they seemed confounded as to what they would consult her for. For a time Millie had filled the room with business cards and supplies and receipts for various expenses in case she ever filed a real tax form. Her daughter and her husband had rolled their eyes and looked, embarrassed, in the other direction.

"Office". Ariel made her quotation marks as four quick slashes, not the careful sixes and nines Millie had been trained long ago to write. There was something a bit spoiled about Ariel, a quiet impudence, which troubled Millie. She had written back to her daughter. 'Your father and I have no real objections, and certainly

77

it will be nice to meet your friend. But you must check with us next time *before* you volunteer *our home*.' She had stressed *our home* with a kind of sternness that lingered regretlessly. 'You mustn't take things for granted.' It was costing them good money to send Ariel abroad. Millie herself had never been to England. Or anywhere, when you got right down to it. Once, as a child, she had been to Florida, but she remembered so little of it. Mostly just the glare of the sky, and some vague and shuddering colors.

People filed out from the Newark customs gate, released and weary, one of them a thin, red-haired boy of about twenty. He lit a cigarette, scanned the crowd, and then, spying Millie, headed towards her. He wore an old, fraying camel hair sports jacket, sneakers of blue, man-made suede, and a baseball cap, which said *Yankees*, an ersatz inscription.

'Are you Mrs Keegan?' he asked, pronouncing it *Kaygan*.

'Um, yes, I am,' Millie said, and blushed as if surprised. She let the sign, which with its crayoned and overblown message now seemed ludicrous, drop to her side. Her other hand she thrust out in greeting. She tried to smile warmly but wondered if she looked 'fakey', something Ariel sometimes accused her of. 'It's like you're doing everything from a magazine article,' Ariel had said. 'It's like you're trying to be happy out of a book.' Millie owned several books about trying to be happy.

John shifted his cigarette into his other hand and shook Millie's. 'John Spee,' he said. He pronounced it *Spay*. His hand was big and bony, like a chicken claw.

'Well, I hope your flight was uneventful,' said Millie.

'Oh, not really,' said John. 'Sat next to a bloke with stories about the Vietnam War and watched two movies about it. *The Deer Hunter* and, uh, I forget the other.' He seemed apprehensive yet proud of himself for having arrived where he'd arrived.

'Do you have any more luggage than that? Is that all you have?'

''Zall I got!' he chirped, holding a small duffel bag and turning around just enough to let Millie see his U.S. Army knapsack.

'You don't want this sign, do you?' asked Millie. She creased it, folded it in quarters like a napkin, and shoved it into her own bag. Over the PA system a woman's voice was repeating, 'Mr Boone, Mr Daniel Boone. Please pick up the courtesy line.'

'Isn't that funny,' said Millie.

On the drive home to Terracebrook, John Spee took out a pack of Johnny Parliaments and chain-smoked. He told Millie about his life in Surrey, his mates at the pub there, in a suburb called Worcester Park. 'Never was much of a student,' he said, 'so there was no chance of me going to university.' He spoke of the scarcity of work and of his 'flash car', which he had sold to pay for the trip. He had worked six years as an auto mechanic, a job that he had quit to come here. 'I may stay in the States a long time,' he said. 'I'm thinking of New York City. Wish I hadn't had to sell me flash car, though.' He looked out at a souped-up Chevrolet zooming by them.

'Yes, that's too bad,' said Millie. What should she say? On the car radio there was news of the garbage barge, and she turned it up to hear. It had been rejected by two states and two foreign countries, and was floating, homeless, toward Texas. 'I used to have a kind of business,' she explained to John. 'It was in garbage and trash recycling. Nothing really came of it, though.' The radio announcer was quoting something now. *The wretched refuse of our teeming shores*, he was saying. *Yeah, yeah, yeah*, he was saying.

'Now I'm taking a college course through the mail,' Millie said, then reddened. This had been her secret. Even Hane didn't know. 'Don't tell my husband,' she added quickly. 'He doesn't know. He doesn't quite approve of my interest in business. He's a teacher. Religious studies at the junior college.'

John gazed out at the snag of car dealerships and the fast-food shacks of Route 22. 'Is he a vicar or something?' He inhaled his cigarette, holding the smoke in like a thought.

'Oh, no,' said Millie. She sighed a little. Hane did go to church every Sunday. He was, she knew, a faithful man. She herself had stopped going regularly over a year ago. Now she went only once in a while, like a visit to an art museum, and it saddened Hane, but she just couldn't help it. 'It's not my thing,' she had said to her husband. It was a phrase she had heard Ariel use, and it seemed a good one, powerful with self-forgiveness, like Ariel herself.

'The traffic on this route is almost always heavy,' said Millie. 'But everyone drives very fast, so it doesn't slow you down.'

John glanced sideways at her. 'You look a little like Ariel,' he said.

'Really?' said Millie brightly, for she had always thought her daughter too pretty to have come from Hane and her. Ariel had the bones and eyes of someone else, the daughter of royalty, or a movie star. Mitzi Gaynor's child. Or the Queen's. Ironically, it had been Michael, their eldest, who had seemed so clearly theirs.

'Oh, yes,' said John. 'You don't think so?'

Usually in spring Millie hurried guests immediately out into the backyard so that they could see her prize tulips – which really weren't hers at all but had belonged to the people who owned the house before them. The woman had purchased prize bulbs and planted them even into the edge of the next-door neighbor's yard. The yards were small, for sure, but the couple had been a young managerial type, and Millie had thought perhaps aggressive gardening went with such people.

Millie swung the car into the driveway and switched off the ignition. 'I'll spare you the tulips for now,' she said to John. 'You probably would like to rest. With jet lag and all.'

'Yeah,' said John. He got out of the car and swung his duffel bag over his shoulder. He surveyed the identical lawns, still a pale, wintry ocher, and the small, boxy split-levels, their stingy porches fronting the entrances like goatees. He looked startled. *He thought we were going to be rich Americans*, thought Millie. 'Are you tired?' she said aloud.

'Not so bad.' He breathed deeply and started to perspire.

Millie went up the steps, took a key out from behind the black metal mailbox, and opened the door. 'Our home is yours,' she said, swinging her arms wide, showing him in.

John stepped in with a lit cigarette between his teeth, his eyes squinting from the smoke. He put his bag and knapsack down and looked about the living room. There were encyclopedias and ceramic figurines. There were some pictures of Ariel placed high on a shelf. Much of the furniture was shredded and old. There was a Bible and a *Time* magazine on the coffee table.

'Let me show you your room,' said Millie, and she took him down a short corridor and opened the door on the right. 'This was once my son's room,' she said, 'but he's — he's no longer with us.' John nodded somberly. 'He's not dead,' Millie hastened to add, 'he's just not with us.' She cleared her throat — there was something in it, a scratch, a bruise of words. 'He left home ten years ago, and we never heard from him again. The police said drugs.' Millie shrugged. 'Maybe it was drugs.'

John was looking for a place to flick his ashes. Millie grabbed a potted begonia from the sill and held it out for him. 'There's a desk and a filing cabinet here, which I was using for my business, so you can just ignore those.' On the opposite wall there was a cot and a blond birch dresser. 'Let me know if you need anything. Oh! Towels are in the bathroom, on the back of the door.'

'Thanks,' said John, and he looked at his watch like a man with plans.

'Leftovers is all we've got tonight!' Millie emerged from the kitchen with quilted pot-holder mittens and a large cast-iron skillet. She beamed like the presenters on the awards shows she sometimes watched; she liked to watch TV when it was full of happiness.

Hane, who had met John coming out of the bathroom and had mumbled an embarrassed how-do-you-do, now sat at the head of the dining room table, waiting to serve the food. John sat kitty-corner, Michael's old place. He regarded the salad bowl, the clover outlines of the peppers, the clock stares of the tomato slices. He had taken a shower and parted his wet hair rather violently on the left.

'You'd think we'd be able to do a little better than this on your first night in America,' said Hane, poking with a serving spoon at the fried pallet of mashed potatoes, turnips, chopped broccoli, and three eggs over easy. 'Millie here, as you probably know already, is devoted to recycling.' His tone was of good-natured mortification, a self-deprecating singsong that was his way of reprimanding his family. He made no real distinction between himself and his family. They were he. They were his feminine, sentimental side and warranted, even required, running commentary.

'It's all very fine,' said John.

'Would you like skim milk or whole?' Millie asked him.

'Whole, I think,' and then, in something of a fluster, he said, 'Water, I mean, please. Don't trouble yourself, Mrs Keegan.'

'In New Jersey, water's as much trouble as milk,' said Millie. 'Have whichever you want, dear.'

'Water, please, then.'

'Are you sure?'

'Milk, then, I guess, thank you.'

Millie went back into the kitchen to get milk. She wondered whether John thought they were poor and milk a little too expensive for them. The neighborhood probably did look shabby. Millie herself had been disappointed when they'd first moved here from the north part of town, after Ariel had started college and

Hane had not been promoted to full professor rank, as he had hoped. It had been the only time she had ever seen her husband cry, and she had started to think of themselves as poor, though she knew that was silly. At least a little silly.

Millie stared into the refrigerator, not looking hungrily for something, anything, to assuage her restlessness, as she had when she was younger, but now forgetting altogether why she was there. *Look in the refrigerator*, was her husband's old joke about where to look for something she'd misplaced. 'Places to look for your mind,' he'd say, and then he'd recite a list. Once she had put a manila folder in the freezer by mistake.

'What did I want?' she said aloud, and the refrigerator motor kicked on in response to the warm air. She had held the door open too long. She closed it and went back and stood in the dining room for a moment. Seeing John's empty glass, she said, 'Milk. That's right,' and promptly went and got it.

'So how was the flight over?' asked Hane, handing John a plate of food. 'If this is too much turnip, let me know. Just help yourself to salad.' It had been years since they'd had a boy in the house, and he wondered if he knew how to talk to one. Or if he ever had. 'Wait until they grow up,' he had said to Millie of their own two children. 'Then I'll know what to say to them.' Even at student conferences he tended to ramble a bit, staring out the window, never, never into their eyes.

'By the time they've grown up it'll be too late,' Millie had said.

But Hane had thought, *No, it won't*. By that time he would be president of the college, or dean of a theological school somewhere, and he would be speaking from a point of achievement that would mean something to his children. He could then tell them his life story. In the meantime, his kids hadn't seemed interested in his attempts at conversation. 'Forget it, Dad,' his son had always said to him. 'Just forget it.' No matter what Hane said, standing in a doorway or serving dinner — 'How was school, son?' – Michael would always tell him just to forget it, Dad. One time, in the living room, Hane had found himself unable to bear it, and had grabbed Michael by the arm and struck him twice in the face.

'This is fine, thank you,' said John, referring to his turnips. 'And the flight was fine. I saw movies.'

'Now, what is it you plan to do here exactly?' There was a gruffness in Hane's voice. This happened often, though Hane rarely intended it, or even heard it, clawing there in the punctuation.

John gulped at some milk and fussed with his napkin.

'Hane, let's save it for after grace,' said Millie.

'Your turn,' said Hane, and he nodded and bowed his head. John Spee sat upright and stared.

Millie began. ' "Bless this food to our use, and us to thy service. And keep us ever needful of the minds of others." Wopes. "Amen." Did you hear what I said?' She grinned, as if pleased.

'We assumed you did that on purpose, didn't we, John?' Hane looked out over his glasses and smiled conspiratorially at the boy.

'Yes,' said John. He looked at the ceramic figurines on the shelf to his right. There was a ballerina and a clown.

'Well,' said Millie, 'maybe I just did.' She placed her napkin in her lap and began eating. She enjoyed the leftovers, the warm, rising grease of them, their taste and ecology.

'It's very good food, Mrs Keegan,' said John, chewing.

'Before you leave, of course, I'll cook up a real meal. Several.'

'How long you staying?' Hane asked.

Millie put her fork down. 'Hane, I told you: three weeks.'

'Maybe only two,' said John Spee. The idea seemed to cheer him. 'But then maybe I'll find a flat in the Big Apple and stay forever.'

Millie nodded. People from out of town were always referring to the Big Apple, like some large forbidden fruit one conquered with mountain gear. It seemed to give them energy, to think of it that way.

'What will you *do*?' Hane studied the food on his fork, letting it hover there, between his fork and his mouth, a kind of ingestive purgatory. Hane's big fear was idleness. Particularly in boys. *What will you do?*

'Hane,' cautioned Millie.

'In England none of me mates have jobs. They're all jealous 'cause I sold the car and came here to New York.'

'This is New Jersey, dear,' said Millie. 'You'll see New York tomorrow. I'll give you a timetable for the train.'

'You sold your car,' repeated Hane. Hane had never once sold a car outright. He had always traded them in. 'That's quite a step.'

The next morning Millie made a list of things for John to do and see in New York. Hane had already left for his office. She sat at the dining room table and wrote:

> *Statue of Liberty*
> *World Trade Center*
> *Times Square*
> *Broadway 2-fors*

She stopped for a moment and thought.

> *Metropolitan Museum of Art*
> *Circle Line Tour*

The door of the 'guest' room was still closed. Funny how it pleased her to have someone in that space, someone really using it. For too long she had just sat in there doodling on her business cards and thinking about Michael. The business cards had been made from recycled paper, but the printers had forgotten to mention that on the back. So she had inked it in herself. They had also forgotten to print Millie's middle initial – Environmental Project Adviser, Mildred *R.* Keegan – and so she had sat in there for weeks, ballpointing the *R* back in, card after card. Later Ariel had told her the cards looked stupid that way, and Millie had had to agree. She then spent days sitting at the desk, cutting the cards into gyres, triangles, curlicues, like a madness, like a business turned madness. She left them, absentmindedly, around the house, and Hane began to find them in odd places – on the kitchen counter, on the toilet tank. He turned to her one night in bed and said, 'Millie, you're fifty-one. You don't have to have a career. Really, you don't,' and she put her hands to her face and wept.

John Spee came out of his room. He was completely dressed, his bright hair parted neat as a crease, the white of his scalp startling as surgery.

'I've made a list of things you'll probably want to do,' said Millie.

John sat down. 'What's this?' He pointed to the Metropolitan Museum of Art. 'I'm not that keen to go to museums. We always went to the British Museum for school. My sister likes that kind of stuff, but not me.'

'These are only suggestions,' said Millie. She placed a muffin and a quartered orange in front of him.

John smiled appreciatively. He picked up a piece of orange, pressed it against his teeth, and sucked it to a damp, stringy mat.

'I can drive you to the station to catch the ten-o-two train, if you want to leave in fifteen minutes,' said Millie. She slid sidesaddle into a chair and began eating a second muffin. Her manner was sprinkled with youthful motions, as if her body were on occasion falling into a memory or a wish.

'That would be lovely, thanks,' said John.

'Did you really not like living in England?' asked Millie, but they were both eating muffins, and it was hard to talk.

At the station she pressed a twenty into his hand and kissed him on the cheek. He stepped back away from her and got on the train. 'See a play,' Millie mouthed at him through the window.

At dinner it was just she and Hane. Hane was talking about Jesus again, the Historical Jesus, how everyone misunderstood Christ's prophetic powers, how Jesus himself had been mistaken.

'Jesus thought the world was going to end,' said Hane, 'but he was wrong. It wasn't just Jerusalem. He was predicting the end of the whole world. Eschatologically, he got it wrong. He said it outright, but he was mistaken. The world kept right on.'

'Perhaps he meant it as a kind of symbol. You know, poetically, not literally.' Millie had heard Hane suggest this himself. They were his words she was speaking, one side of his own self-argument.

'No, he meant it literally,' Hane barked a little fiercely.

'Well, we all make mistakes,' said Millie. 'Isn't the world funny that way.' She always tried to listen to Hane. She knew that few students registered for his courses anymore, and those that did tended to be local fundamentalists, young ignorant people, said Hane, who had no use for history or metaphor. They might as well just chuck the Bible! In class Hane's primary aim was reconciling religion with science and history, but these young 'Pentecostalists,' as Hane referred to them, didn't believe in science or history. 'They're mindless, some of these kids. And if you want your soul nourished – and they do, I think – you've got to have a mind.'

'Cleanliness is next to godliness,' said Millie.

'What are you talking about?' asked Hane. He looked depressed and impatient. There were times when he felt he had married a stupid woman, and it made him feel alone in the world.

'I've been thinking about the garbage barge,' said Millie. 'I

guess my mind's wandering around, just like that heap of trash.'
She smiled. She had been listening to all the reports on the barge,
had charted its course from Islip, where she had relatives, to
Morehead City, where she had relatives. 'Imagine,' she had said
to her neighbor in their backyards, near the prize tulips that
belonged to neither one of them. 'Relatives in both places!
Garbagey relatives!'

Millie wiped her mouth with her napkin. 'It has nowhere to
go,' she said now to her husband.

Hane served himself more leftovers. He thought of Millie and
this interest of hers in ecology. It baffled and awed him, like a
female thing. In the kitchen Millie kept an assortment of boxes
for recycling household supplies. She had boxes marked
Aluminum, *Plastic*, *Dry Trash*, *Wet Trash*, *Garbage*. She had twice
told him the difference between garbage and trash, but the
distinction never meant that much to him, and he always forgot
it. Last night she had told him about swans in the park who were
making their nests from old boots and plastic six-pack rings. 'Laying
their eggs in litter,' she'd said. Then she told him to be more
fatherly toward John Spee, to take a friendly interest in the boy.

'Is this the end of the leftovers?' asked Hane. At his office at
the college he ate very light lunches. Often he just brought a
hard-boiled egg and sprinkled it carefully with salt, shaking the
egg over the wastebasket if he got too much on by mistake.

'This is it,' said Millie, standing. She picked up the skillet, and
taking a serving spoon, scraped and swirled up the hardened,
flat-bottomed remnants. 'Here,' she said, holding it all in front of
Hane. 'Open up.'

Hane scowled. 'Come on, Millie.'

'Just one last spoonful. Tomorrow I cook fresh.'

Hane opened his mouth, and Millie fed him gently, carefully,
because the spoon was large.

Afterward they both sat in the living room and Hane read aloud a passage from 2 Thessalonians. Millie stared off like a child at the figurines, the clown and the ballerina, and thought about Ariel, travelling to foreign countries and meeting people. What it must be like to be young today, with all those opportunities. Once, last semester, before she'd left for England, Ariel had said, 'You know, Mom, there's a girl in my class at Rutgers with exactly your name: Mildred Keegan. Spelled the same and everything.'

'Really?' exclaimed Millie. Her face had lit up. This was interesting.

But Ariel was struck with afterthought. 'Yeah. Only...well, actually she flunked out last week.' Then Ariel began to laugh, and had to get up and leave the room.

At nine o'clock, after she had peeled the labels off an assortment of tin cans, and rinsed and stacked them, Millie went to pick up John Spee at the train station.

'So what all did you do in the city?' asked Millie, slowing for a red light and glancing at the boy. She had left the house in too much of a rush, and now, looking quickly in the rearview mirror, she attempted to smooth the front of her hair, which had fallen onto her forehead in a loose, droopy tangle. 'Did you see a play? I hear there's some funny ones.' Millie loved plays, but Hane didn't so much.

'No, didn't feel like buzzing the bees for a play.' He said *ply*.

'Oh,' said Millie. Her features sagged to a slight frown. Buzzing the bees. Ariel had used this expression once. *Money, honey, bees*, Ariel had explained impatiently. *Get it?* 'Did you go down to Battery Park and see the Statue of Liberty? It's so beautiful since they cleaned it.' Not that Millie had seen it herself, but it was in all the newsmagazines a while back, and the pictures had made it seem very holy and grand.

The light turned green, and she swung the car around the corner. At night this part of New Jersey could seem quiet and sweet as a real hometown.

'I just walked around and looked at the buildings,' said John, glancing away from her, out the car window at the small darkened business district of Terracebrook. 'I went to the top of the Empire State Building, and then I went back and went to the top again.'

'You went twice.'

'Twice, yeah. Twice.'

'Well, good!' Millie exclaimed. And when they pulled into the driveway, she exclaimed it again. 'Well, good!'

'So how was the city?' boomed Hane, rising stiff and hearty, so awkwardly wanting to make the boy feel at home that he lunged at him a bit, big and creaky in the joints from having been sitting and reading all evening.

'Fine, thank you,' said John, who then went quickly to his room.

Millie gave Hane a worried look, then followed and knocked on John's door. 'John, would you like some supper? I've got a can of soup and some bread and cheese for a sandwich.'

'No, thank you,' John called through the door. Millie thought she heard him crying – was he crying? She walked back into the living room toward Hane, who gave her a shrug, helpless, bewildered. He looked at her for some reassuring word.

Millie shrugged back and walked past him into the kitchen. Hane followed her and stood in the doorway.

'I guess I'm not the right sort of person for him,' he said. 'I'm not a friendly man by nature. That's what he needs.' Hane took off his glasses and cleaned them on the hem of his shirt.

'You're a stack of apologies,' said Millie, kissing him on the cheek. 'Here. Squash this can.' She bent over and put a rinsed and label-less can near his shoe. Hane lifted his foot and came down on it with a bang.

The next morning was Friday, and John Spee wanted to go into the city again. Millie drove him to catch the ten-o-two. 'Have a nice time,' she said to him on the platform. 'I'll pick you up tonight.' As the train pulled up, steamy and deafening, she reminded him again about the half-price tickets for Broadway shows.

Back at the house, Millie got out the Hoover and began vacuuming. Hane, who had no classes on Friday, sat in the living room doing a crossword puzzle. Millie vacuumed around his feet. 'Lift up,' she said.

In John Spee's close and cluttered room she vacuumed the sills, even vacuumed the ceiling and the air, before she had to stop. All around the floor there were matchbooks from Greek coffee shops and odd fliers handed out on the street: *Live Eddie*; *Crazy Girls*; *20% off Dinner Specials, now until Easter*. Underwear had been tossed on the floor, and there were socks balled in one corner of the desk.

Millie flicked off the Hoover and began to tidy the desktop. This was at one time to have been her business headquarters, and now look at it. She picked up the socks and noticed a spiral notebook underneath. It looked a little like a notebook she had been using for her correspondence course, the same shade of blue, and she opened it to see.

On the first page was written, *Crazy People I Have Met in America*. Underneath there was a list.

> *1. Asian man in business suit waiting on subway platform. Screaming.*
> *2. Woman in park walking dog. Screaming. Tells dog to walk like a lady.*
> *3. In coffee shop, woman with food spilling out of her mouth. Yells at fork.*

Millie closed the notebook quickly. She was afraid to read on, afraid of what number four might be, or number five. She put the notebook out of her mind and moved away from the desk, unplugged the Hoover, wound up the cord, then collected the odd, inside-out clumps of clothes from under the cot and thought again of her garbage business, how she had hoped to run it out of this very room, how it seemed now to have crawled back in here – her poor little business! – looking a lot like laundry. What she had wanted was garbage, and instead she got laundry. 'Ha!' She laughed out loud.

'What?' called Hane. He was still doing the crossword in the living room.

'Not you,' said Millie. 'I'm just going to put some things in the wash for John.' She went downstairs to the laundry room, with its hampers of recyclable rags, its boxes of biodegradable detergent, its cartons of bottles with the labels soaked off them, the bags of aluminum foil and tins. *This* was an office, in a way, a one-woman room: a stand against the world. Or *for* the world. She meant *for* the world.

Millie flicked on the radio she kept propped on the dryer. She waited through two commercials, and then the news came on: The garbage barge was heading back from Louisiana. 'I'll bet in that garbage there's a lot of trash,' she wagered aloud. This was her distinction between garbage and trash, which she had explained many times to Hane: Garbage was moist and rotting and had to be plowed under. Trash was primmer and papery and could be reused. Garbage could be burned for gas, but trash could be dressed up and reissued. Retissued! Recycled Kleenex, made from cheap, recyclable paper – that was a truly viable thing, that was something she had hoped to emphasise, but perhaps she had not highlighted it enough in her initial materials. Perhaps people thought she was talking about garbage when she was talking about trash. Or vice versa. Perhaps no one had understood.

PLACES TO LOOK FOR YOUR MIND

Certainly, she had neglected to stress her best idea, the one about
subliminal advertising on soap operas: having characters talk about
their diseases and affairs at the same time that they peeled labels
off cans and bundled newspapers. She was sure you could get
programs to do this.

She turned the washer dial to *Gentle* and pushed it in. Warm
water rushed into the machine like a falls, like a honeymoon,
recycled, the same one, over and over.

When Millie picked John up at the station, he told her about the
buildings again.

'You probably didn't get a chance to see a play, then,' said
Millie, but he didn't seem to hear her.

'Going in tomorrow to look some more,' he said. He flicked his
lighter until it lit. He smoked nervously. 'Great cars there, too.'

'Well, wonderful,' said Millie. But when she looked at him there
was a grayness in his face. His life seemed to be untacking itself,
lying loose about him like a blouse. A life could do that. Millie
thought of people in the neighborhood she might introduce him
to. There was a boy of about twenty-two who lived down the
street. He worked at a lawn and seed company and seemed like
the friendly sort.

'There's someone on the street I should introduce you to,'
she said. 'He's a boy about your age. I think you'd like him.'

'Really don't want to meet anyone,' he said. He pronounced it
mate. 'Unless I off to.'

'Oh, no,' said Millie. 'You don't off to.' Sometimes she slipped
accidentally into his accent. She hoped it made him feel more at
home.

In the morning she drove him again to the station for the ten-
o-two train. 'I'm getting fond of this little jaunt every day,' she
said. She smiled and meant it. She threw her arms around the
boy, and this time he kissed her back.

93

At midnight that same day, Ariel phoned from Europe. She was traveling through the Continent – English universities had long spring vacations, a month, and she had headed off to France and to Italy, from where she was calling.

'Venice!' exclaimed Millie. 'How wonderful!'

'That's just great, honey,' said Hane on the bedroom extension. He didn't like to travel much, but he didn't mind it in other people.

'Of course,' said Ariel, 'there's an illusion here that you are separate from the garbage. That the water and food are different from the canal sewage. It's a crucial illusion to maintain. A psychological passport.'

A psychological passport! How her daughter spoke! Children just got so far away from you. 'What's the food like?' asked Millie. 'Are you eating a lot of manicotti?'

'Swamp food. Watercress and dark fishes.'

'Oh, I so envy you,' said Millie. 'Imagine, Hane, being in Venice, Italy.'

'How's John Spee?' asked Ariel, changing the subject. Often when she phoned her parents, they each got on separate extensions and just talked to each other. They discussed money problems and the other's faults with a ferocity they couldn't quite manage face to face.

'All right,' said Millie. 'John is out taking a walk right now around the neighborhood, though it's a little late for it.'

'He is? What time is it?'

'It's about midnight,' said Hane on the other extension. He was in his pajamas, under the covers.

'Gee, I miscalculated the time. I hope I didn't wake you guys up.'

'Of course not, honey,' said Millie. 'You can phone anytime.'

'So it's midnight and John Spee's walking around in that depressing suburban neighborhood? How frightening.' Ariel's voice was staticky but loud. The thoughtless singsong of her words sunk its way into

Millie like something both rusty and honed. 'Is he alone?'

'Yes,' said Millie. 'He probably just wanted some fresh air. He's been spending all his days in the city. He keeps going to the top of the Empire State Building, then just walks around looking at other tall buildings. And the cars. He hasn't been to any plays or anything.'

There was a silence. Hane cleared his throat and said into the phone, 'I suppose I'm not the best sort of person for him. He probably needs a man who is better with kids. Somebody athletic, maybe.'

'Tell us more about Italy, dear,' Millie broke in. She imagined Italy would be like Florida, all colors and light, but with a glorious ruin here and there, and large stone men with no clothes but with lovely pigeons on their heads. Perhaps there were plays.

'It's great,' said Ariel, 'It's hard to describe.'

At twelve-fifteen they hung up. Hane, because he was reading the Scripture the next morning in church, went off to sleep. But Millie was restless and roamed the house, room after room, waiting for John to return. She thought about Ariel again, how much the girl's approval had come to mean to her, and wondered how one's children got so powerful that way. The week before Ariel left for England, the two of them had gone to a movie together. It was something they had not done since Ariel had been little, and so Millie had looked forward to it, like a kind of party. But during the opening credits Millie had started talking. She started to tell Ariel about someone she knew who used to be a garbage man but who was now making short industrial films for different companies. He had taken a correspondence course.

'Mom, you're talking so loudly,' Ariel hissed at her in the dark of the movie theater. Ariel had pressed her index finger to her lips and said, 'Shhhh!' as if Millie were a child. The movie had started, and Millie looked away, her face crumpling, her hand to her eyes so her daughter couldn't see. She tried to concentrate on the movie, the sounds and voices of it, but it all seemed underwater and far away. When afterward, in a restaurant, Ariel wanted to discuss the film, the way she said she always did – an *intellectual* discussion like a college course – Millie had just nodded and shrugged. Occasionally she had tried to smile at her daughter, saying, 'Oh, I agree with you there,' but the smile flickered and trembled and Ariel had looked at her, at a loss, as if her own mother were an idiot who had followed her to the movie theater, hoping only for a kind word or a dime.

Millie looked out the guest room window – John Spee's room – into the night to see whether she might spy John, circling the house or kicking a stone along the street. The moon was full, a porthole of sun, and Millie half expected to glimpse John sitting on someone's front step, not theirs, kneecaps pressed into the soft bulges of his eyes. How disappointing America must seem. To wander the streets of a city that was not yours, a city with its back turned, to be a boy from far away and step ashore here, one's imagination suddenly so concrete and mistaken, how could that not break your heart? But perhaps, she thought, John had dreamed so long and hard of this place that he had hoped it right out of existence. Probably no place in the world could withstand such an assault of human wishing.

She turned away from the window and again opened the blue notebook on the desk.

> *More Crazy People I Have Seen in the States (than anywhere).*
> *11. Woman with white worms on her legs. Flicking off worms.*
> *12. Girl on library steps, the step is her home. Comb and mirror and toothbrush with something mashed in it laid out on step like a dressertop. No teeth. Screaming.*

13. Stumbling man. Arms folded across his chest.
Bumps into me hard. Bumps with hate in his eyes.
I think, 'This bloke hates me, why does he hate me?'
It smells. I run a little until I am away.

The front door creaked open, and shut with a thud. Millie closed the notebook and went out into the living room in just her nightgown. She wanted to say good night and make certain John locked the door.

He seemed surprised to see her. 'Thought I'd just hit the hay,' he said. This was something he'd probably heard Ariel say once. It was something she liked to say.

'Ariel phoned while you were out,' said Millie. She folded her arms across her breasts to hide them, in case they showed through her thin gown.

'That so?' John's face seemed to brighten and fall at the same time. He combed a hand through his hair, and strands dropped back across his part in a zigzag of orange. 'She's coming home soon, is she?' It occurred to Millie that John didn't know Ariel well at all.

'No,' she said. 'She's traveling on the Continent. That's how Ariel says it: *on the Continent*. But she asked about you and says hello.'

John looked away, hung up his coat in the front closet, on a hook next to his baseball cap, which he hadn't worn since his first day. 'Thought she might be coming home,' said John. He couldn't look directly at Millie. Something was sinking in him like a stone.

'Can I make you some warm milk?' asked Millie. She looked in the direction John seemed to be looking: at the photographs of Ariel. There she was at her high school graduation, all formal innocence, lies snapped and pretty. It seemed now to Millie that Ariel was too attractive, that she was careless and hurt people.

'I'll just go to bed, thanks,' said John.

'I put your clean clothes at the foot of it, folded,' said Millie.

'Thank you very much,' he said, and he brushed past her, then apologised. 'So sorry,' he said, stepping away.

'Maybe we can all go into New York together next week,' she blurted. She aimed it at his spine, hoping to fetch him back. He stopped and turned. 'We can go out to eat,' she continued. 'And maybe take a tour of the UN.' She'd seen picture postcards of the flags out front, rippling like sheets, all that international laundry, though she'd never actually been.

'OK,' said John. He smiled. Then he turned back and walked down the hall, trading one room for another, moving through and past, leaving Millie standing there, the way when, having decided anything, once and for all, you leave somebody behind.

In the morning there was just a note and a gift. 'Thank you for lodging me. I decided early to take the bus to California. Please do not think me rude. Yours kindly, John Spee.'

Millie let out a gasp of dismay. 'Hane, the boy has gone!' Hane was dressing for church and came out to see. He was in a shirt and boxer shorts, and had been tying his tie. Now he stopped, as if some ghost that had once been cast from the house had just returned. The morning's Scripture was going to be taken from the third chapter of John, and parts of it were bouncing around in his head, like nonsense or a chant. *For God so loved the world* . . . John Spee was gone. Hane placed his hands on Millie's shoulders. What could he tell her? *For God so loved the world*? He didn't really believe that God loved the world, at least not in the way most people thought. *Love*, in this case, he felt, was a way of speaking. A *metaphor*. Though for what, he didn't exactly know.

'Oh, I hope he'll be OK,' Millie said, and started to cry. She pulled her robe tight around her and placed one hand over her lips to hide their quivering. It was terrible to lose a boy. Girls could make their way all right, but boys went out into the world, limping with notions, and they never came back.

It was a month later when Millie and Hane heard from Ariel that John Spee had returned to England. He had taken the bus to Los Angeles, gotten out, walked around for a few hours, then had climbed back on and ridden six straight days back to Newark Airport. He had wanted to see San Francisco, but a man on the bus had told him not to go, that everyone was dying there. So John went to Los Angeles instead. For three hours. *Can you believe it?* wrote Ariel. She was back in Warwickshire, and John sometimes dropped by to see her when she was very, very busy.

The gift, when Millie unwrapped it, had turned out to be a toaster – a large one that could toast four slices at once. She had never seen John come into the house with a package, and she had no idea when or where he had gotten it.

'Four slices,' she said to Hane, who never ate much bread. 'What will we do with such a thing?'

Every night through that May and June, Millie curled against Hane, one of her hands on his hip, the smells of his skin all through her head. Summer tapped at the bedroom screens, nightsounds, and Millie would lie awake, not sleeping at all. 'Oh!' she sometimes said aloud, though for no reason she could explain. Hane continued to talk about the Historical Jesus. Millie rubbed his shins while he spoke, her palm against the dry, whitening hair of him. Sometimes she talked about the garbage barge, which was now docked off Coney Island, a failed ride, an unamusement.

'Maybe,' she said once to Hane, then stopped, her cheek against his shoulder. How familiar skin flickered in and out of strangeness; how it was yours no matter, no mere matter. 'Maybe we can go someplace someday.'

Hane shifted toward her, a bit plain and a bit handsome without his glasses. Through the window the streetlights shimmered a pale green, and the moon shone woolly and bitten. Hane looked at his wife. She had the round, drying face of someone who once and briefly – a long ago fall, a weekend perhaps – had been very pretty without ever even knowing it. 'You are my only friend,' he said, and he kissed her, hard on the brow, like a sign for her to hold close.

ALONG THE RIVERWALL

COLUM McCANN

Fergus nudges his wheelchair up to the riverwall and watches the Liffey flow quickly along, bloated from an evening rain, a cargo of night sky and neon, all bellying down towards Dublin bay. He remembers his father once heaving a fridge into the river and wonders what else might lie down there. Flakes of gold paint from the Guinness barges perhaps. Blackened shells from British army gunboats. Condoms and needles. Old black kettles. Pennies and prams. History books, harmonicas, fingernails, and baskets full of dead flowers. A billion cigarette butts and bottle caps. Shovels and stovepipes, coins and whistles, horseshoes and footballs. And many an old bicycle, no doubt. Down there with wheels sinking slowly in the mud, handlebars galloping with algae, gear cables rusted into the housing, tiny fish nosing around the pedals.

He adjusts the long black overcoat that hangs in anarchic folds around his legs and wipes the sweat off his forehead with his younger brother's Shamrock Rovers scarf. Half a mile, he reckons, from his house in the Liberties, and the bicycle wheel that he carried in his lap caused all sorts of problems — dropped to the ground as he gently tried to close the front door, smeared his old jeans with a necklace of oil as he negotiated the hill down by Christ Church, and bounced away as he tried to get over the quayside kerb.

The Liffey guides a winter wind along its broadbacked banks. Fergus puts the brake on the wheelchair and lets a gob of phlegm volley out over the river, where it catches and spirals. He wonders what sort of arc the bicycle wheel will make in the air.

The fridge, all those years ago, tumbled head over heels into the water. His father, a leather-faced man with pockets always full of bottles, had taken it down to the river all on his own. He hadn't been able to keep up the payments and wasn't ready to hand it back to the collector. 'That gouger can go for a swim if he wants his Frigidaire.' He nailed a few planks from the coalshed together, screwed some roller skate wheels on the bottom, loaded up the fridge and grunted down towards the quays. Fergus and his brothers tagged behind. Some of the drunks who were belching out of the pubs offered help, but Fergus's father flung his arms in the air. 'Every single one of ya is a horse of a man,' he roared, then stopped and pulled on his cigarette, 'but yez can't shite walking, so I'll do it meself'.

Bottles clinking, he stumbled down to the river, laughing as the huge white fridge cartwheeled into the water, creating a gigantic splash.

The things that fridge must have joined, thinks Fergus. Broken toilets. Flagons of cider. Shirt buttons. High-heeled shoes. A very old pair of crutches. He shivers for a moment in the cold and runs his fingers around through his short curly hair. Or perhaps even a rotating bed, flanked with special syringes, piss bags, rubber gloves, buckets of pills, bottles of Lucozade, a dozen therapy tables, a nurse's pencil with the ends chewed off. Holding on to the axle and the freewheel, Fergus spins the spokes around, peers through them, and listens to the rhythmic click as the river and the quays tumble into slices, then lets another volley from his throat out over the water.

Mangled by a bread truck on the Lansdowne Road, near where the Dodder negotiates low rocks. Bucketfuls of winter sun coming down as he rode back from a delivery, over the bridge by the football stadium, inventing Que Seras and Molly Malones and Ronnie Whelan hitting an eighteen-yard volley from the edge of the box. But there was only a song of tyres and the poor bastard behind the wheel of the bread truck had a heart attack and was found with eclair cream on the front of his white open-neck shirt, brown loaves littered around him on the floor, slumped frontwards on the truck horn, so that it sounded like the cry of a curlew, only constant, with blood in a pattern of feathers on the front windshield.

Fergus was tossed in the air like a stale crust, and woke up in Our Lady of Lourdes Rehabilitation Centre with the doctors in a halo around him. Collarbone broken, thirty forehead stitches, ribs cracked, and the third lumbar on the lower vertebrae smashed to hell. He was put in a ward full of rugby players and motorcycle victims. When his bed was spun he could see out the window to a ripple of trees that curtsied down to the road. Weeks rivered like months. A Cavanman in the bed beside him had a pair of scars that ran like railroad tracks when he held his wrists together. A persistent howl thudded down from the end of the ward. A carrot-haired boy from Sligo tattooed a tricolour on the top of his leg, slamming the needle down hard into a muscle that didn't feel a thing. The months eddied carelessly into one another.

'How d'ya think I feel, I'm marvellous, just fucken marvellous,' Fergus roared at the nurse one afternoon when the knowledge was settling in — no more slipstreaming the 45 down Pearse Street in the rain, or sprinting along by the brewery, slapping at dogs with the bicycle pump, dicing the taxis, swerving the wrong way up the street, no more jokes about women sitting on things other than the crossbar — *that's not me crossbar, love, I'm only happy to see ya* — or slagging matches along the quays with the lorry drivers, or simply just trundling down Thomas Street for a pint of milk.

The bike was at home in the coalshed, a trophy of misery, collected by his father on the day of the accident. He had bought it for Fergus five years before, convinced that his son was good enough to race. Every payday he had rolled up his spare pound notes and stuffed them inside a Pernod bottle. He brought the bike home one Saturday night, carefully wheeling it from the shop on George's Street. It was a red Italian model, all Camagnolo parts. Boys in the neighbourhood whistled when they saw it. Once, on O'Connell Bridge, four youngsters in bomber jackets tried to knock him off and steal it, but he smacked one in the jaw with the kryptonite lock. In the messenger company he was known for the way he salmoned, leaping through the traffic the wrong way up a one-way road. In his first race, in the Wicklow Hills, two months before the accident, he had come in second place. The leather on the saddle had begun to conform to his body. He had learned how to flick it quite easily through the traffic jams up by Christ Church.

After the accident the machine was a ribbon of metal. But, when his father came into the hospital, he would tower over the bed: 'Before y'know it, Fergus, you'll be on her again, and fuck all the begrudgers.' Fergus lay there, nodding.

His mother stayed upstairs in her bedroom, kneeling by red votive lamps and holy pictures. Letters were sent off to Knock and Lourdes. His younger brothers drew pictures of favourite places, Burdocks Chipper, the alleyway down by the Coombe, the front of the Stag's Head, the new graffiti on the schoolyard wall. Fergus's friends from the messenger service sat by the hospital bed and sometimes they'd race off together, radios crackling, *come on ya tosser would ya hurry up for fuck sake*. Old girlfriends wrote short poems that they found in magazines, and occasionally the nurses brought him down to Baker's Corner for a sweet and furtive pint. But when the bed was spun the same trees curtsied down to the road. The boy with the tricolour went berserk with the pins, covering himself in small blue dots and stabbing at his eye with a needle. The Cavanman stroked his wrists. A biker from Waterford shouted that someone had left a pubic hair in the French magazine that had circulated around the ward.

Oranges gathered mould on Fergus's bedside table. The therapy room was full of bright colours and smiling nurses, but at night, back in the ward, the distant low moan wouldn't subside — it became part of the scenery, swallowed up, a hum, a drone, a noise you couldn't sleep without. The months eddied on.

Home from the hospital, his father wheeled him out to the coalshed. It was a Friday and fish was being cooked in the house. The smell drifted. A light drizzle was falling and pigeons were scrapping for food on the rooftops of neighbouring houses. His father opened the lock of the shed slowly. Half a dozen brown boxes waited for Fergus, beside the bicycle. They'd been postmarked in England, sent by mail-order. Fergus opened them slowly. 'The doctors don't know their arses from their elbows, son, go on ahead there now and get cracking.' Fergus stared at the boxes for a long time. 'And they cost a lot fucking more than a miracle,' said his father, chuckling, heading out the door towards the pub, his shoulders ripping at the side of his overcoat. Fergus sat there, the smell of cooking food all around him, fingering a derailleur.

Hitching the scarf up around his neck, he looks at his watch — already three o'clock in the morning — and then lays his head back against the edge of the wheelchair for a moment to look up to the sky. Certain stars are recognisable even through the clouds and the smog. Ten years ago, when he was seven years old, he'd been caught trying to steal a Mini Clubman from outside St Patrick's and his father, after walloping him, took him for a walk down the same river, pointing up at the sky. 'See those stars,' he said, 'let me tell ya something.' The story was that the stars were their own peculiar hell, that all the murderers went to one star where there was nobody left to murder but themselves, all the corrupt politicians went where there was no government, all the child molestors went where there were no children to molest, all the car thieves went where there were no cars, and if that wasn't good enough deterrent for him he'd get another wallop. Fergus rubs his hand over his chest and wonders if there's a star full of bicycle paraphernalia.

The new parts had cost his father the best part of two wage packets. He had even gotten an extra job as a night watchman for a security firm in Tallaght. When he came home at night there wasn't so much as a clink inside his pockets anymore — it was more a persistent clatter of dismissive humphs, an emphatic hope, a nagging insistence that Fergus would get on the bike again.

And out in the coalshed, for two months, in the wheelchair, Fergus sweated over the bicycle. He tightened the nipples of the spokes on the right hand side of the wheel to bring it to the left, took the cotter pin and tapped it until the fat leap came out of the pedals, used the third hand to hold the brakes in place, dropped in the new set of front forks, plied the thin little Phillips head screwdriver to adjust the gears. He overlapped the tape on the handlebars, twisted the ends of the cables where they frayed, bought new decals. His brothers watched and helped. Each night his father would come out to the coalshed, slap the saddle: 'Just a few weeks now, son.'

He offered the bike to his brothers, but they knew better. It was a fossil, and Fergus knew it, and the only thing it could be ridden with was a perfect cadence of the imagination.

First to go were the handlebars and they went down with a small splash. The following night the pedals, the cranks, the front chainwheel and the ball bearings were tossed. It was a Saturday when he wandered down to jettison the brakes, the cables, the saddle, the seatpost, and the derailleur. A crowd of drunks were huffing glue down on the quays, so he sat in the gateway of the Corporation building and waited until they drifted off.

Sunday was the most difficult job of all — it had taken three hours to try and negotiate the frame, and he was about to just leave it alongside the church when a taxi driver, with a cigarette dangling from his mouth, pulled alongside him and asked what the hell he was doing. 'Bringing the bike for a swim,' said Fergus, and the driver just nodded, then offered to put it in the boot and drive it down to the river for him. He balanced the frame on the riverwall. 'Just as well this isn't the bleedin' Ganges,' said the driver, and drove off. Fergus, unsure of what the taximan meant, toppled the frame over the wall and headed home, not even waiting for the ripples to spread out over the water.

And last night, when he went to get rid of the front wheel, he woke his brother, Padraic, as the door of the coalshed swung too far. Padraic came downstairs in his Arsenal jersey: 'Wha' ya doin', Ferg?' 'Mind your own business.' 'Where's the rest of the bike?' Fergus said nothing. 'Da'll cream ya,' said his brother. Later, as Fergus manoeuvred down the street he saw Padraic pull back the curtains and stare. When he got home Padraic was waiting for him on the steps of the house. 'Ya've no fucking right to do that,' Padraic said. 'Da spent all his money on it.'

Fergus pushed past his brother into the house: 'He'll find out soon enough.'

Down along the quays things are still quiet. The exhaust fumes from a couple of lorries make curious shapes in the air, sometimes caught in mid-flight with a streak of neon from a shop or a sign. A couple of pedestrians stroll along on the opposite side of the river, huddled under anorak hoods.

He bends forward in the chair, grabs one of the spokes and hauls the rear wheel up to his chest. He sees a smidgin of oil and dirt on the third cog of the freewheel and runs his finger along it. He daubs the oil on the inside of his jeans, staring at the small smudge the oil makes against the blue.

The water is calmer now, with bits of litter settling on its surface. He wonders if all the pieces that he has flung in over the last few days have settled in the same area of river bottom.

Perhaps one day a storm might blow the whole bike back together again, a freak of nature, the pedals locking on to the cranks, the wheel axle slipping into the frame, the handlebars dropping gently into the housing, the whole damn thing back in one piece. Maybe then he can take a dive to the bottom of the slime and ride it again, slip his feet in the toeclips, curl his fingers around the bars, lean down to touch the gears forward, then pedal all around the river bottom, amongst the ruin of things.

He heaves the wheel out over the Liffey.

It flares out over the river, then almost seems to stop. The wheel appears suspended there in the air, caught by a fabulous lightness, the colours from along the quays whirling in its spin, collecting energy from the push of the sky, reeling outwards, simultaneously serene and violent, a bird ready to burst into flight. For a moment, he thinks of marathons and jerseys, sprints and headbands, tracks and starting guns. Out there trundling through the traffic of Dublin in a wheelchair, racing along with others, maybe even delivering a package or two, parcels and letters that he can fit in his lap, a small paycheck, his father bending down to look at the money, bottles clanking. His younger brothers at some finishing line in colourful shirts, his mother fingering a string of red beads.

In an instant, the wheel turns sideways and falls. The walls of the Liffey curl up to gather it down to its belly as it slices the air with the economy of a stone. Fergus pins his upper body across the chair, leaning against the wall, but loses sight of the wheel about five feet above the water. He listens for the splash, but it is drowned out by the rumble of a lorry coming along the road from the James's Gate Brewery. Down below, on the surface, concentric circles fling themselves outward, reaching for the riverwalls in huge gestures, as if looking for something, galloping outwards, the river itself shifting its circles for another moment, moving its whippled water along, all the time gathering the wheel downwards to the riverfloor, slowly, deliberately, to where it will rest. Fergus tries to remember if the door of the fridge had been flung open as it cartwheeled down into the river all those years ago.

He places his hands on the wheels of the chair, grits his teeth, pushes forward along the riverwall, and rams down the quays, his overcoat flapping in the breeze.

THE TURKEY SEASON

ALICE MUNRO

When I was fourteen I got a job at the Turkey Barn for the Christmas season. I was still too young to get a job working in a store or as a part-time waitress; I was also too nervous.

I was a turkey gutter. The other people who worked at the Turkey Barn were Lily and Marjorie and Gladys, who were also gutters; Irene and Henry, who were pluckers; Herb Abbott, the foreman, who superintended the whole operation and filled in wherever he was needed. Morgan Elliott was the owner and boss. He and his son, Morgy, did the killing.

Morgy I knew from school. I thought him stupid and despicable and was uneasy about having to consider him in a new and possibly superior guise, as the boss's son. But his father treated him so roughly, yelling and swearing at him, that he seemed no more than the lowest of the workers. The other person related to the boss was Gladys. She was his sister, and in her case there did seem to be some privilege of position. She worked slowly and went home if she was not feeling well, and was not friendly to Lily and Marjorie, although she was, a little, to me. She had come back to live with Morgan and his family after working for many years in Toronto, in a bank. This was not the sort of job she was used to. Lily and Marjorie, talking about her when she wasn't there, said she had had a nervous breakdown. They said Morgan made her work in the Turkey Barn to pay for her keep. They also said, with no worry about the contradiction, that she had taken the job because she was after a man, and that the man was Herb Abbott.

All I could see when I closed my eyes, the first few nights after working there, was turkeys. I saw them hanging upside down, plucked and stiffened, pale and cold, with the heads and necks limp, the eyes and nostrils clotted with dark blood; the remaining bits of feathers — those dark and bloody, too — seemed to form a crown. I saw them not with aversion but with a sense of endless work to be done.

Herb Abbott showed me what to do. You put the turkey down on the table and cut its head off with a cleaver. Then you took the loose skin around the neck and stripped it back to reveal the crop, nestled in the cleft between the gullet and the windpipe.

'Feel the gravel,' said Herb encouragingly. He made me close my fingers around the crop. Then he showed me how to work my hand down behind it to cut it out, and the gullet and windpipe as well. He used shears to cut the vertebrae.

'Scrunch, scrunch,' he said soothingly. 'Now, put your hand in.'

I did. It was deathly cold in there, in the turkey's dark insides.

'Watch out for bone splinters.'

Working cautiously in the dark, I had to pull the connecting tissues loose.

'Ups-a-daisy.' Herb turned the bird over and flexed each leg. 'Knees up, Mother Brown. Now.' He took a heavy knife and placed it directly on the knee knuckle joints and cut off the shank.

'Have a look at the worms.'

Pearly-white strings, pulled out of the shank, were creeping about on their own.

'That's just the tendons shrinking. Now comes the nice part!'

He slit the bird at its bottom end, letting out a rotten smell.

'Are you educated?'

I did not know what to say.

'What's that smell?'

'Hydrogen sulfide.'

'Educated,' said Herb, sighing. 'All right. Work your fingers around and get the guts loose. Easy. Easy. Keep your fingers together. Keep the palm inwards. Feel the ribs with the back of

ALICE MUNRO

your hand. Feel the guts fit into your palm. Feel that? Keep going. Break the strings — as many as you can. Keep going. Feel a hard lump? That's the gizzard. Feel a soft lump? That's the heart. OK? OK. Get your fingers around the gizzard. Easy. Start pulling this way. That's right. That's right. Start to pull her out.'

It was not easy at all. I wasn't even sure what I had was the gizzard. My hand was full of cold pulp.

'Pull,' he said, and I brought out a glistening, liverish mass.

'Got it. There's the lights. You know what they are? Lungs. There's the heart. There's the gizzard. There's the gall. Now, you don't ever want to break that gall inside or it will taste the entire turkey.' Tactfully, he scraped out what I had missed, including the testicles, which were like a pair of white grapes.

'Nice pair of earrings,' Herb said.

Herb Abbot was a tall, firm, plump man. His hair was dark and thin, combed straight back from a widow's peak, and his eyes seemed to be slightly slanted, so that he looked like a pale Chinese or like pictures of the Devil, except that he was smooth-faced and benign. Whatever he did around the Turkey Barn — gutting, as he was now, or loading the truck, or hanging the carcasses — was done with efficient, economical movements, quickly and buoyantly. 'Notice about Herb — he always walks like he had a boat moving underneath him,' Marjorie said, and it was true. Herb worked on the lake boats, during the season, as a cook. Then he worked for Morgan until after Christmas. The rest of the time he helped around the poolroom, making hamburgers, sweeping up, stopping fights before they got started. That was where he lived; he had a room above the poolroom on the main street.

In all the operations at the Turkey Barn it seemed to be Herb who had the efficiency and honor of the business continually on his mind; it was he who kept everything under control. Seeing him in the yard talking to Morgan, who was a thick, short man, red in the face, an unpredictable bully, you would be sure that it

112

was Herb who was the boss and Morgan the hired help. But it was not so.

If I had not had Herb to show me, I don't think I could have learned turkey gutting at all. I was clumsy with my hands and had been shamed for it so often that the least show of impatience on the part of the person instructing me could have brought on a dithering paralysis. I could not stand to be watched by anybody but Herb. Particularly, I couldn't stand to be watched by Lily and Marjorie, two middle-aged sisters, who were very fast and thorough and competitive gutters. They sang at their work and talked abusively and intimately to the turkey carcasses.

'Don't you nick me, you old bugger!'

'Aren't you the old crap factory!'

I had never heard women talk like that.

Gladys was not a fast gutter, though she must have been thorough; Herb would have talked to her otherwise. She never sang and certainly she never swore. I thought her rather old, though she was not as old as Lily and Marjorie; she must have been over thirty. She seemed offended by everything that went on and had the air of keeping plenty of bitter judgments to herself. I never tried to talk to her, but she spoke to me one day in the cold little washroom off the gutting shed. She was putting pancake makeup on her face. The color of the makeup was so distinct from the color of her skin that it was as if she were slapping orange paint over a whitewashed, bumpy wall.

She asked me if my hair was naturally curly.

I said yes.

'You don't have to get a permanent?'

'No.'

'You're lucky. I have to do mine up every night. The chemicals in my system won't allow me to get a permanent.'

There are different ways women have of talking about their looks. Some women make it clear that what they do to keep themselves up is for the sake of sex, for men. Others, like Gladys, make the job out to be a kind of housekeeping, whose very difficulties they pride themselves on. Gladys was genteel. I could see her in the bank, in a navy-blue dress with the kind of detachable white collar you can wash at night. She would be grumpy and correct.

Another time, she spoke to me about her periods, which were profuse and painful. She wanted to know about mine. There was an uneasy, prudish, agitated expression on her face. I was saved by Irene, who was using the toilet and called out. 'Do like me, and you'll be rid of all your problems for a while.' Irene was only a few years older than I was, but she was recently — tardily — married, and heavily pregnant.

Gladys ignored her, running cold water on her hands. The hands of all of us were red and sore-looking from the work. 'I can't use that soap. If I use it, I break out in a rash,' Gladys said. 'If I bring my own soap in here, I can't afford to have other people using it, because I pay a lot for it — it's a special anti-allergy soap.'

I think the idea that Lily and Marjorie promoted — that Gladys was after Herb Abbott — sprang from their belief that single people ought to be teased and embarrassed whenever possible, and from their interest in Herb, which led to the feeling that somebody ought to be after him. They wondered about him. What they wondered was: How can a man want so little? No wife, no family, no house. The details of his daily life, the small preferences, were of interest. Where had he been brought up? (Here and there and all over.) How far had he gone in school? (Far enough.) Where was his girlfriend? (Never tell.) Did he drink coffee or tea if he got the choice? (Coffee.)

When they talked about Gladys's being after him they must have really wanted to talk about sex — what he wanted and what he got. They must have felt a voluptuous curiosity about him, as I did. He aroused this feeling by being circumspect and not making the jokes some men did, and at the same time by not being squeamish or gentlemanly. Some men, showing me the testicles from the turkey, would have acted as if the very existence of testicles were somehow a bad joke on me, something a girl could be taunted about; another sort of man would have been embarrassed and would have thought he had to protect me from embarrassment. A man who didn't seem to feel one way or the other was an oddity — as much to older women, probably, as to me. But what was so welcome to me may have been disturbing to them. They wanted to jolt him. They even wanted Gladys to jolt him, if she could.

There wasn't any idea then — at least in Logan, Ontario, in the late forties — about homosexuality's going beyond very narrow confines. Women, certainly, believed in its rarity and in definite boundaries. There were homosexuals in town, and we knew who they were: an elegant, light-voiced, wavy-haired paperhanger who called himself an interior decorator; the minister's widow's fat, spoiled only son, who went so far as to enter baking contests and had crocheted a tablecloth; a hypochondriacal church organist and music teacher who kept the choir and his pupils in line with screaming tantrums. Once the label was fixed, there was a good deal of tolerance for these people, and their talents for decorating, for crocheting, and for music were appreciated — especially by women. 'The poor fellow,' they said. 'He doesn't do any harm.' They really seemed to believe — the women did — that it was the penchant for baking or music that was the determining factor, and that it was this activity that made the man what he was — not any other detours he might take, or wish to take. A desire to play the violin would be taken as more a deviation from manliness than would a wish to shun women. Indeed, the idea was that any manly man would wish to shun women but most of them were caught off guard, and for good.

I don't want to go into the question of whether Herb was

homosexual or not, because the definition is of no use to me. I think that probably he was, but maybe he was not. (Even considering what happened later, I think that.) He is not a puzzle so arbitrarily solved.

The other plucker, who worked with Irene, was Henry Streets, a neighbor of ours. There was nothing remarkable about him except that he was eighty-six years old and still, as he said of himself, a devil for work. He had whiskey in his thermos, and drank it from time to time through the day. It was Henry who had said to me, in our kitchen, 'You ought to get yourself a job at the Turkey Barn. They need another gutter.' Then my father said at once, 'Not her, Henry. She's got ten thumbs,' and Henry said he was just joking — it was dirty work. But I was already determined to try it — I had a great need to be successful in a job like this. I was almost in the condition of a grownup person who is ashamed of never having learned to read, so much did I feel my ineptness at manual work. Work, to everybody I knew, meant doing things I was no good at doing, and work was what people prided themselves on and measured each other by. (It goes without saying that the things I was good at, like schoolwork, were suspect or held in plain contempt.) So it was a surprise and then a triumph for me not to get fired, and to be able to turn out clean turkeys at a rate that was not disgraceful. I don't know if I really understood how much Herb Abbott was responsible for this, but he would sometimes say, 'Good girl,' or pat my waist and say, 'You're getting to be a good gutter — you'll go a long ways in the world,' and when I felt his quick, kind touch through the heavy sweater and bloody smock I wore, I felt my face glow and I wanted to lean back against him as he stood behind me. I wanted to rest my head against his wide, fleshy shoulder. When I went to sleep at night, lying on my side, I would rub my cheek against the pillow and think of that as Herb's shoulder.

I was interested in how he talked to Gladys, how he looked at her or noticed her. This interest was not jealous. I think I wanted something to happen with them. I quivered in curious expectation, as Lily and Marjorie did. We all wanted to see the flicker of sexuality in him, hear it in his voice, not because we thought it would make him seem more like other men but because we knew that with him it would be entirely different. He was kinder and more patient than most women, and as stern and remote, in some ways, as any man. We wanted to see how he could be moved.

If Gladys wanted this, too, she didn't give any signs of it. It is impossible for me to tell with women like her whether they are as thick and deadly as they seem, not wanting anything much but opportunities for irritation and contempt, or if they are all choked up with gloomy fires and useless passions.

Marjorie and Lily talked about marriage. They did not have much good to say about it, in spite of their feeling that it was a state nobody should be allowed to stay out of. Marjorie said that shortly after her marriage she had gone into the woodshed with the intention of swallowing Paris green.

'I'd have done it,' she said. 'But the man came along in the grocery truck and I had to go out and buy the groceries. This was when we lived on the farm.'

Her husband was cruel to her in those days, but later he suffered an accident — he rolled the tractor and was so badly hurt he would be an invalid all his life. They moved to town, and Marjorie was the boss now.

'He starts to sulk the other night and say he don't want his supper. Well, I just picked up his wrist and held it. He was scared I was going to twist his arm. He could see I'd do it. So I say, 'You what?' And he says, "I'll eat it." '

They talked about their father. He was a man of the old school. He had a noose in the woodshed (not the Paris green woodshed — this would be an earlier one, on another farm), and when they got on his nerves he used to line them up and threaten to hang them. Lily, who was the younger, would shake till she fell down. This same father had arranged to marry Marjorie off to a crony of his when she was just sixteen. That was the husband who had driven her to the Paris green. Their father did it because he wanted to be sure she wouldn't get into trouble.

'Hot blood,' Lily said.

I was horrified, and asked, 'Why didn't you run away?'

'His word was law,' Marjorie said.

They said that was what was the matter with kids nowadays — it was the kids that ruled the roost. A father's word should be law. They brought up their own kids strictly, and none had turned out bad yet. When Marjorie's son wet the bed she threatened to cut off his dingy with the butcher knife. That cured him.

They said ninety per cent of the young girls nowadays drank, and swore, and took it lying down. They did not have daughters, but if they did and caught them at anything like that they would beat them raw. Irene, they said, used to go to the hockey games with her ski pants slit and nothing under them, for convenience in the snowdrifts afterward. Terrible.

I wanted to point out some contradictions. Marjorie and Lily themselves drank and swore, and what was so wonderful about the strong will of a father who would ensure you a lifetime of unhappiness? (What I did not see was that Marjorie and Lily were not unhappy altogether — could not be, because of their sense of consequence, their pride and style.) I could be enraged then at the lack of logic in most adults' talk — the way they held to their pronouncements no matter what evidence might be presented to them. How could these women's hands be so gifted, so delicate and clever — for I knew they would be as good at dozens of other jobs as they were at gutting; they would be good at quilting and darning and painting and papering and kneading dough and setting out seedlings — and their thinking so slapdash, clumsy, infuriating?

Lily said she never let her husband come near her if he had been drinking. Marjorie said since the time she nearly died with a hemorrhage she never let her husband come near her, period. Lily said quickly that it was only when he'd been drinking that he tried anything. I could see that it was a matter of pride not to let your husband come near you, but I couldn't quite believe that 'come near' meant 'have sex.' The idea of Marjorie and Lily being sought out for such purposes seemed grotesque. They had bad teeth, their stomachs sagged, their faces were dull and spotty. I decided to take 'come near' literally.

The two weeks before Christmas was a frantic time at the Turkey Barn. I began to go in for an hour before school as well as after school and on weekends. In the morning, when I walked to work, the street lights would still be on and the morning stars shining. There was the Turkey Barn, on the edge of a white field, with a row of big pine trees behind it, and always, no matter how cold and still it was, these trees were lifting their branches and sighing and straining. It seems unlikely that on my way to the Turkey Barn, for an hour of gutting turkeys, I should have experienced such a sense of promise and at the same time of perfect, impenetrable mystery in the universe, but I did. Herb had something to do with that, and so did the cold snap — the series of hard, clear mornings. The truth is, such feelings weren't hard to come by then. I would get them but not know how they were to be connected with anything in real life.

One morning at the Turkey Barn there was a new gutter. This was a boy eighteen or nineteen years old, a stranger named Brian. It seemed he was a relative, or perhaps just a friend, of Herb Abbott's. He was staying with Herb. He had worked on a lake boat last summer. He said he had got sick of it, though, and quit.

What he said was, 'Yeah, fuckin' boats, I got sick of that.'

Language at the Turkey Barn was coarse and free, but this was

119

one word never heard there. And Brian's use of it seemed not careless but flaunting, mixing insult and provocation. Perhaps it was his general style that made it so. He had amazing good looks: taffy hair, bright-blue eyes, ruddy skin, well-shaped body — the sort of good looks nobody disagrees about for a moment. But a single, relentless notion had got such a hold on him that he could not keep from turning all his assets into parody. His mouth was wet-looking and slightly open most of the time, his eyes were half shut, his expression a hopeful leer, his movements indolent, exaggerated, inviting. Perhaps if he had been put on a stage with a microphone and a guitar and let grunt and howl and wriggle and excite, he would have seemed a true celebrant. Lacking a stage, he was unconvincing. After a while he seemed just like somebody with a bad case of hiccups — his insistent sexuality was that monotonous and meaningless.

If he had toned down a bit, Marjorie and Lily would probably have enjoyed him. They could have kept up a game of telling him to shut his filthy mouth and keep his hands to himself. As it was, they said they were sick of him, and meant it. Once, Marjorie took up her gutting knife. 'Keep your distance,' she said. 'I mean from me and my sister and that kid.'

She did not tell him to keep his distance from Gladys, because Gladys wasn't there at the time and Marjorie would probably not have felt like protecting her anyway. But it was Gladys Brian particularly liked to bother. She would throw down her knife and go into the washroom and stay there ten minutes and come out with a stony face. She didn't say she was sick anymore and go home, the way she used to. Marjorie said Morgan was mad at Gladys for sponging and she couldn't get away with it any longer.

Gladys said to me, 'I can't stand that kind of thing. I can't stand people mentioning that kind of thing and that kind of — gestures. It makes me sick to my stomach.'

I believed her. She was terribly white. But why, in that case, did she not complain to Morgan? Perhaps relations between them were too uneasy, perhaps she could not bring herself to repeat or describe such things. Why did none of us complain — if not to Morgan, at least to Herb? I never thought of it. Brian seemed just something to put up with, like the freezing cold in the gutting shed and the smell of blood and waste. When Marjorie and Lily did threaten to complain, it was about Brian's laziness.

He was not a good gutter. He said his hands were too big. So Herb took him off gutting, told him he was to sweep and clean up, make packages of giblets, and help load the truck. This meant that he did not have to be in any one place or doing any one job at a given time, so much of the time he did nothing. He would start sweeping up, leave that and mop the tables, leave that and have a cigarette, lounge against the table bothering us until Herb called him to help load. Herb was very busy now and spent a lot of time making deliveries, so it was possible he did not know the extent of Brian's idleness.

'I don't know why Herb don't fire you,' Marjorie said. 'I guess the answer is he don't want you hanging around sponging on him, with no place to go.'

'I know where to go,' said Brian.

'Keep your sloppy mouth shut,' said Marjorie. 'I pity Herb. Getting saddled.'

On the last school day before Christmas we got out early in the afternoon. I went home and changed my clothes and came into work at about three o'clock. Nobody was working. Everybody was in the gutting shed, where Morgan Elliott was swinging a cleaver over the gutting table and yelling. I couldn't make out what the yelling was about, and thought someone must have made a terrible mistake in his work; perhaps it had been me. Then I saw Brian on the other side of the table, looking very sulky and mean, and standing well back. The sexual leer was not altogether gone from his face, but it was flattened out and mixed with a look of impotent bad temper and some fear. That's it, I thought; Brian is getting fired for being so sloppy and lazy. Even when I made out Morgan saying 'pervert' and 'filthy' and 'maniac', I still thought that was what was happening. Marjorie and Lily, and even brassy Irene, were standing around with downcast, rather pious looks, such as children get when somebody is suffering a terrible bawling out at school. Only old Henry seemed able to keep a cautious grin on his face. Gladys was not to be seen. Herb was standing closer to Morgan than anybody else. He was not interfering but was keeping an eye on the cleaver. Morgy was blubbering, though he didn't seem to be in any immediate danger.

Morgan was yelling at Brian to get out. 'And out of this town — I mean it — and don't you wait till tomorrow if you still want your arse in one piece! Out!' he shouted, and the cleaver swung dramatically towards the door. Brian started in that direction but, whether he meant to or not, he made a swaggering, taunting motion of the buttocks. This made Morgan break into a roar and run after him, swinging the cleaver in a stagy way. Brian ran, and Morgan ran after him, and Irene screamed and grabbed her stomach. Morgan was too heavy to run any distance and probably could not have thrown the cleaver very far, either. Herb watched from the doorway. Soon Morgan came back and flung the cleaver down on the table.

'All back to work! No more gawking around here! You don't get paid for gawking! What are you getting under way at?' he said, with a hard look at Irene.

'Nothing,' Irene said meekly.

'If you're getting under way get out of here.'

'I'm not.'

'All right, then!'

We got to work. Herb took off his blood-smeared smock and put on his jacket and went off, probably to see that Brian got ready to go on the suppertime bus. He did not say a word. Morgan and his son went out to the yard, and Irene and Henry went back to the adjoining shed, where they did the plucking, working knee-deep in the feathers Brian was supposed to keep swept up.

'Where's Gladys?' I said softly.

'Recuperating,' said Marjorie. She, too, spoke in a quieter voice than usual, and 'recuperating' was not the sort of word she and Lily normally used. It was a word to be used about Gladys, with a mocking intent.

They didn't want to talk about what had happened, because they were afraid Morgan might come in and catch them at it and fire them. Good workers as they were, they were afraid of that. Besides, they hadn't seen anything. They must have been annoyed that they hadn't. All I ever found out was that Brian had either done something or shown something to Gladys as she came out of the washroom and she had started screaming and having hysterics.

Now she'll likely be laid up with another nervous breakdown, they said. And he'll be on his way out of town. And good riddance, they said, to both of them.

I have a picture of the Turkey Barn crew taken on Christmas Eve. It was taken with a flash camera that was someone's Christmas extravagance. I think it was Irene's. But Herb Abbott must have been the one who took the picture. He was the one who could be trusted to know or to learn immediately how to manage anything new, and flash cameras were fairly new at the time. The picture was taken about ten o'clock on Christmas Eve, after Herb and Morgy had come back from making the last delivery and we had washed off the gutting table and swept and mopped the cement floor. We had taken off the bloody smocks and heavy sweaters and gone into the little room called the lunchroom, where there was a table and a heater. We still wore our working clothes: overalls and shirts. The men wore caps and the women kerchiefs, tied in the wartime style. I am stout and cheerful and comradely in the picture, transformed into someone I don't ever remember being or pretending to be. I look years older than fourteen. Irene is the only one who has taken off her kerchief, freeing her long red hair. She peers out from it with a meek, sluttish, inviting look, which would match her reputation but is not like any look of hers I remember. Yes, it must have been her camera; she is posing for it, with that look, more deliberately than anyone else is. Marjorie and Lily are smiling, true to form, but their smiles are sour and reckless. With their hair hidden, and such figures as they have bundled up, they look like a couple of tough and jovial but testy workmen. Their kerchiefs look misplaced; caps would be better. Henry is in high spirits, glad to be part of the work force, grinning and looking twenty years younger than his age. Then Morgy, with his hangdog look, not trusting the occasion's bounty, and Morgan very flushed and bosslike and satisfied. He has just given each of us our bonus turkey. Each of these turkeys has a leg or a wing missing, or a malformation of some kind, so none of them are salable at the full price. But Morgan has been at pains to tell us that you often get the best meat off the gimpy ones, and he has shown us that he's taking one home himself.

We are all holding mugs or large, thick china cups, which contain not the usual tea but rye whiskey. Morgan and Henry have been drinking since suppertime. Marjorie and Lily say they only want a little, and only take it at all because it's Christmas Eve and they are dead on their feet. Irene says she's dead on her feet as well but that doesn't mean she only wants a little. Herb has poured quite generously not for her but for Lily and Marjorie, too, and they do not object. He has measured mine and Morgy's out at the same time, very stingily, and poured in Coca-Cola. This is the first drink I have ever had, and as a result I will believe for years that rye-and-Coca-Cola is a standard sort of drink and will always ask for it, until I notice that few other people drink it and that it makes me sick. I didn't get sick that Christmas Eve, though; Herb had not given me enough. Except for an odd taste, and my own feeling of consequence, it was like drinking Coca-Cola.

I don't need Herb in the picture to remember what he looked like. That is, if he looked like himself, as he did all the time at the Turkey Barn and the few times I saw him on the street — as he did all the times in my life when I saw him except one.

The time he looked somewhat unlike himself was when Morgan was cursing out Brian and, later, when Brian had run off down the road. What was this different look? I've tried to remember, because I studied it hard at the time. It wasn't much different. His face looked softer and heavier then, and if you had to describe the expression on it you would have to say it was an expression of shame. But what would he be ashamed of? Ashamed of Brian, for the way he had behaved? Surely that would be late in the day; when had Brian ever behaved otherwise? Ashamed of Morgan, for carrying on so ferociously and theatrically? Or of himself, because he was famous for nipping fights and displays of this sort in the bud and hadn't been able to do it here? Would he be ashamed that he hadn't stood up for Brian? Would he have expected himself to do that, to stand up for Brian?

All this was what I wondered at the time. Later, when I knew more, at least about sex, I decided that Brian was Herb's lover, and that Gladys really was trying to get attention from Herb, and that was why Brian had humiliated her — with or without Herb's connivance and consent. Isn't it true that people like Herb — dignified, secretive, honorable people — will often choose somebody like Brian, will waste their helpless love on some vicious, silly person who is not even evil, or a monster, but just some importunate nuisance? I decided that Herb, with all his gentleness and carefulness, was avenging himself on us all — not just on

Gladys but on us all — with Brian, and that what he was feeling when I studied his face must have been a savage and gleeful scorn. But embarrassment as well — embarrassment for Brian and for himself and for Gladys, and to some degree for all of us. Shame for all of us — that is what I thought then.

Later still, I backed off from this explanation. I got to a stage of backing off from the things I couldn't really know. It's enough for me now just to think of Herb's face with that peculiar, stricken look; to think of Brian monkeying in the shade of Herb's dignity; to think of my own mystified concentration on Herb, my need to catch him out, if I could ever get the chance, and then move in and stay close to him. How attractive, how delectable, the prospect of intimacy is, with the very person who will never grant it. I can still feel the pull of a man like that, of his promising and refusing. I would still like to know things. Never mind facts. Never mind theories, either.

When I finished my drink I wanted to say something to Herb. I stood beside him and waited for a moment when he was not listening to or talking with anyone else and when the increasingly rowdy conversation of the others would cover what I had to say.

'I'm sorry your friend had to go away.'

'That's all right.'

Herb spoke kindly and with amusement, and so shut me off from any further right to look at or speak about his life. He knew what I was up to. He must have known it before, with lots of women. He knew how to deal with it.

Lily had a little more whiskey in her mug and told how she and her best girlfriend (dead now, of liver trouble) had dressed up as men one time and gone into the men's side of the beer parlor, the side where it said 'Men Only', because they wanted to see what it was like. They sat in a corner drinking beer and keeping their eyes and ears open, and nobody looked twice or thought a thing about them, but soon a problem arose.

'Where were we going to go? If we went around to the other side and anybody seen us going into the ladies', they would scream bloody murder. And if we went into the men's somebody'd be sure to notice we didn't do it the right way. Meanwhile the beer was going through us like a bugger!'

'What you don't do when you're young!' Marjorie said.

Several people gave me and Morgy advice. They told us to enjoy ourselves while we could. They told us to stay out of trouble. They said they had all been young once. Herb said we were a good crew and had done a good job but he didn't want to get in bad with any of the women's husbands by keeping them there too late. Marjorie and Lily expressed indifference to their husbands, but Irene announced that she loved hers and that it was not true that he had been dragged back from Detroit to marry her, no matter what people said. Henry said it was a good life if you didn't weaken. Morgan said he wished us all the most sincere Merry Christmas.

When we came out of the Turkey Barn it was snowing. Lily said it was like a Christmas card, and so it was, with the snow whirling around the street lights in town and around the colored lights people had put up outside their doorways. Morgan was giving Henry and Irene a ride home in the truck, acknowledging age and pregnancy and Christmas. Morgy took a shortcut through the field, and Herb walked off by himself, head down and hands in his pockets, rolling slightly, as if he were on the deck of a lake boat. Marjorie and Lily linked arms with me as if we were old comrades.

'Let's sing,' Lily said. 'What'll we sing?'

' "We Three Kings?" said Marjorie. ' "We Three Turkey Gutters"?'

' "I'm Dreaming of a White Christmas." '

'Why dream? You got it!'

So we sang.

THE BRAT

ANNE ENRIGHT

She was a brat. It wasn't that she was good-looking – she could be, but she wasn't. She wore her ugliness like a badge. Her clothes were tight in all the worst places, but she pushed her body forward as she spoke. She had fat arms and small breasts. She wore bovver boots and cheap pink cotton trousers. She was all wrong. Her eyebrows were plucked bare and a thin, brown line was pencilled in over the stubble. There was a flicker in her eye that told you she knew that she was being watched, and every gesture took on the slight edge of performance. It made her unpopular, except with new acquaintances, whom she seduced casually and then annoyed.

Clare was fifteen. She had been drunk once in her life, with a girl from school who had filled two pint glasses with the top of every bottle on her parents' cupboard. They drank it all in one go and Clare noticed nothing until she sat down in the bus and discovered that her legs were numb. The rest of the night was spent throwing up in the queue for a toilet, and kissing a boy who took her home. When she woke up her eyes were swollen, and her father had left without his breakfast.

Clare's father makes his way from the Customs House to O'Beirne's on the Quays, crosses the Liffey by means of a bridge, so sited as to add to the distance between the two buildings a length of nearly three hundred yards.

'If I could swim now, I'd be right.' He is a man much given to speaking aloud when company is absent, and to silence when the nicer of social obligations might urge him into speech. Those contributions he does make are as counterpoint to the sounds of liquid consumption only, the sweetest of which is the sound of a pint drawing creamily at the bar, a music only those born with the gift, or those who spend a minimum of three thousand hours acquiring the gift, can hear.

O'Donnel was doubly blessed. He was born with a magic thumb, the sucking of which enabled him to discern the music of a good pint from the discord of a bad, before a head had even begun to form; but being a man of diligence and application (those same qualities which, combined with tenacity, ensured his promotion to the rank of Under-Manager, Grade Two of Dublin Corporation, Sanitation Section, despite the vagaries of political influence, which was never behind him, the unenlightened reservations of his superiors, cognisant as they were of his talents, and thence careful of their own interests and tenure, and the constant, whingeing begrudgery of his fellow workers, craven in the envy of a magnitude only the true culchie could muster, with the smell of dung still clinging to their boots, the stripes of the diocesan fathers still stinging their palms and the sly post-colonialism still giving the edge of flattery to every utterance of a personal nature that crossed their lips), he distrusted the gifts of nature and concentrated the subtle power of his intelligence on discerning, without the aid of his cool, Fenian thumb, that crystalline hum, that black, creamy noise, of a pint just waiting to be drunk.

The river is at an ebb, its green is black in the early evening. 'It's not green. See?' he says to a passing young woman, who ignores both him and the complexity of his literary allusion. He pivots his body and fixes his eyes on her receding back, its cheap, smart blue coat, her black hair and the hurried motion of her tights, with a pattern of skin disease, arranged in bows, along the seam.

'Golden stockings she had on,' he says loudly, in the interests of the general good. A sharp sniff, and the air stings his nose, outside and in. Three fingers he counts, tapping them one after the other on the interstice of his right nostril.

'Most high, most pure, most sweet . . . ' Black hair, blue coat, and flesh-coloured legs – don't forget the bows. He stands, swaying slightly against the flood of people crossing the river to the northside of the city and strains to hear the broken clack of her shoes on the pavement. He sees her opening cans in a bedsit in Drumcondra. The shoes are loose, and a raw, reddened heel emerges at every step.

'There will be peace in the valley,' he assures her and all the other backs now interrupting his view of her, as a benediction, then turns to square himself against the tide.

'I wouldn't spit now,' he says, 'at a pint. If it was handed to me.' He was a man who could not abide spit.

O'Donnel avoids the snug in O'Beirne's, likely as it is to contain Elements. He takes his place with the dockers at the bar.

'Stevedores.'

There is no need for another word, his order is known. The brown suit strains tightly against the yoke of his back as he places the elbows, long stained with old porter, carefully on two beer-mats equidistant from the apex of his nose. His head is loosely cupped in two large hands.

'There's one for the drip,' says the barman, slapping a mat under the point of his snout. O'Donnel stares at the wood of the counter, his feet broadly placed on the brass rail. His air could be interpreted as one of dignified rebuke.

'Larry,' he says, from the cavern of his crouched torso, 'would you ever hinge that elbow in the way God intended.' And not wishing to disturb the barman by his tone, he adds the phrase, 'he says,' to allow a proper distance from the remark.

'Does he so?' says Larry, and places a small preliminary Bushmills on the central mat.

After many hours of similar silences, the air is punctuated by the single word 'Nevermore'.

The barman gives the wink to a man in the snug, the long-suffering recipient of countless memos on the subject of parking meters: the cleaning thereof, embellished in O'Donnel's hand by the appropriate quotations from the Latin.

'So they finally gave the old codger the push, eh?' The final syllable is terse, sympathetic, way-of-the-worldish; harsh, without interrogative cadence or function.

'Resigned, Larry. For God's sake, the word is "resigned".' He salutes the barman with his pint, and with one finger he taps, three times, on the interstice of his left nostril.

Clare was late home again. A boy came up to her at the dance and started asking questions. 'How are you?' 'What did the Da say?' It was the one she had kissed some weeks before and she found herself answering quite sweetly because of the shame she felt. She must have told him everything. 'You were crying,' he told her, 'and you said that you wanted to die.'

'I wanted to throw up,' she said.

'You did.'

'Well, that didn't stop you, anyway.'

'Shush,' he said, although the music was making them shout, and she started to kiss him again.

He had a good, strong accent and spoke very carefully. When the slow songs came on he just stood back and looked at her face. They only kissed again when the music changed.

Apart from that he had green eyes. 'Don't fucking worry about me,' Clare said, 'I'm clever.'

'I know you're clever.'

'My father is clever.'

'My Da's an arsehole,' he said, 'So what?' He was like a doctor, he asked questions that no one else asked. Whatever it was that made him sad made him kind as well and so she took his sympathy. He was a nice man. She felt obliged to tell him things, like she would tell any unicorn she met in the street.

Clare's father was sitting in front of the television when she got home, with his eyes closed. He looked away from her when she came in, and examined the curtains. 'Words,' he said, 'are for the radio. They should have stuck to silent films. Where were you?'

'Where were you?' she asked back.

'Your mother never left, you know . . . ' his voice trailed after her as she left the room, 'you have her accusatory tone to perfection.'

There was a smell in the house. Clare had never realised that the disinfectants, the carpet cleaners, the plastic boxes that were hung up in the toilet did any good. She had hated their stink, like an industrial version of all the fluids, lotions, perfumes and bathsalts that made it her mother's house. A stink of unnecessary work and hours spent in front of the mirror, of cleaning windows in pink fluffy slippers, of fits of hysteria when towels were folded the wrong way. Now the kitchen smelt of old fat, the hall of damp and urine, her bedroom of clothes come out of the rain, like the top deck of the bus on a bad morning.

She went across to pull the curtains and was shocked to see that the boy was still outside, his arms folded and leaning on top of the wall. He saw her, smiled and walked away.

Her brother came into the room, and she let the curtain drop. 'The old man got the sack,' he said. 'Where were you?'

Your honour, on this, the second occasion, the victim spent some hours with the accused outside her house. Interglottal activity was engaged upon and some saliva was exchanged. The couple embraced warmly and muscular tissue from the sacral region of the crown of the head was palpated. This was followed by both visual and tactile exploration of the upper limbs and face of the accused and there was a Verbal Exchange. On the evening in question the victim had his back to a wall and indentations made from the ornamental gravel in his buttocks and upper back took thirty minutes to diffuse.

A girl from up the road told Clare that she had seen her mother in town, walking down the street 'and Dressed To Kill'.

Kill what?

It was on the third occasion that the alleged murder took place. I will not offend the court with details save that there were several breaks for cigarettes, which were smoked in a car, the windows of which, much to the amusement of the accused, became steamed up, in the manner of comic sketches which can be seen from time to time on the television set. I have the assurance of the victim that no reproductive processes were engaged, although they were vigorously and callously primed by the frotteur.

(Objection your honour! The term 'frottage' implies guilt, I will not have my client tried by lexiphanicism, at the hands of a coprolalomaniac!)

(Objection sustained.) The appalling psychological damage suffered by the victim even before the fatal blow was struck, can only be imagined, and in happier times this frustration of biology might be viewed in the light which it deserves and sentence passed commensurate with the enormity of the crime.

He had left school young. He had a car and a job. He had taken his hand off the wheel and crossed his middle finger over his index and said 'I'm like that. You see? You can trust me. I'm like that.' The streetlamp outside the house made slits of his eyes, and Clare was shocked by the freedoms she took. She was violent and tender and made herself cry again. He absorbed it all without surprise.

At three o'clock in the morning, she heard the sound of a dog barking and her father's voice. He was walking down the street with a Jack Russell at his heel. As she watched she saw that he was not kicking the dog but playing with it. He emerged from Mrs Costello's forsythia bush with only a few leaves in his hands, but he threw them defiantly, shouting 'Fetch!' The dog was confused and he bent down over it, flinging his arm out and repeating the command. Then he straightened up and addressed the street and its dog, in the grand manner: 'Bitch!' He buttoned up his coat and walked on.

'That's the old man,' she said to the boy in the car, who smiled.

'Does he have a shotgun?'

Clare had never seen her father look monumental. He staggered in and out of the light from the streetlamp and she lost all sympathy. He was not in any way normal.

'You should see mine on a good night,' said the boy in the car. He straightened his jumper.

'Do you want to go?'

Mr O'Donnel reached the car and vented a stream of buff-coloured puke on the bonnet, which was fresh and decorative against the biscuit-brown of the paintwork and the chrome. His meditation on the effect was disturbed by the cognisance that the vehicle was occupied and by intimations of a possible unpleasantness to come. He hinged his torso into the upright and carefully aligned the cuffs of his shirt below the line of his coat-sleeves, a gesture he had admired in his long observation of the British Royal Family, and one he reserved for the petty and the punctilious. His relief on finding the face that peered out from behind the windscreen familiar, mitigated to a great extent the indignation he felt on finding that she was not alone: that uncomfortably close to his daughter was a hairy young skelp. The contrasting paleness of his daughter's countenance, and the bar of shadow that fell from the framework of the car and caressed her mouth, made his throat constrict alarmingly, and the tragedy of generation burst in his chest. This was the entrance to eternity. No sound or movement greeted his thoughts as they took wing, but beneath his hand he could sense the dormant miracle of the internal combustion engine, and above his head stars, that had seen the continents rip, one from the other, wheeled and waited the light years it would take before they could witness his shame. He stood back. The moment cried out for expression. With the flat of his palm, he banged the bonnet of the car.

  ' "I will tell you.

The barge she sat in, like a burnish'd throne,
Burn'd on the water; the poop was beaten gold,
Purple the sails, and so perfumed, that
The winds were love-sick with them, the oars were silver
Which to the tune of flutes kept stroke, and made
The water which they beat to follow faster,
As amorous of their strokes. For her own person,
It beggar'd all description . . ." '

And so beggar'd, he left the lovers, opened the gate with a creak and entered his house.

Clare came into the kitchen at four o'clock in the morning and found her father sitting at the kitchen table. There was a smell of drink in the room but she couldn't see any bottles. The record player in the living room was left on and the record on the turntable was finished. The sound of the needle going round and round reminded her of the scene in the car and the feeling in her insides.

'Your mother never left, you know. You have her guilty look to perfection.'

She left her father where he was and went into her room where she took down all the posters and started to write on the walls. She wrote all the poems from the school curriculum so that she would be able to study them every night, and so know them off by heart.

'Had I the heaven's embroidered cloths.'

'Golden stockings she had on.'

'I wonder, by my troth, what thou and I
Did, til we loved?'

No more dancing. On the other wall, she copied all her theorems and the basic laws of Physics. Then she lay on the bed and promised herself that she would not sleep for three days and three nights before she closed her eyes and cried.

GRAVITY

DAVID LEAVITT

Theo had a choice between a drug that would save his sight and a drug that would keep him alive, so he chose not to go blind. He stopped the pills and started the injections — these required the implantation of an unpleasant and painful catheter just above his heart — and within a few days the clouds in his eyes started to clear up; he could see again. He remembered going into New York City to a show with his mother, when he was twelve and didn't want to admit he needed glasses. 'Can you read that?' she'd shouted, pointing to a Broadway marquee, and when he'd squinted, making out only one or two letters, she'd taken off her own glasses — harlequins with tiny rhinestones in the corners — and shoved them onto his face. The world came into focus, and he gasped, astonished at the precision around the edges of things, the legibility, the hard, sharp, colorful landscape. Sylvia had to squint through *Fiddler on the Roof* that day, but for Theo, his face masked by his mother's huge glasses, everything was as bright and vivid as a comic book. Even though people stared at him, and muttered things, Sylvia didn't care; he could *see*.

Because he was dying again, Theo moved back to his mother's house in New Jersey. The DHPG injections she took in stride — she'd seen her own mother through *her* dying, after all. Four times a day, with the equanimity of a nurse, she cleaned out the plastic tube implanted in his chest, inserted a sterilised hypodermic and slowly dripped the bag of sight-giving liquid into his veins. They endured this procedure silently, Sylvia sitting on the side of the hospital bed she'd rented for the duration of Theo's stay — his life, he sometimes thought — watching reruns of *I Love Lucy* or the news, while he tried not to think about the hard piece of

137

pipe stuck into him, even though it was a constant reminder of how wide and unswimmable the gulf was becoming between him and the ever-receding shoreline of the well. And Sylvia was intricately cheerful. Each day she urged him to go out with her somewhere — to the library, or the little museum with the dinosaur replicas he'd been fond of as a child — and when his thinness and the cane drew stares, she'd maneuver him around the people who were staring, determined to shield him from whatever they might say or do. It had been the same that afternoon so many years ago, when she'd pushed him though a lobbyful of curious and laughing faces, determined that nothing should interfere with the spectacle of his seeing. What a pair they must have made, a boy in ugly glasses and a mother daring the world to say a word about it!

This warm, breezy afternoon in May they were shopping for revenge. 'Your cousin Howard's engagement party is next month,' Sylvia explained in the car. 'A very nice girl from Livingston. I met her a few weeks ago, and really, she's a superior person.'

'I'm glad,' Theo said. 'Congratulate Howie for me.'

'Do you think you'll be up to going to the party?'

'I'm not sure. Would it be okay for me just to give him a gift?'

'You already have. A lovely silver tray, if I say so myself. The thank-you note's in the living room.'

'Mom,' Theo said, 'why do you always have to —'

Sylvia honked her horn at a truck making an illegal left turn. 'Better they should get something than no present at all, is what I say,' she said. 'But now, the problem is, *I* have to give Howie something, to be from me, and it better be good. It better be very, very good.'

'Why?'

'Don't you remember that cheap little nothing Bibi gave you for your graduation? It was disgusting.'

'I can't remember what she gave me.'

'Of course you can't. It was a tacky pen-and-pencil set. Not even a real leather box. So naturally, it stands to reason that I have to get something truly spectacular for Howard's engagement. Something that will make Bibi blanch. Anyway, I think I've found just the thing, but I need your advice.'

'Advice? Well, when my old roommate Nick got married, I gave him a garlic press. It cost five dollars and reflected exactly how much I felt, at that moment, our friendship was worth.'

Sylvia laughed. 'Clever. But my idea is much more brilliant, because it makes it possible for me to get back at Bibi *and* give Howard the nice gift he and his girl deserve.' She smiled, clearly pleased with herself. 'Ah, you live and learn.'

'You live,' Theo said.

Sylvia blinked. 'Well, look, here we are.' She pulled the car into a handicapped-parking place on Morris Avenue and got out to help Theo, but he was already hoisting himself up out of his seat, using the door handle for leverage. 'I can manage myself,' he said with some irritation. Sylvia stepped back.

'Clearly one advantage to all this for you,' Theo said, balancing on his cane, 'is that it's suddenly so much easier to get a parking place.'

'Oh Theo, please,' Sylvia said. 'Look, here's where we're going.'

She leaned him into a gift shop filed with porcelain statuettes of Snow White and all seven of the dwarves, music boxes which, when you opened them, played 'The Shadow of Your Smile', complicated-smelling potpourris in purple wallpapered boxes, and stuffed snakes you were supposed to push up against drafty windows and doors.

'Mrs Greenman,' said an expansive, gray-haired man in a cream-colored cardigan sweater. 'Look who's here, Archie, it's Mrs Greenman.'

Another man, this one thinner and balding, but dressed in an identical cardigan, peered out from the back of the shop. 'Hello there!' he said, smiling. He looked at Theo, and his expression changed.

'Mr Sherman, Mr Baker. This is my son, Theo.'

'Hello,' Mr Sherman and Mr Baker said. They didn't offer to shake hands.

'Are you here for that item we discussed last week?' Mr Sherman asked.

'Yes,' Sylvia said. 'I want advice from my son here.' She walked over to a large ridged crystal bowl, a very fifties sort of bowl, stalwart and square-jawed. 'What do you think? Beautiful, isn't it?'

'Mom, to tell the truth, I think it's kind of ugly.'

'Four hundred and twenty-five dollars,' Sylvia said admiringly. 'You have to feel it.'

Then she picked up the big bowl and tossed it to Theo, like a football.

The gentlemen in the cardigan sweaters gasped and did not exhale. When Theo caught it, it sank his hands. His cane rattled as it hit the floor.

'That's heavy,' Syliva said, observing with satisfaction how the bowl had weighted Theo's arms down. 'And where crystal is concerned, heavy is impressive.'

She took the bowl back from him and carried it to the counter. Mr Sherman was mopping his brow. Theo looked at the floor, still surprised not to see shards of glass around his feet.

Since no one else seemed to be volunteering, he bent over and picked up the cane.

'Four hundred and fifty-nine, with tax,' Mr Sherman said, his voice still a bit shaky, and a look of relish came over Sylvia's face as she pulled out her checkbook to pay. Behind the counter, Theo could see Mr Baker put his hand on his forehead and cast his eyes to the ceiling.

It seemed Sylvia had been looking a long time for something like this, something heavy enough to leave an impression, yet so fragile it could make you sorry.

GRAVITY

They headed back out to the car.

'Where can we go now?' Sylvia asked, as she got in. 'There must be someplace else to go.'

'Home,' Theo said. 'It's almost time for my medicine.'

'Really? Oh. All right.' She pulled on her seat belt, inserted the car key in the ignition and sat there.

For just a moment, but perceptibly, her face broke. She squeezed her eyes shut so tight the blue shadow on the lids cracked.

Almost as quickly she was back to normal again, and they were driving. 'It's getting hotter,' Sylvia said. 'Shall I put on the air?'

'Sure,' Theo said. He was thinking about the bowl, or more specifically, about how surprising its weight had been, pulling his hands down. For a while now he'd been worried about his mother, worried about what damage his illness might secretly be doing to her that of course she would never admit. On the surface things seemed all right. She still broiled herself a skinned chicken breast for dinner every night, still swam a mile and a half a day, still kept used teabags wrapped in foil in the refrigerator. Yet she had also, at about three o'clock one morning, woken him up to tell him she was going to the twenty-four-hour supermarket, and was there anything he wanted. Then there was the gift shop: She had literally pitched that bowl toward him, pitched it like a ball, and as that great gleam of flight and potential regret came sailing his direction, it had occurred to him that she was trusting his two feeble hands, out of the whole world, to keep it from shattering. What was she trying to test? Was it his newly regained vision? Was it the assurance that he was there, alive, that he hadn't yet slipped past all her caring, a little lost boy in rhinestone-studded glasses? There are certain things you've already done before you even think how to do them — a child pulled from in front of a car, for instance, or the bowl, which Theo was holding before he could even begin to calculate its brief trajectory. It had pulled his arms down, and

141

from that apish posture he'd looked at his mother, who smiled broadly, as if, in the war between heaviness and shattering, he'd just helped her win some small but sustaining victory.

ALL FALL DOWN

HELEN LUCY BURKE

There was not an ounce of innate prejudice against me in the heart of Miss O'Leary. Every now and then she took us on 'Nature Walks' to point us out interesting weeds and mushrooms that would clarify the botanical bits in our reader. In the same way she used me and my family to illustrate her thesis on alcohol.

By disposition she was very strong against the drink. The Parish Priest urged her to still greater extremities of zeal – our parish was a horror for alcohol. Who could blame her for her enthusiasm when daily, opposite her very window, she was presented with a text-book example?

Who but me?

Each day at half-past two came my moment of torture: for that was the time when my father, chased out of the pub for the regulation hour, went staggering home past the windows of the school.

'See, children,' Miss O'Leary would cry, all professional interest, 'how alcohol depresses the brain, causing loss of muscular control.'

My father was a long, thin man. His legs wobbled about as awkwardly as the legs of a newly-dropped colt. There was a bit of a rise in the boreen outside the school, and there he always fell. It used to take him a long time to get up. He would throw one leg out in front of him, stiff as the fork of a compass: but then the other leg pivoted away, and there he was again, sprawling in the mud. His face was very calm and serious all the time. None of us ever attempted to help him. Miss O'Leary instructed us that drunks had terrible tempers and that we were not to trust ourselves near them, any more than we would go beside a ram or a bull.

Of course the other kids had fathers who got drunk – there

was not an abstainer in the whole parish — but they did it in a jollier way altogether, at fairs and card-parties: and afterwards they went home and beat the tar out of their wives and children, which was thought nicer and more natural.

Basically, the great local failing was not alcohol but excess. The women never touched a drop of fermented liquor, but instead got their release in exaggerated fervour of church-going. They practised bowings before the altar, daily Communion, weekly Confession at which they accused themselves of interesting faults like over-zealousness and scruples, and all sorts of other religious *bonne-bouches* in the style of Sodalities and Leagues against Swearing. At night while their husbands were out drinking and gambling, they cautioned their huge families against marriage and did their best to turn their minds in the direction of monasteries and nunneries.

Among this crew my father was an oddity. He did not beat my mother or me. He drank alone. He showed no loud enjoyment of his drink — poor man, what was wine to them was blood to him. Worst of all he was a sort of gentleman, and the wrong sort, the quiet standoffish kind. If he had turned out for the first meet of the season and galloped his half-mile with the hounds there would have been no animosity. Even attendance now and then at a point-to-point would have been better than nothing.

Quite simply, I hated him. At night, lying with the blankets drawn over my head and tucked in the far side of the pillow, I used to scheme how I would kill him before I was eighteen. A push down the stairs from the top landing — now that would be a fine thing!

Most of the time I think he did not know I was there. If by chance he noticed me, I embarrassed him so much that he gave me all his loose change.

One night, coming home from the village, my father was knocked down by a straying cow who rolled him into the ditch.

There he lay, all the freezing night. When he was found next morning his condition was grave. My mother had him conveyed to the hospital forty miles away. So that she might be free to sit at his bedside – his death was expected – she sent me by train to Dublin as a boarder in a convent school. I believe she was quite fond of him.

I was ten years old.

For the next two days I cried steadily, more because it was expected of me than from grief. After this purge I settled down into the bliss of a life that I could build to my own specifications.

There are strange paradises in this world. Mine was compounded of long dark corridors smelling of paraffin polish and disinfectant, a playground paved with cinders, staircases hollowed out of the mouldering walls, a corner of the nuns' garden where we dug plots for seeds.

Oh, the strangeness of the customs! The nuns bowed as they passed each other in the corridors. If they were alone they swept down the middle of the passages, majestic in their white starched bonnets as ships in full sail; and we pupils crowded in against the walls and bowed humbly with hands folded. Impassive, they never returned our reverences but floated rapidly on, their faces adorned with little mysterious smiles.

They filled me with awe. Nature must have moulded them from a different clay. Surely they were not of the same make as the harried red and brown women of Kilanore. I remember my horror when one day, peeping from a forbidden window, I saw the nuns' knickers hanging like great white spinnakers from the clothes-line. I told my infamy later in Confession.

We went to bed at nine o'clock and we rose at six. Once a month we had a bath. Hair-washing was not permitted for the whole length of the term. Some abandoned girls secretly used to wash their hair after the lights were out, and dried it on their pillows; but we were told that God had His eyes on them and sooner or later He would punish them by striking them deaf.

A number of the girls had lice. When this was spotted – we were watched pretty sharply for undue scratching – they were combed over an enamel basin with a fine comb dipped in paraffin. For weeks these victims went round smelling of paraffin and howling for grief that their shame had been exposed.

All this was paradise because my father was not near. In fact I spread it around that I had no father. Died while I was small, I said, and basked in the caressing sympathy of the older girls.

I never heard from him, of course, and when my mother wrote it was just dry little notes saying that things were going well, or things could be better, or things were not so well. The nuns opened the letters and read them before we got them, but that did not disturb me. I did not even wonder what would happen if they got to hear of my fictions. Life was taking place on two planes, and the plane of the imagination was the more real. Religion helped. Sin was all around us, we were told, lurking like a worm at the heart of an apple, invisible until you got to the ruined core. Opportunities for virtue were offered as plentifully. At lunch in the refectory one day Frances Boylan got a decayed human tooth in her stew. She wept and complained, but the refectarian pointed out the great opportunity she had missed for gaining grace by 'offering it up' and saying nothing. Next day they read to us from the *Lives of the Saints* about a French lady who developed her sanctity by eating spits off the ground.

Heaven lay about us, and so did Hell, and the school was an infinite wonder, a battleground of forces contending for possession of us; and yet pure, unsensual, unworldly, a place where everything including sin could take place in the mind.

Kilanore and its grossness became a memory.

Easter came, making a dent in the routine. Christ died. Prayerbooks banged with sinister noise in the darkened chapel at Tenebrae. He rose again from the dead. We were allowed to attend

146

three Masses on Easter Sunday. Afterwards there were boiled eggs for breakfast, and in the afternoon there was a film about the Missions. A number of girls, including myself, did not go home for the Easter holidays. We all cried a little each night, and the other girls petted me and stroked me because my father was dead and I was so brave. Frances Boylan, who was two months older than me, said she would be my best friend. The sun shone and my whole body seemed to blossom and send out green shoots. I knew at last that God lived and loved me.

I prepared with fervour for my Confirmation.

Not long after term started again my mother wrote to say that himself was out of hospital. The two of them planned to attend my Confirmation.

It was my sentence of death.

Closing my eyes tightly to shut out the pictures that presented themselves I could see them all the more clearly. My father lurching over the parquet floor . . . the fall and the sprawl and the dreadful efforts to get up . . . the girls turning kindly away so as not to see and not to know that I had lied.

I wrote to him for the first time in my life, told him what I had done, and demanded that he stay his distance. A few days later I got a letter from my mother saying that she and my uncle would be arriving for the Confirmation.

I had no uncle.

We walked – no, proceeded, slowly up the aisle, heads bent in reverence. Our white dresses creaked over layers of petticoats. The weather had turned cold, but none of us wore a coat that might hide the glory of our rows of picot-edged frills. Frances Boylan beside me had only four rows of frills: I had six, and this was a triumph that made me love her even more. When the Bishop tapped us on the cheek with a withered hand that rustled like paper she grabbed my arm and held it tightly, not daring to look up, while I stared boldly into the beaky face, lemon-coloured under the mitre, and the Bishop stared back at me the way an angry cock does.

Later, we promised to abide by the truths of our religion and to refrain from alcohol under the age of twenty-one. We chorused this in unison, and no voice was stronger than mine.

Parents and children met afterwards in the Middle Parlour. Awkwardly, on the chill expanse of waxed parquet, the family groups talked in low embarrassed voices. Even Frances Boylan's father, who was a stout red-faced bookmaker, planed the rough race-course edges off his voice and fluted out his conversation in a genteel treble.

My father seemed at ease. He did not come forward to meet me but stood quietly waiting, as if he were ready to be disowned without making a fuss.

My mother and he kissed me. I noticed at once that he did not smell of drink. There was a carnation in the buttonhole of his suit. It was a new suit, dark-brown fine tweed with a little hair in it that scratched my cheek when he pressed me against him.

'Your uncle came out of hospital a fortnight ago,' said my mother.

I nodded my head politely up and down. 'I hope you're better,' I said.

'Not too bad.' He spoke in a sort of ghost voice, that seemed to come with great effort from a great distance. His face had got smaller and was a funny clear colour, a bit like the tracing paper we used for making maps, but greyer. His moustache was gone, so that it was easier to see his mouth, and to see that his lips trembled slightly but continually. Each time he caught my eye he tried to smile, but could not quite make it. I left them and went to the table where tea and sandwiches and seedcake were set out.

Frances Boylan and Una Sheedy asked me was that my uncle.

'It is,' I said. 'He's just after coming out of hospital.'

'He's lovely looking,' said Frances. Flabbergasted, I realised that she meant it; and that she was comparing his emaciated elegance with her stout common father. And I realised that she too was ashamed of her father. Did all children hate their parents, I wondered? It seemed a new strong bond. I led them over to be introduced.

'This is my mother and my Uncle Matthew,' I said.

He stood up at once and shook hands. Then he asked their permission to smoke. Reverent in their awe for his politeness they assured him that they did not mind. My mother stood in the background with a shut-off expression on her face. Presently she said that they must go. My father gave me a five-pound note, and bowed to Una and Frances.

We left the parlour all five of us together, like a family, or like a herd of does with the stag. No, that was not it either, for he deferred to us so lightly and gently that it was more like a king with a group of young queens, his equals in rank, but younger.

Worshipping, Frances and Una drifted forward beside him, while my mother and I as proprietors hung back a little and let them have their fill. He told them to call him uncle, and they did so. He took the carnation from his buttonhole and presented it to them jointly, regretting that roses were not in season. We came to the head of the marble stairs. Frances and Una drew back, I moved forward to escort my visitors down to the door.

The saints smiled at us from the walls. He turned back to wave to my friends and his footing went. His stick tumbled before him down to the foot of the stairs. Behind it he rolled, threshing with his arms for a hold to save himself. There was a dull sound from each stair as he struck, then silence when he reached the bottom. We stared down at him, an insect on its back, waving its legs. There was no power in them, like tentacles they moved. His head came up several times and turned vaguely about.

'He's killed,' screamed Frances and Una. They started down

the stairs. I ran past them and picked up his stick.

It took the combined strength of my mother and two nuns to get me away from him. As I struck, his eyes looked up at me for each blow and winced away as the stick fell. He said nothing, although his mouth writhed. He did not cry out.

They sent me to the sickroom with hot milk and aspirin. Later the priest came. He sat at the end of my bed for a long time. All I would say in answer to his questioning was: 'He fell down again.'

A few weeks afterwards I got word that my father had died. It was alcohol poisoning, I learned later.

NICE DAY AT SCHOOL

WILLIAM TREVOR

Eleanor lay awake, thinking in advance about the day. The face of Miss Whitehead came into her mind, the rather pointed nose, eyes set wide apart, a mouth that turned up at the corners and gave the impression that Miss Whitehead was constantly smiling, although it was a widely held view among the girls whom she taught that Miss Whitehead had little to smile over, having missed out. The face of Liz Jones came into Eleanor's mind also, a pretty, wild face with eyes that were almost black, and black hair hanging prettily down on either side of it, and full lips. Liz Jones claimed to have gypsy blood in her, and another girl, Mavis Temple, had once remarked to Eleanor that she thought Liz Jones's lips were negroid. 'A touch of the tar brush,' Mavis Temple had said. 'A seaman done her mum.' She'd said it three years ago, when the girls had all been eleven, in Miss Homber's class. Everything had been different then.

In the early morning gloom Eleanor considered the difference, regretting, as always, that it had come about. It had been nice in Miss Homber's class, the girls' first year at Springfield Comprehensive: they'd all had a crush on Miss Homber because Miss Homber, who'd since become Mrs George Spaxton and a mother, had been truly beautiful and intelligent. Miss Homber told them it was important to wash all the parts of the body once per day, including you knew where. Four girls brought letters of complaint after that and Miss Homber read them out to the class, commenting on the grammar and the spelling errors and causing the girls to become less carefree about what they repeated to their mums. 'Remember, you can give birth at thirteen,' Miss Homber warned, and she added that if a boy ever said he was too embarrassed to go into a chemist's for preventatives he could always get them in a slot machine that was situated in the Gents at the filling station on the Portsmouth Road, which was something her own boyfriend had told her.

It had been nice in those days because Eleanor didn't believe that any boy would try stuff like that on when she was thirteen, and the girls of the first year all agreed that it sounded disgusting, a boy putting his thing up you. Even Liz Jones did, although she was constantly hanging about the boys of the estate and twice had had her knickers taken down in the middle of the estate playground. There were no boys at Springfield Comprehensive, which was just as well, Eleanor had always considered, because boys roughened up a school so.

But in spite of their physical absence boys had somehow penetrated, and increasingly, as Eleanor passed up through the school, references to them infiltrated all conversation. At thirteen, in Miss Croft's class, Liz Jones confessed that a boy called Gareth Swayles had done her in the corner of the estate playground, at eleven o'clock one night. She'd been done standing up, she reported, leaning against the paling that surrounded the playground. She said it was fantastic.

Lying in bed, Eleanor remembered Liz Jones saying that and saying a few months later that a boy called Rogo Pollini was twice as good as Gareth Swayles, and later that a boy called Tich Ayling made Rogo Pollini seem totally laughable. Another girl, Susie Crumm, said that Rogo Pollini had told her that he'd never enjoyed it with Liz Jones because Liz Jones put him off with all her wriggling and pinching. Susie Crumm, at the time, had just been done by Rogo Pollini.

By the time they reached Class 2 it had become the fashion to have been done and most of the girls, even quiet Mavis Temple, had succumbed to it. Many had not cared for the experience and had not repeated it, but Liz Jones said that this was because they had got it from someone like Gareth Swayles, who was no better on the job than a dead horse. Eleanor hadn't ever been done nor did she wish to be, by Gareth Swayles or anyone else. Some of the girls said it had hurt them: she knew it would hurt her. And she'd heard that even if Gareth Swayles, or whoever it was, went to the slot machine in the filling station it sometimes happened that the preventative came asunder, a disaster that would be followed by weeks of worry. That, she knew, would be her fate too.

'Eleanor's prissy,' Liz Jones said every day now. 'Eleanor's prissy like poor prissy Whitehead.' Liz Jones went on about it all the time, hating Eleanor because she still had everything in store for her. Liz Jones had made everyone else think that Eleanor would grow into a Miss Whitehead, who was terrified of men, so Liz Jones said. Miss Whitehead had hairs on her chin and her upper lip that she didn't bother to do anything about. Quite often her breath wasn't fresh, which was unpleasant if she was leaning over you, explaining something.

Eleanor, who lived on the estate with her parents, hated being identified with Miss Whitehead and yet she felt, especially when she lay awake in the early morning, that there was something in Liz Jones's taunting. 'Eleanor's waiting for Mr Right,' Liz Jones would say. 'Whitehead waited forever.' Miss Whitehead, Liz Jones said, 'never had a fellow for long because she wouldn't give herself wholly and in this day and age a girl had to be sensible and natural over a matter like that. Everyone agreed that this was probably so, because there was no doubt about it that in her time Miss Whitehead had been pretty. 'It happens to you,' Liz Jones said, 'left solitary like that: you grow hairs on your face; you get stomach trouble that makes your breath bad. Nervous frustration, see.'

Eleanor gazed across her small bedroom, moving her eyes from the pink of the wall to her school uniform, grey and purple, hanging over the back of a chair. In the room there was a teddy-bear she'd had since she was three, and a gramophone, and records by the New Seekers and the Pioneers and Diana Ross, and photographs of such performers. In her vague, uninterested manner her mother said she thought it awful that Eleanor should waste money on these possessions, but Eleanor explained that everyone at Springfield Comprehensive did so and that she herself did not consider it a waste of money.

'You up?' Eleanor heard her mother calling now, and she replied that she was. She got out of bed and looked at herself in a looking-glass on her dressing-table. Her night-dress was white with small sprigs of violets on it. Her hair had an auburn tinge, her face was long and thin and was not afflicted with spots, as were a few of the faces of her companions at Springfield Comprehensive. Her prettiness was delicate, and she thought as she examined it now that Liz Jones was definitely right in her insinuations: it was a prettiness that could easily disappear overnight. Hairs would appear on her chin and her upper lip, a soft down at first, later becoming harsher. 'Your sight, you know,' an oculist would worriedly remark to her, and tell her she must wear glasses. Her teeth would lose their gleam. She'd have trouble with dandruff.

Eleanor slipped her night-dress over her head and looked at her naked body. She didn't herself see much beauty in it, but she knew that the breasts were the right size for the hips, that arms and legs nicely complemented each other. She dressed and went into the kitchen, where her father was making tea and her mother was reading the *Daily Express*. Her father hadn't been to bed all night. He slept during the day, being employed by night as a doorman in a night-club called Daisy's, in Shepherd Market. Once upon a time her father had been a wrestler, but in 1961 he'd injured his back in a bout with a Japanese and had since been unfit for the ring. Being a doorman of a night-club kept him in touch, so he claimed, with the glamorous world he'd been used to in the past. He often saw familiar faces, he reported, going in and out of Daisy's, faces that once had been his audience. Eleanor felt embarrassed when he talked like that, being unable to believe much of what he said.

'You're in for a scorcher,' he said now, placing a pot of tea on the blue formica of the table. 'No end to the heatwave, they can't see.'

He was a large, red-faced man with closely cut grey hair and no lobe to his right ear. He'd put on weight since he'd left the wrestling ring and although he moved slowly now, as though in some way compensating for years of nimbleness on the taut canvas, he was still, in a physical sense, a formidable opponent, as occasional troublemakers at the night-club had painfully discovered.

Eleanor knocked Special K into a dish and added milk and sugar.

'That's a lovely young girl,' her father said. 'Mia Farrow. She was in last night, Eleanor.'

His breakfast-time conversation was always the same. Princess Margaret had shaken him by the hand and Anthony Armstrong-Jones had asked if he might take his photograph for a book about London he was doing. The Burtons came regularly, and Rex Harrison, and the Canadian Prime Minister whenever he was in London. Her father had a way of looking at Eleanor when he made such statements, his eyes screwed up, almost lost in the puffed red flesh of his face: he stared unblinkingly and beadily, as if defying her to reply that she didn't for a moment accept that Princess Margaret's hand had ever lain in his or that Anthony Armstrong-Jones had addressed him.

'Faceful of innocence,' he said. 'Just a faceful of innocence, Eleanor. ' "Good night, Miss Farrow," I said, and she turned the little face to me and said to call her Mia.'

Eleanor nodded. Her mother's eyes were fixed on the *Daily*

Express, moving from news item to news item, her lips occasionally moving also as she read. 'Liz Jones,' Eleanor wanted to say. 'Could you complain to the school about Liz Jones?' She wanted to tell them about the fashion in Class 2, about Miss Whitehead, and how everyone was afraid of Liz Jones. She imagined her voice speaking across the breakfast table, to her father who was still in his doorman's uniform and her mother who mightn't even hear her. There'd be embarrassment as her father listened, her own face would be as hot as fire. He'd turn his head away in the end, like the time she'd had to ask him for money to buy sanitary towels.

'Lovely little fingers,' he said, 'like a baby's fingers, Eleanor. Little wisps of things. She touched me with the tips.'

'Who?' demanded her mother, suddenly sharp, looking up. 'Eh, then?'

'Mia Farrow,' he said. 'She was down in Daisy's last night. Sweetest thing; sweetest little face.'

'Ah, yes, *Peyton Place*,' her mother said, and Eleanor's father nodded.

Her mother had spectacles with swept-up, elaborately bejewelled frames. The jewels were made of glass, but they glittered, especially in strong sunlight, just like what Eleanor imagined diamonds must glitter like. Her mother, constantly smoking, had hair which she dyed so that it appeared to be black. She was a thin woman with bones that stuck out awkwardly at the joints, seeming as though they might at any moment break through the surface of taut, anaemic skin. In Eleanor's opinion her mother had suffered, and once she had had a dream in which her mother was fat and married to someone else, a man, as far as Eleanor could make out, who ran a vegetable shop.

Her mother always had breakfast in her night-dress and an old fawn-coloured dressing-gown, her ankles below it as white as paper, her feet stuck into tattered slippers. After breakfast, she would return to bed with Eleanor's father, obliging him, Eleanor knew, as she had obliged him all her life. During the school holidays, and on Saturdays and Sundays when Eleanor was still in the flat, her mother continued to oblige him: in the bedroom he made the same kind of noise as he'd made in the wrestling ring. The Prince of Hackney he'd been known as.

Her mother was a shadow. Married to a man who ran a vegetable shop or to any other kind of man except the one she'd chosen, Eleanor believed she'd have been different: she'd have had more children, she'd have been a proper person with proper flesh on her bones, a person you could feel for. As she was, you could hardly take her seriously. She sat there in her night-clothes, waiting for the man she'd married to rise from the table and go into their bedroom so that she might follow. Afterwards she cleared up the breakfast things and washed them, while he slept. She shopped in the Express Dairy Supermarket, dropping cigarette ash over tins of soup and peas and packets of crisps, and at half past eleven she sat in the corner of the downstairs lounge of the Northumberland Arms and drank a measure of gin and water, sometimes two.

'Listen to this,' her mother said in her wheezy voice. She quoted a piece about a fifty-five-year-old woman, a Miss Margaret Sugden, who had been trapped in a bath for two days and three nights. '*It ended*,' read Eleanor's mother, '*with two burly policemen – eyes carefully averted – lifting her out. It took them half an hour of gentle levering, for Miss Sugden, a well-rounded sixteen stone, was helplessly stuck.*'

He laughed. Her mother stubbed her cigarette out on her saucer and lit a fresh one. Her mother never ate anything at breakfast-time. She drank three cups of tea and smoked the same number of cigarettes. He liked a large breakfast, eggs and bacon, fried bread, a chop sometimes.

'*History's longest soak*,' her mother said, still quoting from the *Daily Express*. Her father laughed again.

Eleanor rose and carried the dish she'd eaten her Special K out of to the sink, with her cup and her saucer. She rinsed them under the hot tap and stacked them on the red, plastic-covered rack to dry. Her mother spoke in amazed tones when she read pieces out of the newspaper, surprised by the activities of people and animals, never amused by them. Some part of her had been smashed to pieces.

She said goodbye to both of them. Her mother kissed her as she always did. Winking, her father told her not to take any wooden dollars, an advice that was as regular and as mechanical as her mother's embrace.

'Netball is it?' her mother vaguely asked, not looking up from the newspaper. There wasn't netball, Eleanor explained, as she'd explained before, in the summer term: she wouldn't be late back.

She left the flat and descended three flights of concrete stairs. She passed the garages and then the estate's playground, where Liz Jones had first of all been done. 'Good morning, Eleanor,' a woman said to her, an Irish woman called Mrs Rourke. 'Isn't it a great day?'

Eleanor smiled. The weather was lovely, she said. Mrs Rourke was a lackadaisical woman, middle-aged and fat, the mother of eight children. On the estate it was said that she was no better than she should be, that one of her sons, who had a dark tinge in his pallor, was the child of a West Indian railway porter. Another of Mrs Rourke's children and suspect also, a girl of Eleanor's age called Dolly, was reputed to be the daughter of Susie Crumm's father. In the dream Eleanor had had in which her own mother was fat rather than thin it had seemed that her mother had somehow become Mrs Rourke, because in spite of everything Mrs Rourke was a happy woman. Her husband had a look of happiness about him also, as did all the Rourke children, no matter where they'd come from. They regularly went to Mass, all together in a family outing, and even if Mrs Rourke occasionally obliged Susie Crumm's father and others it hadn't taken the same toll of her as the obliging of Eleanor's father by her mother had. For years, ever since she'd listened to Liz Jones telling the class the full facts of life, Eleanor had been puzzled by the form the facts apparently took when different people were involved. She'd accepted quite easily the stories about Mrs Rourke and had thought no less of the woman, but when Dolly Rourke had said, about a month ago, that she'd been done by Rogo Pollini, Eleanor had felt upset, not caring to imagine the occasion, as she didn't care to imagine the occasion that took place every morning after breakfast in her parents' bedroom. Mrs Rourke didn't matter because she was somehow remote, like one of the people her mother read about in the *Daily Express* or one of the celebrities her father told lies about: Mrs Rourke didn't concern her, but Dolly Rourke and Rogo Pollini did because they were close to her, being the same as she was and of the same generation. And her parents concerned her because they were close to her also. You could no longer avoid any of it when you thought of Dolly Rourke and Rogo Pollini, or your parents.

She passed a row of shops, Len Parrish the baker, a dry cleaner's, the Express Dairy Supermarket, the newsagent's and post office, the off-licence attached to the Northumberland Arms. Girls in the grey-and-purple uniform of Springfield Comprehensive alighted in numbers from a bus. A youth whistled at her. 'Hi, Eleanor,' said Gareth Swayles, coming up behind her. In a friendly manner he put his hand on her back, low down, so that, as though by accident, he could in a moment slip it over her buttocks.

There's a new boy in Grimes the butcher's, Liz Jones wrote on a piece of paper. *He's not on the estate at all*. She folded the paper and addressed it to Eleanor. She passed it along the row of desks.

'*Je l'ai vu qui travaillait dans la cour*,' said Miss Whitehead.

I saw him in Grimes, Eleanor wrote. *Funny-looking fish*. She passed the note back and Liz Jones read it and showed it to her neighbour, Thelma Joseph. *Typical Eleanor*, Liz Jones wrote and Thelma Joseph giggled slightly.

'*Un anglais qui passait ses vacances en France*,' said Miss Whitehead.

Miss Whitehead lived in Esher, in a bed-sitting-room. Girls had sometimes visited her there and those who had done so described for others what Miss Whitehead's residence was like. It was very clean and comfortable and neat. White paint shone on the window ledges and the skirting-boards, lace curtains hung close to sparkling glass. On the mantelpiece there were ornaments in delicate ceramic, Highland sheep and cockerels, and a chimney sweep with his brushes on his back. A clock ticked on the mantelpiece, and in the fireplace – no longer used – Miss Whitehead had stood a vase of dried flowers. Her bed was in a recess, not at all obtrusive in the room, a narrow divan covered in cheerful chintz.

'*Le pêcheur*,' said Miss Whitehead, '*est un homme qui* . . . Eleanor?'

'*Pêche?*'

'*Très bien. Et la blanchisseuse est une femme qui* . . . ?'

'*Lave le linge*.'

Liz Jones said it must be extraordinary to be Miss Whitehead, never to have felt a man's hand on you. *Gareth Swayles said he'd give it to her*, she'd written on one of the notes she was constantly passing round the class. *Imagine Swayles in bed with Whitehead!*

'*La mère n'aime pas le fromage*,' said Miss Whitehead, and Liz Jones passed another note to Eleanor. *The new boy in Grimes is called Denny Price*, it said. *He wants to do you*.

'Eleanor,' said Miss Whitehead.

She looked up from the elaborately looped handwriting of Liz Jones. In their bedroom her father would be making the noises he used to make in the wrestling ring. Her mother would be lying there. Once, when she was small, she'd gone in by mistake and her father had been standing without his clothes on. Her mother had pulled a sheet up to cover her own nakedness.

'Why are you writing notes, Eleanor?'

'She didn't, Miss Whitehead,' Liz Jones said. 'I sent her – '

'Thank you, Elizabeth. Eleanor?'

'I'm sorry, Miss Whitehead.'

'Were you writing notes, Eleanor?'

'No, I – '

'I sent her the note, Miss Whitehead. It's a private matter – '

'Not private in *my* class, Elizabeth. Pass me the note, Eleanor.'

Liz Jones was sniggering: Eleanor knew that she'd wanted this to happen. Miss Whitehead would read the note out, which was her rule when a note was found.

'The new boy in Grimes is called Denny Price,' Miss Whitehead said. 'He wants to do you.'

The class laughed, a muffled sound because the girls' heads were bent over their desks.

'He wants to have sexual relations with Eleanor,' Liz Jones explained, giggling more openly. 'Eleanor's a – '

'Thank you, Elizabeth. The future tense, Elizabeth: *s'asseoir.*'

Her voice grated in the classroom. Her voice had become unattractive also, Eleanor thought, because she'd never let herself be loved. In her clean bed-sitting-room she might weep tonight, recalling the insolence of Liz Jones. She'd punish Liz Jones when the bell went, the way she always inflicted punishment. She'd call her name out and while the others left the room she'd keep the girl longer than was necessary, setting her a piece of poetry to write out ten times and explaining, as if talking to an infant, that notes and conversation about sexual matters were not permitted in her classroom. She'd imply that she didn't believe that the boy in Grimes had said what Liz Jones had reported he'd said. She'd pretend it was all a fantasy, that no girl from Springfield Comprehensive had ever been done in the playground of the estate or anywhere else. It was easy for Miss Whitehead, Eleanor thought, escaping to her bed-sitting-room in Esher.

'It's your bloody fault,' Liz Jones said afterwards in the washroom. 'If you weren't such a curate's bitch – '

'Oh, for heaven's sake, shut up about it!' Eleanor cried.

'Denny Price wants to give you his nine inches – '

'I don't want his bloody nine inches. I don't want anything to do with him.'

'You're under-sexed, Eleanor. What's wrong with Denny Price?'

'He's peculiar-looking. There's something the matter with his head.'

'Will you listen to this!' Liz Jones cried, and the girls who'd gathered round tittered. 'What's his head got to do with it for God's sake? It's not his head that's going to – ' She broke off, laughing, and all the girls laughed also, even though several of them didn't at all care for Liz Jones.

'You'll end like Whitehead,' Liz Jones said. 'Doing yourself in Esher.' The likes of Whitehead, she added, gave you a sickness in your kidneys. Eleanor had the same way of walking as Whitehead had, which was a way that dried-up virgins acquired because they were afraid to walk any other way in case a man touched their dried-up bottoms.

Eleanor went away, moving through the girls of other classes, across the washroom.

'Liz Jones is a nasty little tit,' a girl called Eileen Reid whispered, and Joan Moate, a fair-haired girl with a hint of acne, agreed. But Liz Jones couldn't hear them. Liz Jones was still laughing, leaning against a wash-basin with a cigarette in her mouth.

For lunch that day at Springfield Comprehensive there was stew and processed potatoes and carrots, with blancmange afterwards, chocolate and strawberry.

'Don't take no notice,' Susie Crumm said to Eleanor. The way Liz Jones went on, she added, it wouldn't surprise her to hear that she'd contracted syphilis.

'What's it like, Susie?' Eleanor asked.

'Syphilis? You get lesions. If you're a girl you can't tell sometimes. Fellas get them all over their equipment – '

'No, I mean what's it like being done?'

''Sall right. Nice really. But not like Jones goes for it. Not all the bloody time.'

They ate spoonfuls of blancmange, sucking it through their teeth.

''Sall right,' Susie Crumm repeated when she'd finished. ''Sall right for an occasion.'

Eleanor nodded. She wanted to say that she'd prefer to keep it for her wedding night, but she knew that if she said that she'd lose Susie Crumm's sympathy. She wanted it to be special, not just a woman lying down waiting for a man to finish taking his clothes off; not just fumbling in the dark of the estate playground, or something behind the Northumberland Arms, where Eileen Reid had been done.

'My dad said he'd gut any fella that laid a finger on me,' Susie Crumm said.

'Jones's said the same.'

'He done Mrs Rourke. Jones's dad.'

'They've all done Mrs Rourke.' For a moment she wanted to tell the truth: to add that Susie Crumm's dad had done Mrs. Rourke also, that Dolly Rourke was Susie's half-sister.

'You've got a moustache growing on you,' Liz Jones said, coming up behind her and whispering into her hair.

The afternoon of that day passed without incident at Springfield Comprehensive, while on the estate Eleanor's father slept. He dreamed that he was wrestling again. Between his knees he could feel the ribs of Eddie Rodriguez; the crowd was calling out, urging him to give Eddie Rodriguez the final works. Two yards away, in the kitchen, Eleanor's mother prepared a meal. She cut cod into pieces, and sliced potatoes for chips. He liked a crisply fried meal at half past six before watching a bit of television. She liked cod and chips herself, with tinned peas, and maybe a tin of pears. She'd bought a tin of pears in the Express Dairy: they might as well have them with a tin of Carnation cream. She'd get everything ready and then she'd run an iron over his uniform, sponging off any spots there were. She thought about *Crossroads* on the television, wondering what would happen in the episode today.

'I'd remind you that the school photographs will be taken on Tuesday,' Miss Whitehead said. 'Clean white blouses, please.'

They would all be there: Eleanor, Liz Jones, Susie Crumm, Eileen Reid, Joan Moate, Mavis Temple, and all the others: forty smiling faces, and Miss Whitehead standing at the end of the middle row. If you kept the photograph it would be a memory for ever, another record of the days at Springfield Comprehensive. 'Who's that with the bow legs?' her father had asked a few years ago, pointing at Miss Homber.

'Anyone incorrectly dressed on Tuesday,' Miss Whitehead said, 'will forfeit her place in the photo.'

The bell rang for the end of school. 'Forfeit her bloody knickers,' said Liz Jones just before Miss Whitehead left the classroom.

The girls dispersed, going off in twos and threes, swinging the briefcases that contained their school books.

'Walk with you?' Susie Crumm suggested to Eleanor, and together they left the classrooms and the school. 'Baking, innit?' Susie Crumm remarked.

They walked slowly, past concrete buildings, the Eagle Star Insurance Company, Barclays Bank, the Halifax Building Society.

Windows were open, the air was chalky dry. Two girls in front of them had taken off their shoes but now, finding the pavement too hot to walk on, had paused to put them on again. The two girls shrieked, leaning on one another. Women pushed prams around them, irritation in their faces.

'I want to get fixed in a Saxone,' Susie Crumm said. 'Can't wait to leave that bloody place.'

An *Evening Standard* van swerved in front of a bus, causing the bus-driver to shout and blow his horn. In the cab of the van the driver's mate raised two fingers in a gesture of disdain.

'I fancy selling shoes,' Susie Crumm said. 'Fashion shoes type of thing. You get them at cost if you work in a Saxone.'

Eleanor imagined the slow preparation of the evening meal in her parents' flat, and the awakening of her father. He'd get up and shave himself, standing in the bathroom in his vest, braces hanging down, his flies half open. Her mother spent ages getting the evening meal, breaking off to see to his uniform and then returning to the food. He couldn't bear not being a wrestler any more.

'What you going to do, Eleanor?'

She shook her head. She didn't know what she was going to do. All she wanted was to get away from the estate and from Springfield Comprehensive. She wondered what it would be like to work in the Eagle Star Insurance Company, but at the moment that didn't seem important. What was important was the exact present, the afternoon of a certain day, a day that was like others except for the extreme heat. She'd go back and there the two of them would be, and in her mind there'd be the face of Miss Whitehead and the voice of Liz Jones. She'd do her homework and then there'd be *Crossroads* on the TV and then the fried meal and the washing-up and more TV and then he'd go, saying it was time she was in bed. 'See you in the morning,' he'd say and soon after he'd gone they'd both go to bed, and she'd lie there thinking of being married in white lace in a church, to a delicate man who wouldn't hurt her, who'd love the virginal innocence that had been kept all these years for him alone. She'd go away in a two-piece suit on an autumn afternoon when the leaves in London were yellow-brown. She'd fly with a man whose fingers were long and thin and gentle, who'd hold her hand in the aeroplane, Air France to Biarritz. And afterwards she'd come back to a flat where the curtains were the colour of lavender, the same as the walls, where gas fires glowed and there were rugs on natural-wood floors, and the telephone was pale blue.

'What's matter?' Susie Crumm asked.

'Nothing.'

They walked past Len Parrish the baker, the dry cleaner's, the Express Dairy Supermarket, the newsagent's and post office, the off-licence attached to the Northumberland Arms.

'There's that fella,' Susie Crumm said. 'Denny Price.'

His head was awkwardly placed on his neck, cocked to one side. His hair was red and long, his face small in the midst of it. He had brown eyes and thick, blubbery lips.

'Hullo,' he said.

Susie Crumm giggled.

'Like a fag?' he said, holding out a packet of Anchor. 'Smoke, do you, girls?'

Susie Crumm giggled again, and then abruptly ceased. 'Oh God!' she said, her hand stretched out for a cigarette. She was looking over Denny Price's shoulder at a man in blue denim overalls. The man, seeing her in that moment, sharply called at her to come to him.

'Stuff him,' she said before she smiled and obeyed.

'Her dad,' said Denny Price, pleased that she had gone. 'You want a fag, Eleanor?'

She shook her head, walking on. He dropped into step with her.

'I know your name,' he said. 'I asked Liz Jones.'

'Yes.'

'I'm Denny Price. I work in Grimes'.'

'Yes.'

'You're at the Comprehensive.'

'Yes.'

She felt his fingers on her arm, squeezing it just above the elbow. 'Let's go for a walk,' he said. 'Come down by the river, Eleanor.'

She shook her head again and then, quite suddenly, she didn't care what happened. What harm was there in walking by the river with a boy from Grimes'? She looked at the fingers that were still caressing her arm. All day long they had handled meat; the fingernails were bitten away, the flesh was red from scouring. Wasn't it silly, like an advertisement, to imagine that a man would come one day to marry her in white lace in a church and take her, Air France, to Biarritz?

'We'll take a bus to the bridge,' he said. 'A thirty-seven.'

He sat close to her, paying her fare, pressing a cigarette on her. She took it and he lit it for her. His eyes were foxy, she noticed; she could see the desire in them.

'I saw you a week back,' he said.

They walked by the river, away from the bridge, along the tow-path. He put his arm around her, squeezing a handful of underclothes and flesh. 'Let's sit down here,' he said.

They sat on the grass, watching barges going by and schoolboys rowing. In the distance traffic moved, gleaming, on the bridge they'd walked from. 'God,' he said, 'you have fantastic breasts.'

His hands were on them and he was pushing her back on to the grass. She felt his lips on her face, and his teeth and his tongue, and saliva. One hand moved down her body. She felt it under her skirt, on the bare flesh of her thigh, and then on her stomach. It was like an animal, a rat gnawing at her, prodding her and poking.

There was no one about; he was muttering, his voice thickly slurred. 'Take down your knickers,' he said.

She pushed at him and for a moment he released his hold, imagining she was about to undo some of her clothing. Instead she ran away, tearing along the tow-path, saying to herself that if he caught up with her she'd hit him with the briefcase that contained her school books.

But he didn't follow her and when she looked back he was lying where she had left him, stretched out as though wounded on the grass.

Her father talked of who might come that night to Daisy's. He mentioned Princess Margaret. Princess Margaret had seem him wrestling, or if it hadn't been Princess Margaret it had been a face almost identical to hers. The Burtons might come tonight; you never knew when the Burtons were going to pop in.

Her mother placed the fried fish, with chips and peas, in front of him. She never really listened to him when he went on about the night-club because her mind was full of what had happened on *Crossroads*. She put her cigarette on a saucer on the draining-board, not extinguishing it. She remembered the news items she'd read at breakfast-time and wondered about them all over again.

Tomorrow would be worse, Eleanor thought. Even at this very moment Denny Price's blubber lips might be relating the incident to Liz Jones, how Eleanor had almost let him and then had drawn back. 'I went down by the river with a boy,' she wanted to say. 'I wanted to get done because it's the Class 2 fashion. I'm tired of being mocked by Liz Jones.' She could say it with her eyes cast down, her fork fiddling with a piece of cod on her plate. She wouldn't have to see the embarrassment in her father's face, like she'd seen it when she'd asked for money for sanitary towels. Her mother wouldn't hear at first, but she'd go on saying it, repeating herself until her mother did hear. She longed for the facts to be there in the room, how it disgusted her to imagine her father taking off his uniform in the mornings, and Rogo Pollini doing Dolly Rourke. She wanted to say she'd been disgusted when Denny Price had told her to take down her knickers.

'Extraordinary, that woman,' her mother said. 'Fancy two days stuck in a bath.'

Her father laughed. It could be exaggerated, he said: you couldn't believe everything you read, not even in the newspapers.

'Extraordinary,' her mother murmured.

Her mother was trapped, married to him, obliging him so that she'd receive housekeeping money out of which she could save for her morning glass of gin. He was trapped himself, going out every night in a doorman's uniform, the Prince of Hackney with a bad back. He crushed her mother because he'd been crushed himself. How could either of them be expected to bother if she spoke of being mocked, and then asked them questions, seeking reassurance?

They wouldn't know what to say - even if she helped them by explaining that she knew there was no man with delicate hands who'd take her away when the leaves in London were yellow-brown, that there were only the blubber lips of Denny Price and the smell of meat that came off him, and Susie Crumm's father doing Mrs Rourke, and Liz Jones's father doing her also, and the West Indian railway porter, and Mr Rourke not aware of a thing. They wouldn't know what she was talking about if she said that Miss Whitehead had divorced himself from all of it by lying solitary at night in a room in Esher where everything was clean and neat. It was better to be Miss Whitehead than a woman who was a victim of a man's bad back. In her gleaming room Miss Whitehead was more successful in her pretence than they were in theirs. Miss Whitehead was complete and alone, having discarded what she wished to discard, accepting now that there was no Mr Right.

'Nice day at school?' her mother inquired suddenly in her vague manner, as though mistily aware of a duty.

Eleanor looked up from her fish and regarded both of them at once. She smiled, forcing herself to, feeling sorry for them because they were trapped by each other; because for them it was too late to escape to a room in which everything was clean.

THE CYPRESS TREES

MARY BECKETT

Gavin hurried home from school, half running, lopsided with the heavy schoolbag under one arm. Beyond the roundabout the whole sky was black and down the road to the west the big new church in another estate stood out against the cloud like the prow of an ocean-going liner. At the corner of his own road he stopped and searched in the front pocket of his jeans until he felt the comfort of the door key and kept it clenched in his hand. He had another key in his pencil case to be on the safe side but he never liked to delay on the doorstep. That woman who had come to live in the 'granny flat' in the house opposite was forever at her window, watching with her pale-blue eyes in that very white face. She made Gavin uncomfortable. Anyway, he never relaxed when neighbour women asked him to come in and wait in their houses until his parents came home from work. The children who lived nearby were either younger than his eleven years, or girls, and although he didn't mind playing with them outside it was a different matter indoors. Their mothers had a habit of making them do their homework when he was there, or they gave him things to eat he didn't like — bread with margarine, for instance, or tea with too much milk in it. He liked to close his own front door behind him.

He stopped in the hall to pick up the post — a couple of business envelopes and a strange crumpled-looking letter with unfamiliar writing addressed to his mother. He put them on the hall table and stood looking in the mirror above it. 'Your writing, Gavin Mac Evoy, is atrocious!' he told his reflection, imitating his teacher. 'You'll never pass the test into St Mark's College at this rate.' Trouble showed in his grey eyes for a moment but he shrugged off his worry, pulled off his hat and with his hand smoothed his light hair back into shape. The last time that had come up — when his Christmas report arrived — he had said to his parents, 'What will happen if I don't get into St Mark's? What am I going to do?'

His father had said, 'Of course you'll get in. You have plenty of ability,' and his mother had said, 'We have two pay-packets in this house and only one of a family — we can afford to pay for you in one of the colleges outside the free scheme.'

'My friends will all be going to St Mark's but I'll not know anybody in these other places.'

'If your friends can get in, you can get in if you put your mind to it,' his mother snapped.

'It's not like that, Mum,' he explained. 'The teacher draws names out of a hat.'

'Don't be ridiculous,' his mother said. 'You can't expect us to believe that.'

'It's true,' he insisted. 'I'm telling you. That's what happened last year. We all do the exam and if forty pass and there's only room for twenty they pull twenty names out of a hat.'

'How, then,' his mother asked, 'are your friends any more certain than you of getting in?'

'Ah, well they're different,' he said. 'If you have a brother already in St Mark's you get in all right. They all have brothers.'

His father had looked miserable then, and his mother cross, because they all remembered the time not so long ago that he had raged and cried and banged his head on the door when he heard that his friend Brian's mother had a new baby boy, giving him three brothers, when he, Gavin, had none. Later that night he had heard his mother shouting that she would not be having any more children, she didn't care about Gavin or his father or anybody else, nor would she adopt any either. She was happy going out to work and she wasn't changing. She wasn't going to be like *her* mother, having seven one after the other and slaving away at dressmaking in that poky little front room in a corporation house because her father had a 'bad back' and would only work occasionally. Gavin rarely saw any of these people because his mother, having pushed herself away from their poverty, wanted to have nothing to do with them.

His own house was warm and comfortable. He knew there would be food left for him in the kitchen but he didn't really want it. He wasn't interested in food. He was thin, especially his legs, so that he would never wear shorts, even on hot days, but sweltered in his jeans. The sudden blatter of rain on the window brought him into the front room to look out at the long rods of rain scudding the road. Some straggling homecomers turned their backs to the force of it and put their schoolbags on their heads. There'd be no football for a while. As the concrete darkened the road emptied. There used to be a bus rattling down at irregular intervals until the chairman of the residents' committee asked to have it diverted. Gavin liked the whoosh it used to make as it tore down if the road was clear. He liked it even better if it couldn't pass parked cars and sat hooting until someone appeared from a house half running, rattling car keys and contrived a space. Now there was no excitement and since that Christmas report he wasn't allowed to turn on the television except at weekends. He was to do his homework after school and they would hear his tables, spellings, etc. after dinner. Sometimes they did and sometimes they forgot. Sometimes they were quite sharp with him and sometimes they said, yawning, 'Oh I suppose it'll do.'

The room held nothing for him as he turned from the window. The mushroom-coloured couch and chairs at one end and the glass-topped dining table beyond the sliding doors were all immaculate. His own feet had made slight scuffmarks on the pale carpet. His mother tidied and polished every night before she went to bed. He trailed up to his own room with his schoolbag and put out his homework. He did a sum but his pen began to leak messily. He put it down and leaned his chair backwards, trying to see how far he could tilt before having to grab at the table to prevent falling. When that palled he banged around the small room in time to his transistor and then flung himself on his bed to bounce.

He jumped up when he heard his parents' car and straightened the Manchester United duvet. At the window he was just in time to glimpse his mother's shiny brown hair and shiny brown boots. He was always proud looking at her compared to some of the mothers he saw wearing slippers in the house, sometimes rollers in their hair. She was frowning over her letter as he came down the stairs smiling. She lifted her eyes and glared at Gavin and passed the letter to his father who read it quickly and then said, 'The thing to do with anonymous letters is put them in the fire.'

'Let Gavin read it first and see what he says,' his mother said.

Gavin took the blue lined notepaper and puzzled over the writing with its long unfamiliar loops. When he got used to that, the message was clear enough: this person signed 'The Watcher' was accusing him of stealing from shops. The recollection, never far from his mind, of talking a Yorkie bar in the shop beside the school for no reason except the impulse of the moment made his mother point to his face. 'Look at him! Just look at him. He's the picture of guilt.' She grabbed his shoulder and shook him. 'What have you stolen? How long has this been going on? Where did you take these things?' When he staggered back and sat down on the stairs she hit his head and when he put his hands up over his head for protection she hit his hands and arms.

His father said, 'Angela, go easy. You'll hurt him. I'm sure it's not serious.'

His father was a fool. Of course it was serious, he thought — the trouble he'd had putting it back afterwards.

His mother stepped back and straightened her suit. 'Do you

want a thief for a son?' she demanded. 'What did you steal, you little runt?'

Gavin closed his lips tight and wouldn't answer either her ranting or his father's pleading. She threatened to tell the police, the school, the shops, so that they would all know he was a thief. Then suddenly she turned her back on him and shouted, 'Oh get out of my sight. Go to your room and don't let me see you again. Go, go, go!' He ran up the stairs, tripping at the top, stumbled into his room and closed the door.

He stood for a long time in the middle of the small room with his hands up to his head. 'She hit me,' he said to himself, enraged. There was no space in him for any other thought.

He had taken the bar of chocolate on a February day that had started fine and had turned windy and grey. He had shivered without hat or gloves waiting to pay for the bunch of parsley his mother had asked him to buy on the way home from school. He put the chocolate in his pocket and ran home laughing to himself. When he took it out in the house and looked at it in the palm of his hand he wondered what had come over him. He had plenty of pocket money; if he had wanted to buy chocolate there was nothing to prevent him. He was not tempted to eat it. In fact he felt if he ate it he would be sick. He put it into his schoolbag, meaning to put it back on the shelf the next day. He knew about restitution from his grandfather — his father's father.

He had been a bricklayer and one of his favourite stories was about a man from the country who went to Confession and said, 'Father, I stole a house,' because he'd taken bricks, blocks, tiles and cement from his employer and suppliers over the months and built his house with his own labour. His grandfather used to chuckle, telling about the difficulties the man had encountered for the rest of his life, saving up and buying materials and smuggling them back until his conscience was clear and he'd said, 'Now I won't have to go to God arguing.'

So Gavin knew he had to put the chocolate back but he hadn't realised how hard it would be to slip away by himself without his schoolfriends, to poke down under his books for the hidden bar, becoming daily more battered, only to be prevented by the shopowners or hovering customers from going near the sweet stand. After each attempt he felt more like a thief, he felt everybody knew to look at him that he was a thief, and he slunk home in distress. Eventually he had managed and then he avoided the shop completely. He wished that his grandfather could have turned it into just a funny story but his grandfather had had a heart attack, or, as his mother put it, 'a massive coronary', and took no further interest in the world outside his own chest.

Not that his grandfather had ever talked to Gavin. When Gavin and his father had gone across the town to visit him, as they did some Sunday afternoons, he had shaken hands and said, 'Hello, young man. How are you?' Gavin said, 'Well,' and that was the end of the conversation. After that Gavin sat listening, snug in the old-fashioned kitchen with a coal fire and a red shiny floor and a table and chairs, unlike his mother's with its breakfast bar and stools and units. His grandfather had a wooden armchair at one side of the fire, his grandmother a lumpy cushioned one at the other. She sat Gavin at the table and gave him lemonade and biscuits. His father and grandfather each had a bottle of stout although his grandmother frequently urged them not to drink that terrible stuff but to have a nice glass of whiskey instead. They would all laugh and she would show photographs of her daughters' children and tell how well they were doing in their exams and at their music and dancing lessons. Gavin's mother complained that his grandmother took no interest in him, caring only for her daughters' children, but Gavin loved hearing about these wonderful cousins. He relished his connection with their successes. After his grandfather came home from hospital he sat sunk in himself, listening to his own breathing, sighing, while his wife sat on the edge of her shapeless chair, watching him, ready to jump if he needed her. Their visits were curtailed; they were too tiring for his grandfather, it was no place for a child.

Because his arms were aching in their strained position Gavin took his hands from his head but he still stood in the middle of the floor. Cooking smells reached his room. His mother was quick and skilled at contriving the meal — she did much of the preparation the night before. He could hear her voice, sharp at times, and his father's, lower, placating. He expected them to call him down any minute and he tried to make up his mind if he should tell them what had happened or stay silent. He had no guarantee they would believe him. Eventually he realised they were leaving him alone. They would not have him at the table. They would not eat with him. He curled up on the bed with his boots out over the side, and because he shivered he pulled the cover over himself and fell asleep.

His father at his own bedtime peeped in and, seeing the child's sleeping face on the pillow but not the boots still on, decided that Gavin had taken himself to bed and that it would be better not to disturb him. The closing door wakened Gavin although he didn't know what woke him or for a moment what he was doing in bed, hot and sticky in his clothes. He thought at first he had flu, but then he remembered. He lay wide awake in the darkness listening to his parents talking companionably together, laughing a little now and then. When the house was silent except for the clicking of contracting heat he felt a pain in his stomach. He thought it was likely hunger so he got up and went down to the fridge, not taking any particular care to keep quiet. He took out a pint of milk and drank straight from the bottle, a habit that his mother said belonged to 'the lowest of the low'. He ate a banana and left the skin lying on the counter. Then he opened the back door and went out.

The rain had stopped during the evening and the air was sweet, perfumed by the apple blossoms in one garden and lilac and wallflowers in another. The sky was clear, moonlit, showing the unbroken lawn in his own garden as smooth as the sitting-room carpet. He walked along the high end wall that separated the gardens of his road from those of the back road. He held his arms out to balance like a tightrope walker, except when he could catch on to trees or bushes that people had planted to hide the bare concrete blocks. A grey cat met him, then turned and went ahead of him on the wall with its tail erect. Gavin smiled, following it over a garage and down with a jump to the road. He kept to the shady part of the footpath, aware that if he met one of the policemen who patrolled the district he would have to account for himself. At the foot of the back road there were new houses, half a dozen of them unoccupied. He headed for them. They were expensive houses but just before they were finished the builder had disappeared, bankrupt, leaving them without plumbing or fireplaces. They had deep sheltered porches and Gavin knew that, night after night, bigger boys went there to smoke and play cards while their parents thought they were at the youth club. He had watched the group in fascination the previous summer and they had repeatedly chased him. They were all gone home to bed now, so he pressed himself into a corner among their litter of cigarette ends and empty bottles. Even in the shelter he was cold without a jacket. The milk and banana were cold in his stomach. An animal howl of misery gathered in him but he checked it and ran.

He took a different wall home, hugging his arms round his cold jersey, leaving his balance to luck. When he staggered and fell off into someone's rhubarb bed he picked himself up. The house was in darkness. He got as far as the kitchen window but he found it too high for him to reach so he pulled the dustbin over underneath the sill. Fat red worms wriggled in the exposed wet circle. He stood on the bin lid and surveyed the window. He had heard that if you tapped persistently with the heel of your shoe on the metal frame of the little top window it would spring open. But his were expensive French padded boots with thick spongy soles, useless for that purpose. He jumped down and hunted on the ground for an implement. The worms were disappearing behind the coal bunker. He saw the head of a small hammer, possibly a child's. It had no handle but he climbed back with it and tapped awkwardly. He thought the blows were far too light to have any effect, and almost laughed out loud when the window sprang and he was able to catch the opening and haul himself close to the glass. He stretched his right arm in until he could knock open the handle of the bigger window and he stood there looking in, the whole room at his mercy in the moonlight. He pushed aside a teapot and an egg-timer and put his foot in on the painted wood. There was still warmth in the kitchen and he thought of coming in until he could face the cold again. A dark armchair had a comfortable bulk.

Then the floorboards upstairs creaked and a light went on in the window above him. He stayed without moving. On the ledge beside his foot was a metal tea-caddy and the lid held three magnets, two little fancy ones with handles and the other a solid horseshoe, worn, partly red. He pulled it off and the tin rattled slightly. He held the magnet in the palm of his hand, liking it, and then closed his fingers over it so that it felt like his door key, only heavier. Someone was struggling with the upstairs window but he was able to hide in the only shadow near the house before the bathroom window was flung wide and a stout woman in a dressing-gown looked out, craning from one side to the other. His shelter was given by a cordon of branchy slanting trees, trained along wires held by poles. The ground where he crouched had been recently dug and black soil mulched in. A mixture of terror and excitement had Gavin's bowel in a ferment so that he pushed down his trousers and emptied it on the ground. He hunkered in the same place, disgust in abeyance, even though the window had been shut again and the light was switched off.

Two motorbikes roared, one after the other, on the main road. The noise and the speed vibrated through his head. He'd get a motorbike as soon as he could. There'd be more scope with a motorbike. His father would buy it for him to make up for his unhappiness. Listening as the machines faded in the distance he had a wild hope that he'd find release in hurtling power and swinging light and ringing sound. He became aware of his squatting position and he straightened up, fixing his clothes carefully, and stepped to one side. He looked at the magnet on his open hand. He was keeping that. He wasn't giving it back. He took out his door key and laid it beside the magnet. They remained separate. Disappointed, he put them both in his pocket. He'd go home, in the back door, wash himself and go to bed. If his parents asked him any questions he'd stay silent. He plotted out the best way to his house.

All along the back walls of these gardens people had planted cypress trees to give them privacy from newer, cheaper bungalows on the road behind. The trees cut into the moonlit sky. One section was carefully clipped and tended, to form a manageable light-green hedge. Other trees soared, pristine, pointed, giving a dark nesting-room for magpies or a swaying perch for pigeons. But, from where Gavin stood in the soft soil among the cordons, the row that blocked his view had been carelessly hacked and chopped, irremediably mutilated.

STAR FOOD

ETHAN CANIN

The summer I turned eighteen I disappointed both my parents for the first time. This hadn't happened before, since what disappointed one usually pleased the other. As a child, if I played broom hockey instead of going to school, my mother wept and my father took me outside later to find out how many goals I had scored. On the other hand, if I spent Saturday afternoon on the roof of my parents' grocery store staring up at the clouds instead of counting cracker cartons in the stockroom, my father took me to the back to talk about work and discipline, and my mother told me later to keep looking for things that no one else saw.

This was her theory. My mother felt that men like Leonardo da Vinci and Thomas Edison had simply stared long enough at regular objects until they saw new things, and thus my looking into the sky might someday make me a great man. She believed I had a worldly curiosity. My father believed I wanted to avoid stock work.

Stock work was an issue in our family, as were all the jobs that had to be done in a grocery store. Our store was called Star Food and above it an incandescent star revolved. Its circuits buzzed, and its yellow points, as thick as my knees, drooped with the slow melting of the bulb. On summer nights flying insects flocked in clouds around it, droves of them burning on the glass. One of my jobs was to go out on the roof, the sloping, eaved side that looked over the western half of Arcade, California, and clean them off the star. At night, when their black bodies stood out against the glass, when the wind carried in the marsh smell of the New Jerusalem River, I went into the attic, crawled out the dormer window onto the peaked roof, and slid across the shingles

181

to where the pole rose like a lightning rod into the night. I reached with a wet rag and rubbed away the June bugs and pickerel moths until the star was yellow-white and steaming from the moisture. Then I turned and looked over Arcade, across the bright avenue and my dimly lighted high school in the distance, into the low hills where oak trees grew in rows on the curbs and where girls drove to school in their own convertibles. When my father came up on the roof sometimes to talk about the store, we fixed our eyes on the red tile roofs or the small clouds of blue barbecue smoke that floated above the hills on warm evenings. While the clean bulb buzzed and flickered behind us, we talked about loss leaders or keeping the elephant-ear plums stacked in neat triangles.

The summer I disappointed my parents, though, my father talked to me about a lot of other things. He also made me look in the other direction whenever we were on the roof together, not west to the hills and their clouds of barbecue smoke, but east toward the other part of town. We crawled up one slope of the roof, then down the other so that I could see beyond the back alley where wash hung on lines in the moonlight, down to the neighborhoods across Route 5. These were the neighborhoods where men sat on the curbs on weekday afternoons, where rusted, wheel-less cars lay on blocks in the yards.

'*You're* going to end up on one of those curbs,' my father told me.

Usually I stared farther into the clouds when he said something like that. He and my mother argued about what I did on the roof for so many hours at a time, and I hoped that by looking closely at the amazing borders of clouds I could confuse him. My mother believed I was on the verge of discovering something atmospheric, and I was sure she told my father this, so when he came upstairs, made me look across Route 5, and talked to me about how I was going to end up there, I squinted harder at the sky.

'You don't fool me for a second,' he said.

He was up on the roof with me because I had been letting someone steal from the store.

From the time we first had the star on the roof, my mother believed her only son was destined for limited fame. Limited because she thought that true vision was distilled and could not be appreciated by everybody. I discovered this shortly after the star was installed, when I spent an hour looking out over the roofs and chimneys instead of helping my father stock a shipment of dairy. It was a hot day and the milk sat on the loading dock while he searched for me in the store and in our apartment next door. When he came up and found me, his neck was red and his footfalls shook the roof joists. At my age I was still allowed certain mistakes, but I'd seen the dairy truck arrive and knew I should have been downstairs, so it surprised me later, after I'd helped unload the milk, when my mother stopped beside me as I was sprinkling the leafy vegetables with a spray bottle.

'Dade, I don't want you to let anyone keep you from what you ought to be doing.'

'I'm sorry,' I said. 'I should have helped with the milk earlier.'

'No,' she said, 'that's not what I mean.' Then she told me her theory of limited fame while I sprayed the cabbage and lettuce with the atomiser. It was the first time I had heard her idea. The world's most famous men, she said, presidents and emperors, generals and patriots, were men of vulgar fame, men who ruled the world because their ideas were obvious and could be understood by everybody. But there was also limited fame. Newton and Galileo and Enrico Fermi were men of limited fame, and as I stood there with the atomiser in my hand my mother's eyes watered over and she told me she knew in her heart that one day I was going to be a man of limited fame. I was twelve years old.

After that day I found I could avoid a certain amount of stock work by staying up on the roof and staring into the fine layers of stratus clouds that floated above Arcade. In the *Encyclopedia Americana* I read about cirrus and cumulus and thunderheads, about inversion layers and currents like the currents at sea, and in the afternoons I went upstairs and watched. The sky was a changing thing, I found out. It was more than a blue sheet. Twirling with pollen and sunlight, it began to transform itself.

Often as I stood on the roof my father came outside and swept the sidewalk across the street. Through the telephone poles and crossed power lines he looked up at me, his broom strokes small and fierce as if he were hoeing hard ground. It irked him that my mother encouraged me to stay on the roof. He was a short man with direct habits and an understanding of how to get along in the world, and he believed that God rewarded only two things, courtesy and hard work. God did not reward looking at the sky. In the car my father acknowledged good drivers and in restaurants he left good tips. He knew the names of his customers. He never sold a rotten vegetable. He shook hands often, looked everyone in the eye, and on Friday nights when we went to the movies he made us sit in the front row of the theater. 'Why should I pay to look over other people's shoulders?' he said. The movies made him talk. On the way back to the car he walked with his hands clasped behind him and greeted everyone who passed. He smiled. He mentioned the fineness of the evening as if he were the admiral or aviator we had just seen on the screen. 'People like it,' he said. 'It's good for business.' My mother was quiet, walking with her slender arms folded in front of her as if she were cold.

I liked the movies because I imagined myself doing everything the heroes did — deciding to invade at daybreak, swimming half the night against the seaward current — but whenever we left the theater I was disappointed. From the front row, life seemed like a clear set of decisions, but on the street afterward I realised that the world existed all around me and I didn't know what I wanted.

The quiet of evening and the ordinariness of human voices startled me.

Sometimes on the roof, as I stared into the layers of horizon, the sounds on the street faded into this same ordinariness. One afternoon when I was standing under the star my father came outside and looked up at me. 'You're in a trance,' he called. I glanced down at him, then squinted back at the horizon. For a minute he waited, and then from across the street he threw a rock. He had a pitcher's arm and could have hit me if he wanted, but the rock sailed past me and clattered on the shingles. My mother came right out of the store anyway and stopped him. 'I wanted him off the roof,' I heard my father tell her later in the same frank voice in which he explained his position to vegetable salesmen. 'If someone's throwing rocks at him he'll come down. He's no fool.'

I was flattered by this, but my mother won the point and from then on I could stay up on the roof when I wanted. To appease my father I cleaned the electric star, and though he often came outside to sweep, he stopped telling me to come down. I thought about limited fame and spent a lot of time noticing the sky. When I looked closely it was a sea with waves and shifting colors, wind seams and denials of distance, and after a while I learned to look at it so that it entered my eye whole. It was blue liquid. I spent hours looking into its pale wash, looking for things, though I didn't know what. I looked for lines or sectors, the diamond shapes of daylight stars. Sometimes, silver-winged jets from the air force base across the hills turned the right way against the sun and went off like small flash bulbs on the horizon. There was nothing that struck me and stayed, though, nothing with the brilliance of white light or electric explosion that I thought came with discovery, so after a while I changed my idea of discovery. I just stood on the roof and stared. When my mother asked me, I told her that I might be seeing new things but that seeing change took time. 'It's slow,' I told her. 'It may take years.'

The first time I let her steal I chalked it up to surprise. I was working the front register when she walked in, a thin, tall woman in a plaid dress that looked wilted. She went right to the standup display of cut-price, nearly expired breads and crackers, where she took a loaf of rye from the shelf. Then she turned and looked me in the eye. We were looking into each other's eyes when she walked out the front door. Through the blue-and-white Look Up To Star Food sign on the window I watched her cross the street.

There were two or three other shoppers in the store, and over the tops of the potato chip packages I could see my mother's broom. My father was in back unloading chicken parts. Nobody else had seen her come in; nobody had seen her leave. I locked the cash drawer and walked to the aisle where my mother was sweeping.

'I think someone just stole.'

My mother wheeled a trash receptacle when she swept, and as I stood there she closed it, put down her broom, and wiped her face with her handkerchief. 'You couldn't get him?'

'It was a her.'

'A lady?'

'I couldn't chase her. She came in and took a loaf of rye and left.'

I had chased plenty of shoplifters before. They were kids usually, in sneakers and coats too warm for the weather. I chased them up the aisle and out the door, then to the corner and around it while ahead of me they tried to toss whatever it was — Twinkies, freeze-pops — into the sidewalk hedges. They cried when I caught them, begged me not to tell their parents. First time, my father said, scare them real good. Second time, call the law. I took them back with me to the store, held them by the collar as we walked.

Then I sat them in the straight-back chair in the stockroom and gave them a speech my father had written. It was printed on a blue index card taped to the door. DO YOU KNOW WHAT YOU HAVE DONE? it began. DO YOU KNOW WHAT IT IS TO STEAL? I learned to pause between the questions, pace the room, check the card. 'Give them time to get scared,' my father said. He was expert at this. He never talked to them until he had dusted the vegetables or run a couple of women through the register. 'Why should I stop my work for a kid who steals from me?' he said. When he finally came into the stockroom he moved and spoke the way policemen do at the scene of an accident. His manner was slow and deliberate. First he asked me what they had stolen. If I had recovered whatever it was, he took it and held it up to the light, turned it over in his fingers as if it were of large value. Then he opened the freezer door and led the kid inside to talk about law and punishment amid the frozen beef carcasses. He paced as he spoke, breathed clouds of vapor into the air.

In the end, though, my mother usually got him to let them off. Once when he wouldn't, when he had called the police to pick up a third-offense boy who sat trembling in the stockroom, my mother called him to the front of the store to talk to a customer. In the stockroom we kept a key to the back door hidden under a silver samovar that had belonged to my grandmother, and when my father was in front that afternoon my mother came to the rear, took it out, and opened the back door. She leaned down to the boy's ear. 'Run,' she said.

The next time she came in it happened the same way. My father was at the vegetable tier, stacking avocados. My mother was in back listening to the radio. It was afternoon. I rang in a customer, then looked up while I was putting the milk cartons in the bottom of the bag, and there she was. Her gray eyes were looking into mine. She had two cans of pineapple juice in her hands, and on the way out she held the door for an old woman.

That night I went up to clean the star. The air was clear. It was warm. When I finished wiping the glass I moved out over the edge of the eaves and looked into the distance where little turquoise squares — lighted swimming pools — stood out against the hills.

'Dade —'

It was my father's voice from behind the peak of the roof.

'Yes?'

'Come over to this side.'

I mounted the shallow-pitched roof, went over the peak, and edged down the other slope to where I could see his silhouette against the lights on Route 5. He was smoking. I got up and we stood together at the edge of the shingled eaves. In front of us trucks rumbled by on the interstate, their trailers lit at the edges like the mast lights of ships.

'Look across the highway,' he said.

'I am.'

'What do you see?'

'Cars.'

'What else?'

'Trucks.'

For a while he didn't say anything. He dragged a few times on his cigarette, then pinched off the lit end and put the rest back in the pack. A couple of motorcycles went by, a car with one headlight, a bus.

'Do you know what it's like to live in a shack?' he said.

'No.'

'You don't want to end up in a place like that. And it's damn easy to do if you don't know what you want. You know how easy it is?'

'Easy,' I said.

'You have to know what you want.'

For years my father had been trying to teach me competence and industry. Since I was nine I had been squeeze-drying mops before returning them to the closet, double-counting change, sweeping under the lip of the vegetable bins even if the dirt there was invisible to customers. On the basis of industry, my father said, Star Food had grown from a two-aisle, one-freezer corner store to the largest grocery in Arcade. When I was eight he had bought the failing gas station next door and built additions, so that now Star Food had nine aisles, separate coolers for dairy, soda, and beer, a tiered vegetable stand, a glass-fronted butcher counter, a part-time butcher, and, under what used to be the rain roof of the failing gas station, free parking while you shopped. When I started high school we moved into the apartment next door, and at meals we discussed store improvements. Soon my father invented a grid system for easy location of foods. He stayed up one night and painted, and the next morning there was a new coordinate system on the ceiling of the store. It was a grid, A through J, 1 through 10. For weeks there were drops of blue paint in his eyelashes.

A few days later my mother pasted up fluorescent stars among the grid squares. She knew about the real constellations and was accurate with the ones she stuck to the ceiling, even though she also knew that the aisle lights in Star Food stayed on day and night, so that her stars were going to be invisible. We saw them only once, in fact, in a blackout a few months later, when they lit up in hazy clusters around the store.

'Do you know why I did it?' she asked me the night of the blackout as we stood beneath their pale light.

'No.'

'Because of the idea.'

She was full of ideas, and one was that I was accomplishing something on the shallow-pitched section of our roof. Sometimes she sat at the dormer window and watched me. Through the glass I could see the slender outlines of her cheekbones. 'What do you see?' she asked. On warm nights she leaned over the sill and pointed out the constellations. 'They are the illumination of great minds,' she said.

After the woman walked out the second time I began to think a lot about what I wanted. I tried to discover what it was, and I had an idea it would come to me on the roof. In the evenings I sat up there and thought. I looked for signs. I threw pebbles down into the street and watched where they hit. I read the newspaper, and stories about ballplayers or jazz musicians began to catch my eye. When he was ten years old, Johnny Unitas strung a tire from a tree limb and spent afternoons throwing a football through it as it swung. Dizzy Gillespie played with an orchestra when he was seven. There was an emperor who ruled China at age eight. What could be said about me? He swept the dirt no one could see under the lip of the vegetable bins.

The day after the woman had walked out the second time, my mother came up on the roof while I was cleaning the star. She usually wore medium heels and stayed away from the shingled roof, but that night she came up. I had been over the glass once when I saw her coming through the dormer window, skirt hem and white shoes lit by moonlight. Most of the insects were cleaned off and steam was drifting up into the night. She came through the window, took off her shoes, and edged down the roof until she was standing next to me at the star. 'It's a beautiful night,' she said.

'Cool.'

'Dade, when you're up here do you ever think about what is in the mind of a great man when he makes a discovery?'

The night was just making its transition from the thin sky to the thick, the air was taking on weight, and at the horizon distances were shortening. I looked out over the plain and tried to think of an answer. That day I had been thinking about a story my father occasionally told. Just before he and my mother were married he took her to the top of the hills that surround Arcade. They stood with the New Jerusalem River, western California, and the sea on their left, and Arcade on their right. My father has always planned things well, and that day as they stood in the hill pass a thunderstorm covered everything west, while Arcade, shielded by hills, was lit by the sun. He asked her which way she wanted to go. She must have realised it was a test, because she thought for a moment and then looked to the right, and when they drove down from the hills that day my father mentioned the idea of a grocery. Star Food didn't open for a year after, but that was its conception, I think, in my father's mind. That afternoon as they stood with the New Jerusalem flowing below them, the plains before them, and my mother in a cotton skirt she had made herself, I think my father must have seen right through to the end of his life.

I had been trying to see right through to the end of my life, too, but these thoughts never led me in any direction. Sometimes I sat and remembered the unusual things that had happened to me. Once I had found the perfect, shed skin of a rattlesnake. My mother told my father that this indicated my potential for science. I was on the roof another time when it hailed apricot-size balls of ice on a summer afternoon. The day was hot and there was only one cloud, but as it approached from the distance it spread a shaft of darkness below it as if it had fallen through itself to the earth, and when it reached the New Jerusalem the river began throwing up spouts of water. Then it crossed onto land and I could see the hailstones denting parked cars. I went back inside the attic and watched it pass, and when I came outside again and picked up the ice balls that rolled between the corrugated roof spouts, their prickly edges melted in my fingers. In a minute they were gone. That was the rarest thing that had ever happened to me. Now I waited for rare things because it seemed to me that if you traced back the lives of men you arrived at some sort of sign, rainstorm at one horizon and sunlight at the other. On the roof I waited for mine. Sometimes I thought about the woman and sometimes I looked for silhouettes in the blue shapes between the clouds.

'Your father thinks you should be thinking about the store,' said my mother.

'I know.'

'You'll own the store some day.'

There was a carpet of cirrus clouds in the distance, and we watched them as their bottom edges were gradually lit by the rising moon. My mother tilted back her head and looked up into the stars. 'What beautiful names,' she said. 'Cassiopeia, Lyra, Aquila.'

'The Big Dipper,' I said.

'Dade?'

'Yes?'

'I saw the lady come in yesterday.'

'I didn't chase her.'

'I know.'

'What do you think of that?'

'I think you're doing more important things,' she said. 'Dreams are more important than rye bread.' She took the bobby pins from her hair and held them in her palm. 'Dade, tell me the truth. What do you think about when you come up here?'

In the distance there were car lights, trees, aluminum power poles. There were several ways I could have answered.

I said, 'I think I'm about to make a discovery.'

After that my mother began meeting me at the bottom of the stairs when I came down from the roof. She smiled expectantly. I snapped my fingers, tapped my feet. I blinked and looked at my canvas shoe-tips. She kept smiling. I didn't like this so I tried not coming down for entire afternoons, but this only made her look more expectant. On the roof my thoughts piled into one another. I couldn't even think of something that was undiscovered. I stood and thought about the woman.

Then my mother began leaving little snacks on the sill of the dormer window. Crackers, cut apples, apricots. She arranged them in fan shapes or twirls on a plate, and after a few days I started working regular hours again. I wore my smock and checked customers through the register and went upstairs only in the evenings. I came down after my mother had gone to sleep. I was afraid the woman was coming back, but I couldn't face my mother twice a day at the bottom of the stairs. So I worked and looked up at the door whenever customers entered. I did stock work when I could, stayed in back where the air was refrigerated, but I sweated anyway. I unloaded melons, tuna fish, cereal. I counted the cases of freeze-pops, priced the cans of All-American ham. At the swinging door between the stockroom and the back of the store my heart went dizzy. The woman knew something about me.

In the evenings on the roof I tried to think what it was. I saw mysterious new clouds, odd combinations of cirrus and stratus. How did she root me into the linoleum floor with her gray stare? Above me on the roof the sky was simmering. It was blue gas. I knew she was coming back.

It was raining when she did. The door opened and I felt the wet breeze, and when I looked up she was standing with her back to me in front of the shelves of cheese and dairy, and this time I came out from the counter and stopped behind her. She smelled of the rain outside.

'Look,' I whispered, 'why are you doing this to me?'

She didn't turn around. I moved closer. I was gathering my words, thinking of the blue index card, when the idea of limited fame came into my head. I stopped. How did human beings understand each other across huge spaces except with the lowest of ideas? I have never understood what it is about rain that smells, but as I stood there behind the woman I suddenly realised I was smelling the inside of clouds. What was between us at that moment was an idea we had created ourselves. When she left with a carton of milk in her hand I couldn't speak.

On the roof that evening I looked into the sky, out over the plains, along the uneven horizon. I thought of the view my father had seen when he was a young man. I wondered whether he had imagined Star Food then. The sun was setting. The blues and oranges were mixing into black, and in the distance windows were lighting up along the hillsides.

'Tell me what I want,' I said then. I moved closer to the edge of the eaves and repeated it. I looked down over the alley, into the kitchens across the way, into living rooms, bedrooms, across slate rooftops. 'Tell me what I want,' I called. Cars pulled in and out of the parking lot. Big rigs rushed by on the interstate. The air around me was as cool as water, the lighted swimming pools like pieces of the daytime sky. An important moment seemed to be rushing up. 'Tell me what I want,' I said again.

Then I heard my father open the window and come out onto the roof. He walked down and stood next to me, the bald spot on top of his head reflecting the streetlight. He took out a cigarette, smoked it for a while, pinched off the end. A bird fluttered around the light pole across the street. A car crossed below us with the words JUST MARRIED on the roof.

'Look,' he said, 'your mother's tried to make me understand this.' He paused to put the unsmoked butt back in the pack. 'And maybe I can. You think the gal's a little down and out; you don't want to kick her when she's down. Okay, I can understand that. So I've decided something, and you want to know what?'

He shifted his hands in his pockets and took a few steps toward the edge of the roof.

'You want to know what?'

'What?'

'I'm taking you off the hook. You mother says you've got a few thoughts, that maybe you're on the verge of something, so I decided it's okay if you let the lady go if she comes in again.'

'What?'

'I said it's okay if you let the gal go. You don't have to chase her.'

'You're going to let her steal?'

'No,' he said. 'I hired a guard.'

He was there the next morning in clothes that were all dark blue. Pants, shirt, cap, socks. He was only two or three years older than I was. My father introduced him to me as Mr Sellers. 'Mr Sellers,' he said, 'this is Dade.' He had a badge on his chest and a ring of keys the size of a doughnut on his belt. At the door he sat jingling them.

I didn't say much to him, and when I did my father came out from the back and counted register receipts or stocked impulse items near where he sat. We weren't saying anything important, though. Mr Sellers didn't carry a gun, only the doughnut-size key ring, so I asked him if he wished he did.

'Sure,' he said.

'Would you use it?'

'If I had to.'

I thought of him using his gun if he had to. His hands were thick and their backs were covered with hair. This seemed to go along with shooting somebody if he had to. My hands were thin and white and the hair on them was like the hair on a girl's cheek.

During the days he stayed by the front. He smiled at customers and held the door for them, and my father brought him sodas every hour or so. Whenever the guard smiled at a customer I thought of him trying to decide whether he was looking at the shoplifter.

And then one evening everything changed.

I was on the roof. The sun was low, throwing slanted light. From beyond the New Jerusalem and behind the hills, four air force jets appeared. They disappeared, then appeared again, silver dots trailing white tails. They climbed and cut and looped back, showing dark and light like a school of fish. When they turned against the sun their wings flashed. Between the hills and the river they dipped low onto the plain, then shot upward and toward me. One dipped, the others followed. Across the New Jerusalem they turned back and made two great circles, one inside the other, then dipped again and leveled off in my direction. The sky seemed small enough for them to fall through. I could see the double tails, then the wings and the jets. From across the river they shot straight toward the shore, angling up so I could see the V-wings and camouflage and rounded bomb bays, and I covered my ears, and in a moment they were across the water and then they were above me, and as they passed over they barrel-rolled and flew upside down and showed me their black cockpit glass so that my heart came up into my mouth.

I stood there while they turned again behind me and lifted back toward the hills, trailing threads of vapor, and by the time their booms subsided I knew I wanted the woman to be caught. I had seen a sign. Suddenly the sky was water-clear. Distances moved in, houses stood out against the hills, and it seemed to me that I had turned a corner and now looked over a rain-washed street. The woman was a thief. This was a simple fact and it presented itself to me simply. I felt the world dictating its course.

I went downstairs and told my father I was ready to catch her.

He looked at me, rolled the chewing gum in his cheek. 'I'll be damned.'

'My life is making sense,' I said.

When I unloaded potato chips that night I laid the bags in the aluminum racks as if I were putting children to sleep in their beds. Dust had gathered under the lip of the vegetable bins, so I swept and mopped there and ran a wet cloth over the stalls. My father slapped me on the back a couple of times. In school once I had looked through a microscope at the tip of my own finger, and now as I looked around the store everything seemed to have been magnified in the same way. I saw cracks in the linoleum floor, speckles of color in the walls.

This kept up for a couple of days, and all the time I waited for the woman to come in. After a while it was more than just waiting; I looked forward to the day when she would return. In my eyes she would find nothing but resolve. How bright the store seemed to me then when I swept, how velvety the skins of the melons beneath the sprayer bottle. When I went up to the roof I scrubbed the star with the wet cloth and came back down. I didn't stare into the clouds and I didn't think about the woman except with the thought of catching her. I described her perfectly for the guard. Her gray eyes. Her plaid dress.

After I started working like this my mother began to go to the back room in the afternoons and listen to music. When I swept the rear I heard the melodies of operas. They came from behind the stockroom door while I waited for the woman to return, and when my mother came out she had a look about her of disappointment. Her skin was pale and smooth, as if the blood had run to deeper parts.

'Dade,' she said one afternoon as I stacked tomatoes in a pyramid, 'it's easy to lose your dreams.'

'I'm just stacking tomatoes.'

She went back to the register. I went back to stacking, and my father, who'd been patting me on the back, winking at me from behind the butcher counter, came over and helped me.

'I notice your mother's been talking to you.'

'A little.'

We finished the tomatoes and moved on to the lettuce.

'Look,' he said, 'it's better to do what you have to do, so I wouldn't spend your time worrying frontwards and backwards about everything. Your life's not so long as you think it's going to be.'

We stood there rolling heads of butterball lettuce up the shallow incline of the display cart. Next to me he smelled like Aqua Velva.

'The lettuce is looking good,' I said.

Then I went up to the front of the store. 'I'm not sure what my dreams are,' I said to my mother. 'And I'm never going to discover anything. All I've ever done on the roof is look at the clouds.'

Then the door opened and the woman came in. I was standing in front of the counter, hands in my pockets, my mother's eyes watering over, the guard looking out the window at a couple of girls, everything revolving around the point of calm that, in retrospect, precedes surprises. I'd been waiting for her for a week, and now she came in. I realised I never expected her. She stood looking at me, and for a few moments I looked back. Then she realised what I was up to. She turned around to leave, and when her back was to me I stepped over and grabbed her.

I've never liked fishing much, even though I used to go with my father, because the moment a fish jumps on my line a tree's length away in the water I feel as if I've suddenly lost something. I'm always disappointed and sad, but now as I held the woman beneath the shoulder I felt none of this disappointment. I felt strong and good. She was thin, and I could make out the bones and tendons in her arm. As I led her back toward the stockroom, through the bread aisle, then the potato chips that were puffed and stacked like a row of pillows, I heard my mother begin to weep behind the register. Then my father came up behind me. I didn't turn around, but I knew he was there and I knew the deliberately calm way he was walking. 'I'll be back as soon as I dust the melons,' he said.

I held the woman tightly under her arm but despite this she moved in a light way, and suddenly, as we paused before the stockroom door, I felt as if I were leading her onto the dance floor. This flushed me with remorse. Don't spend your whole life looking backward and forwards, I said to myself. Know what you want. I pushed the door open and we went in. The room was dark. It smelled of my whole life. I turned on the light and sat her down in the straight-back chair, then crossed the room and stood against the door. I had spoken to many children as they sat in this chair. I had frightened them, collected the candy they had tried to hide between the cushions, presented it to my father when he came in. Now I looked at the blue card. DO YOU KNOW WHAT YOU HAVE DONE? it said. DO YOU KNOW WHAT IT IS TO STEAL? I tried to think of what to say to the woman. She sat trembling slightly. I approached the chair and stood in front of her. She looked up at me. Her hair was gray around the roots.

'Do you want to go out the back?' I said.

She stood up and I took the key from under the silver samovar. My father would be there in a moment, so after I let her out I took my coat from the hook and followed. The evening was misty. She crossed the lot, and I hurried and came up next to her. We walked fast and stayed behind cars, and when we had gone a distance I turned and looked back. The stockroom door was closed. On the roof the star cast a pale light that whitened the aluminum-sided eaves.

It seemed we would be capable of a great communication now, but as we walked I realised I didn't know what to say to her. We went down the street without talking. The traffic was light, evening was approaching, and as we passed below some trees the streetlights suddenly came on. This moment has always amazed me. I knew the woman had seen it too, but it is always a disappointment to mention a thing like this. The streets and buildings took on their night shapes. Still we didn't say anything to each other. We kept walking beneath the pale violet of the lamps, and after a few more blocks I just stopped at one corner. She went on, crossed the street, and I lost sight of her.

I stood there until the world had rotated fully into the night, and for a while I tried to make myself aware of the spinning of the earth. Then I walked back toward the store. When they slept that night, my mother would dream of discovery and my father would dream of low-grade crooks. When I thought of this and the woman I was sad. It seemed you could never really know another person. I felt alone in the world, in the way that makes me aware of sound and temperature, as if I had just left a movie theater and stepped into an alley where a light rain was falling, and the wind was cool, and, from somewhere, other people's voices could be heard.

LIKE ALL OTHER MEN

JOHN McGAHERN

He watched her for a long time among the women across the dancefloor in the half-light of the afternoon. She wasn't tall or beautiful, but he couldn't take his eyes away. Some of the women winced palpably and fell back as they were passed over. Others stood their ground and stared defiantly back. She seemed quietly indifferent, taking a few steps back into the thinning crowd each time she found herself isolated on the floor. When she was asked to dance, she behaved exactly the same. She flashed no smile, gave no giddy shrug of triumph to betray the tension of the wait, the redeemed vanity.

Nurses, students, actors and actresses, musicians, some prostitutes, people who worked in restaurants and newspapers, nightwatchmen, a medley of the old and very young, came to these afternoon dances. Michael Duggan came every Saturday and Sunday. He was a teacher of Latin and history in a midlands town forty miles from Dublin, and each Friday he came in on the evening bus to spend the whole weekend round the cinemas and restaurants and dancehalls of O'Connell Street. A year before he had been within a couple of months of ordination.

When he did cross to ask her to dance, she followed him with the same unconcern on to the floor as she had showed just standing there. She danced beautifully, with a strong, easy freedom. She was a nurse in the Blanchardstown Chest Hospital. She came from Kerry. Her father was a National Teacher near Killarney. She had been to these afternoon dances before, but not for a couple of years. Her name was Susan Spillane.

'I suppose everybody asks you these questions,' he said.

'The last one did anyhow.' She smiled. 'You'd better tell me about yourself as well.' She had close curly black hair, an intelligent face, and there was something strange about her eyes.

'Are your eyes two different colours?'

'One eye is brown, the other grey. I may have got the grey eye by mistake. All the others in the house have brown eyes.'

'They are lovely.' The dance had ended. He had let her go. It was not easy to thread a way through these inanities of speech.

A girl could often stand unnoticed a long time, and then it was enough for one man to show an interest to start a rush. When the next two dances were called, though he moved quickly each time, he was beaten to her side. The third dance was a ladies' choice, and he withdrew back into the crowd of men. She followed him into the crowd, and this time he did not let her slip away when the dance ended. It was a polite convention for women to make a show of surprise when invited for a drink, of having difficulty making up their minds, but she said at once she'd love a drink, and asked for whiskey.

'I hardly drink at all, but I like the burnt taste,' and she sipped the small measure neat for the two hours that were left of the dance. 'My father loves a glass of whiskey late at night. I've often sat and had a sip with him.'

They danced again and afterwards came back to the table, sipped the drinks, sat and talked, and danced again. Time raced.

'Do you have to go on night duty tonight?' he asked as it moved near the time when the band would stand and play the anthem. He was afraid he would lose her then.

'No. I'm on tomorrow night.'

'Maybe you'd eat something with me this evening?'

'I'd like that.'

There was still some daylight left when they came from the dancehall, and they turned away from it into a bar. They both had coffee. An hour later, when he knew it was dark outside, he asked awkwardly, 'I suppose it's a bit outrageous to suggest a walk before we look for a place to eat,' his guilty smile apologising for such a poor and plain admission of the sexual.

'I don't see why not.' She smiled. 'I'd like a walk.'

'What if it's raining?' He gave them both the excuse to draw back.

'There's only one way to find out,' she said.

It was raining very lightly, the street black and shining under the lamps, but she didn't seem to mind the rain, nor that the walk led towards the dark shabby streets west of O'Connell Street. There they found a dark doorway and embraced. She returned his kisses with the same directness and freedom with which she had danced, but people kept continually passing in the early evening dark, until they seemed to break off together to say, 'This is useless,' and arm in arm to head back towards the light.

'It's a pity we haven't some room or place of our own,' he said.

'Where did you spend last night?' she asked.

'Where I stay every weekend, a rooming house in North Earl Street, four beds to the room.'

It was no place to go. A dumb man in the next bed to his had been very nearly beaten up the night before. The men who took the last two beds had been drinking. They woke the dumb man while they fumbled for the light, and he sat up in his bed and gestured towards the partly open window as soon as the light came on. Twice he made the same upward movement with his thumb: he wanted them to try to close the window because of the cold wind blowing in. The smaller of the two men misinterpreted the gesture and with a shout fell on the man. They realised that he was dumb when he started to squeal. She didn't laugh at the story.

'It's not hard to give the wrong signals in this world.'

'We could go to a hotel,' she said. He was stopped dead in his tracks. 'That's if you want to, and only – only – if I can pay half.'

'Which hotel?'

'Are you certain you'd want that? It doesn't matter to me.' She was looking into his face.

'There's nothing I want more in the world, but where?' He stood between desire and fear.

'The Clarence across the river is comfortable and fairly inexpensive.'

'Will we see if we can get a room before we eat or afterwards?' He was clumsy with diffidence in the face of what she had proposed.

'We might as well look now, but are you certain?'

'I'm certain. And you?'

'As long as you agree that I can pay half,' she said.

'I agree.'

They sealed one another's lips and crossed the river by the Halfpenny Bridge.

'Do you think we will have any trouble?' he asked as they drew close to the hotel.

'We'll soon find out. I think we both look respectable enough,' and for the first time he thought he felt some nervousness in her handclasp, and it made him feel a little easier.

There was no trouble. They were given a room with a bath on the second floor.

'I liked very much that you gave your real name,' she said when they were alone.

'Why?'

'It seemed more honest . . . '

'It was the only name I could think of at the time,' and their nervousness found release in laughter.

The bathroom was just inside the door. The bed and bedside lamp and table were by the window, a chair and writing table in the opposite corner, two armchairs in the middle of the room. The window looked down on the night city and the river. He drew the curtains and took her in his arms.

'Wait,' she said. 'We've plenty of time before going out to eat.'

While she was in the bathroom he turned off the light, slipped from his clothes, and got into the bed to wait for her.

'Why did you turn out the light?' she asked sharply when she came from the bathroom.

'I thought you'd want it out.'

'I want to see.'

It was not clear whether she wanted the light for the practical acts of undressing or if she wanted these preliminaries to what is called the act of darkness to be free of all furtiveness, that they should be noted with care like the names of places passed on an important journey.

'I'm sorry,' he said, and turned on the bedside lamp. He watched her slow, sure movements as she stepped from her clothes, how strong and confident and beautiful she was. 'Do you still want the light on?' he asked as she came towards him.

'No.'

'You are beautiful.' He wanted to say that her naked beauty took his breath away, was almost hurtful.

What he had wanted so much that it had become frightening she made easy, but it was almost impossible to believe that he now rested in the still centre of what had long been a dream. After long deprivation the plain pleasures of bed and table grow sadly mystical.

'Have you slept with anyone before?' he asked.

'Yes, with one person.'

"Were you in love with him?'

'Yes.'

'Are you still in love with him?'

'No. Not at all.'

'I never have.'

'I know.'

They came again into one another's arms. There was such peace afterwards that the harsh shrieking of the gulls outside, the even swish of the traffic along the quays, was more part of that peace.

Is this all? Common greed and restlessness rose easily to despise what was so hard come by as soon as it was gained, so luckily, so openly given. Before it had any time to grow there was the grace of dressing, of going out to eat together in the surety that they were coming back to this closed room. He felt like a young husband as he waited for her to finish dressing.

The light drizzle of the early evening had turned into a downpour by the time they came down, the hotel lobby crowded with people in raincoats, many carrying umbrellas.

'We're guaranteed a drowning if we head out in that.'

'We don't need to. We can eat here. The grill is open.'

It was a large, very pleasant room with light wood panelling and an open fire at its end. She picked the lamb cutlets, he the charcoaled steak, and they each had a glass of red wine.

'This has to be split evenly as well,' she said.

'I don't see why. I'd like to take you.'

'That was the bargain. It must be kept.' She smiled. 'How long have you been teaching?'

'Less than a year. I was in Maynooth for a long time.'

'Were you studying for the priesthood?'

'That's what people mostly do there,' he said drily. 'I left with only a couple of months to go. It must sound quite bad.'

'It's better than leaving afterwards. Why did you leave?' she asked with formidable seriousness. It could not be turned aside with sarcasm or irony.

'Because I no longer believed. I could hardly lead others to a life that I didn't believe in myself. When I entered Maynooth at eighteen I thought the whole course of my life was settled. It wasn't.'

'There must be something,' she insisted.

'There may well be, but I don't know what it is.'

'Was it because you needed . . . to be married?'

'No, not sex,' he said. 'Though that's what many people think. If anything, the giving up of sex – renunciation was the word we used – gave the vocation far more force. We weren't doing anything easy. That has its own pride. We were giving up an idea of pleasure for a far greater good. That is . . . until belief started to go . . . and then all went.'

'You don't believe in anything at all, then?' she said with a gravity that both charmed and nettled.

'I have no talent for profundity.' He had spoken more than he had intended and was beginning to be irritated by the turn of the conversation.

'You must believe in something?' she insisted.

''Tis most certain. Have not the schoolmen said it?' he quoted to tease gently, but saw she disliked the tone. 'I believe in honour, decency, affection, in pleasure. This, for instance, is a very good steak.'

'You don't seem bitter.' This faint praise was harder to take than blame.

'That would be stupid. That would be worst of all. How is the lamb?'

'It's good, but I don't like to be fobbed off like that.'

'I wouldn't do that. I still find it painful, that's all. I'm far too grateful to you. I think you were very brave to come here.' He started to fumble again, gently, diffidently.

'I wasn't brave. It was what I wanted.'

'Not many women would have the courage to propose a hotel.'

'They might be the wise ones.'

It was her turn to want to change the direction of the conversation. A silence fell that wasn't silence. They were unsure, their minds working furiously behind the silence to find some safe way to turn.

'That man you were in love with,' he suggested.

'He was married. He had a son. He travelled in pharmaceuticals.'

'That doesn't sound too good for you.'

'It wasn't. It was a mess.'

They had taken another wrong turning.

It was still raining heavily when they came from the grill. They had one very slow drink in the hotel bar, watching the people drink and come and go before the room and night drew them.

In the morning he asked, 'What are you doing today?'

'I'll go back to the hospital, probably try to get some sleep. I'm on night duty at eight.'

'We didn't get much sleep last night.'

'No, we didn't,' she answered gently enough, but making it plain that she had no interest in the reference. "What are you doing?' she changed the subject.

'There are three buses back. I'll have to get one of them.'

'Which one?'

'Probably the twelve o'clock, since you're going back to the hospital. When will we meet again?' he asked in a tone that already took the meeting for granted.

She was half dressed. The vague shape of her thighs shone through the pale slip as she turned towards him. 'We can't meet again.'

'Why not?' The casualness changed. 'Is there something wrong?'

'Nothing. Nothing at all. The very opposite.'

'What's the matter, then?' Why can't we meet?'

'I was going to tell you last night and didn't. I thought it might spoil everything. After all, you were in Maynooth once. I'm joining an Order.'

'You must be joking.'

'I was never more serious in my life. I'm joining next Thursday . . . the Medical Missionaries.' She had about her that presence that had attracted him in the dancehall; she stood free of everything around her, secure in her own light.

'I can't believe you.'

'It's true,' she said.

'But the whole thing is a lie, a waste, a fabrication.'

'It's not for me and it wasn't once for you.'

'But I believed then.'

'Don't you think I do?' she said sharply.

'To mouth Hail Marys and Our Fathers all of your life.'

'You know that's cheap. It'll be mostly work. I'll nurse as I nurse now. In two years' time I'll probably be sent to medical school. The Order has a great need of its own doctors.'

'Wasn't last night a strange preparation for your new life?'

'I don't see much wrong with it.'

'From your point of view, wasn't it a sin?' He was angry now.

'Not much of a one, if it was. I've known women who spent the night before their marriage with another man. It was an end to their free or single life.'

'And I was the goodbye, the shake-hands?'

'I didn't plan it. I was attracted to you. We were free. That's the way it fell. If I did it after joining, it would be different. It would be a very great sin.'

'Perhaps we could be married?' he pressed blindly.

'No. You wouldn't ask so lightly if we could.'

'We wouldn't have much at first but we would have one another and we could work,' he pursued.

'No. I'm sorry. I like you very much, but it cannot be. My mind has been made up for a long time.'

'Well, one last time, then,' he cut her short.

'Hadn't we the whole night?'

'One last time.' His hands insisted: and as soon as it was over he was sorry, left with less than if it had never taken place.

'I'm sorry,' he said.

'It doesn't matter.'

After they had paid downstairs, they did not want to eat in the hotel, though the grill room was serving breakfast. They went to one of the big plastic and chrome places on O'Connell Street. They ate slowly in uneasy silence.

'I hope you'll forgive me, if there's anything to forgive,' she said after a long time.

'I was going to ask the same thing. There's nothing to forgive. I wanted to see you again, to go on seeing you. I never thought I'd have the luck to meet someone so open...so unafraid.' He was entangled in his own words before he'd finished.

'I'm not like that at all.' She laughed as she hadn't for a long time. 'I'm a coward. I'm frightened of next week. I'm frightened by most things.'

'Why don't you take an address that'll always find me in case you change your mind?'

'I'll not change.'

'I thought that once too.'

'No. I'll not. I can't,' she said, but he still wrote the address and slipped it in her pocket.

'You can throw it away as soon as I'm out of sight.'

As they rose he saw that her eyes were filled with tears.

They now leaned completely on those small acts of ceremony that help us better out of life than any drug. He paid at the cash desk and waited afterwards while she fixed her scarf, smiled ruefully as he stood aside to allow her the inside of the stairs, opened the large swing-door at the bottom of the steps. They walked slowly to the bus stop. At the stop they tried to foretell the evening's weather by the dark cloudy appearance of the sky towards the west. The only thing that seemed certain was that there'd be more rain. They shook hands as the bus came in. He waited until all the passengers had got on and it had moved away.

The river out beyond the Custom House, the straight quays, seemed to stretch out in the emptiness after she had gone. In my end is my beginning, he recalled. In my beginning is my end, his and hers, mine and thine. It seemed to stretch out, complete as the emptiness, endless as a wedding ring. He knew it like his own breathing. There might well be nothing, but she was still prepared to live by that one thing, to will it true.

Thinking of her, he found himself walking eagerly towards the Busáras . . . but almost as quickly his walking slowed. His steps grew hesitant, as if he was thinking of turning back. He knew that no matter how eagerly he found himself walking in any direction it could only take him to the next day and the next.

TRAIN TRACKS

AIDAN MATHEWS

Timmy leans across the arm-rest of his window seat and tells the airhostess that he's sick. He might have told the cabin steward, the one who brought him the magnetic chess set with the missing bishop ten minutes before, but he didn't; he may be only twelve, twelve and a bit, but he's learned already from his mother and his sister that secrets are best shared with women.

The hostess smiles at him. Her smile is brisk, professional; her eyes are tired. A little fluid is oozing from her left earlobe where the pearl stud ought to be. He wonders whether it's tender, remembers his sister having her ears pierced by the ex-nun on her thirteenth birthday. Did the Germans take the earrings as well as the gold fillings from the men and women they killed in the camps he couldn't pronounce?

'Sick?'

'A bit.'

'In your head or your tummy?'

'In my stomach,' he says.

'Maybe you drank that Coke too fast. Would you feel better if you put your seat back? Or if you got sick? Sick into the bag.'

'No.' He has already stowed the sick-bag and the in-flight magazine and the sugar sachet from the lunch that was served, in the pocket of his school blazer as souvenirs of the flight.

'We'll be in Dusseldorf soon,' she tells him; and she reaches across the other, elderly passenger to rumple his hair with her red fingernails.

Now that she's touched him, he has to confess. He hopes the other passenger won't overhear, but the man seems to be asleep, his mouth open, a dental brace on his bottom teeth as if he were a child again, and a slight smell of hair-oil from his button-down collar.

'I can't go,' Timmy tells the airhostess. 'I've tried to go ever since I woke up at home this morning. I tried at the airport, in the departure lounge, and I've tried twice since the plane took off, but I had to stop because I was afraid that there'd be other people waiting outside. And it gets more sore all the time.'

She laughs; it's meant kindly.

'That's only constipation,' she tells him. 'It'll pass. And now you know how women feel when they're having babies.'

She begins to move away as the elderly passenger comes to.

'I could report her,' he says to Timmy. 'I could report her for saying things like that.'

Timmy doesn't answer. Instead, he stares out the window, tilting his glasses slightly on the bridge of his nose to bring the countryside beneath him into sharper definition. What do women feel when they're having babies, and why is it wrong to say so? His stomach tightens again, the pressure to pass a motion makes him gasp.

'Are you all right?'

'Yes. Thank you.'

The elderly passenger in the next seat holds a Ventolin inhaler to his mouth, and sucks sharply on it. After ten or fifteen seconds, he exhales again slowly, as if he were blowing invisible smoke rings. He glances at Timmy.

'The good life,' he says.

'Were you in the army during the war?'

'Yes. I was.'

Timmy's delighted. He puts the bottoms of two pawn pieces together, and their magnets meet precisely.

'In the commandos?'

'In catering.' The boy's face falls. 'Don't despise it. An army marches on its stomach.'

But Timmy looks away at the window. Far below him, he can see a river that must be the Rhine, a thin tapeworm the colour of concrete; and near it a road, perhaps an autobahn, a relic of the Reich. But where are the train tracks? Surely there must be train tracks between Dusseldorf and the city of Krefeld where the Sterms have their home. After all, there are train tracks everywhere in this strange, sinister land; and the train tracks lead from the cities through the country to the concentration camps, and everybody knew that they did, knew at the time, and said nothing.

The boy thinks of the depots, of the huddled deportees. He thinks of the chemists, the teachers, the mezzo-sopranos, squeezed into stifling cattle-trucks, sealed carriages; men with beards who had lectured in anatomy, artists and actresses whose dressing-rooms were lavish with insect-eating plants from Argentina; people who could talk in three languages, yet who had to pull their dresses up or their trousers down and squat over straw while the train roared towards the watchtowers.

'Would you like to see the cockpit?'

The hostess beams at him. She seems revived. Or is she coming back because of what the elderly man said? Could she lose her job because of him?

'No, thank you.'

'Don't you want to be a pilot when you grow up?'

He looks at her, at the weeping earlobe, a wisp of brown hair black at the roots.

'No,' he says. 'I want to be a Jew.'

She frowns, the elderly passenger turns to stare at him; and the plane begins its descent.

His classmates troop through the shallow chlorine pools back into the men's dressing-room. They peel off their swimming togs, and wring them out over the basins, excitedly chattering in this vast wooden space with its lockers like baskets. One of them whistles the theme song from *The Monkees*; another pushes a hair-clip up his nostril to scrape out a scab.

'I'm dying for a drink. Water, water.'

One of the boys, pretending to be thirsty, lets his tongue loll. A taller child volunteers the tiny pink nipple on his chest, and the thirsty one nibbles greedily at it.

'There you go, my child. Suck away.'

Timmy twists his regulation gym shorts, twists and tightens them until the last little strings of water drip down on to the floor. He'll have to wear them again on the bus journey back to the school, because he forgot his togs today, for the third time in a single term. As a penalty, he has to write out the Our Father twelve times, once for each year of his life.

'Into the showers! Into the showers! Quickly, quickly!'

It's Mr Madden, standing in the doorframe, shouting. He's carrying the large Tayto crisps carton where he puts the boys' glasses and watches for safe-keeping while they're in the pool. Timmy hurries into the shower, jostling, being jostled in turn, the hips and buttocks of the other boys grazing against him. He lifts his face to the hard hail of the water.

'Do it now, Hardiman. Come on. Do it now.'

One voice, two, then many, all of them. Timmy joins in, though he doesn't quite know what it is that Hardiman must do. The boy beside him lifts his wrist. There's a phone number written on it, a five-letter phone number; it looks like a camp tattoo, it looks like—

'You all have to pay me sixpence. All of you.'

They nod solemnly; they're hushed now. Hardiman folds his arms across his chest, and stares at his penis. One of the boys stops the shower; the others surround Hardiman to shield him from the door. Outside they can hear the shrieks of the prep class, dog-paddling on their yellow floats, and a distant whistle. Timmy wishes he had his glasses. Things are blurred without them.

He has to squeeze the edges of his eyelids with his fingers in order to make anything out.

'You look a bit Chinese that way,' says the boy beside him.

'Do I?'

'A bit. Listen, Tim, when you go to Germany next week, will you bring me back some Hitler stamps?'

'Any moment now,' says Hardiman; and, sure enough, his penis begins to grow: slowly at first, then more swiftly, it stiffens, straightens, and stands up. The boys stare at it in silence, at its beauty, its lack of embarrassment.

'And I didn't even have to stroke it,' says Hardiman. 'Most people have to stroke it. But I can make it big just by thinking.'

'Thinking what?' says Timmy. 'What do you think?'

'Never you mind,' Hardiman says.

They've left the airport, arrived at the station, boarded the train and found a compartment, before Timmy has an opportunity to examine Frau Sterm closely. Modest and mild, she doesn't much mind such inspection. Instead, she smiles benignly out the window, watching the long, low barges on the river.

'The Rhine,' she tells him. 'The Rhine.' And she laughs, laughs because this strawberry-blond boy is looking at her so seriously, as if she were an ichthyosaurus or some other creepie-crawlie in the Natural History Museum where she brings her own son, Claus, on rainy Saturdays. She laughs, and lifts her hands to her forehead to flick back her fringe. The two boys will hit it off, she thinks: they're different, and difference, despite what universities may say, is the fountainhead of friendship. That was the aim and outcome of these programmes, a pairing of peers, of boys whose fathers had fought as enemies but whose sons, she thinks, whose sons will build rabbit hutches together.

Timmy's intrigued by the hair under her arms. He's never seen it before. Neither his mother nor his sister have anything like it.

He hasn't even come across it in the *National Geographic* or in his father's large, forbidden volume called *Diseases of the Breast*. Is it restricted to Germans or to German-speaking countries? Or is it found in Italy and France as well? Frau Sterm doesn't seem shy or secretive. After all, she's wearing a sleeveless dress. Besides, Europeans are different. In Spain, his sister wouldn't be allowed out without an escort; in Greece, she'd have to wear a black frock if her husband went and died. The world is peculiar.

'Are you afraid?'

She grins at him, showing her teeth. She has many gold fillings. If she were a Jew when she was little, they would have torn the gold out of her mouth with mechanics' tools. But she can't be Jewish, and not because the Jews are dead now, but because she's married to a man who served in the Wehrmacht, to a man who got frostbite in Russia. So perhaps the gold is from a Jew, perhaps it's migrated from one mouth to another; perhaps it was used to the sound of Lithuanian, to the taste of kosher sweetbread, and now it hears German greetings, and chews sausage.

'No,' he says. 'I'm not afraid.' And then, because he can't bear her to look at him without speaking, he decides to tell her about the presents.

'I have duty-free bottles for you,' he says. He can't remember what they are; his parents chose them. 'I have a model airplane for Claus. I have a Heinkel, a Heinkel bomber. There are a hundred and fifty bits. Do you know Heinkels?'

'Yes,' she tells him. 'Yes, I know Heinkels.' She becomes silent again.

Timmy's got to go to the toilet. It's the same problem, the need to shit something strong and solid that seems stuck inside him, the inability to shift it. He leaves the compartment, squeezes past a woman holding a hat-stand like a stag's antler in the passageway. He excuses himself as the two of them manoeuvre, excuses himself and wonders whether she'll think he's English, and, if so, whether she'll hate him, remembering perhaps a charred torso under masonry.

'Thank you,' he says.

'You're welcome.'

In the toilet, he's alone. The seat is plastic, not wooden like at home. And the lever for flushing is attached to the cistern behind; it doesn't hang from a chain. Timmy lowers his trousers, studies his underpants to ensure that they're not stained, but they are, slightly. How is he going to clean them without Frau Sterm finding out; and if she does, what can he tell her? His mother's warned him twice, three times that a boy is judged by the state of his shirt-collar and the condition of his underpants. He sits and strains, sits and strains. He feels behind him with his fingers, between his cheeks, to where the tip of the shit is wedged, but he can't pass it. The pain is too much.

The toilet is dry. Timmy can see down through it, though there's a loop in the exit pipe. Sleeper after sleeper after sleeper, thin strips of gravel and grass, a whirling monochrome, a rush of field-grey greyness. They would have seen the same, the ballerinas and the butchers, their eyes pressed to the chinks in the shoddy wooden goods trains.

The boy tears the identification tag from the lapel of his blazer, the one with his name and flight number on it, the one the air-hostess with the red fingernails had written. He holds it over the bowl for a moment, feels it flap in the uprush of the breeze, and then he lets it go.

'*Voilà*,' says Mr McDonagh; and he whisks the sheet away. '*Voilà*. That's German, I think, or maybe it's French.'

Timmy fumbles with his glasses, blows the short hairs from the lenses, and puts the glasses on. Mr McDonagh has followed his father's instructions to the letter. His hair is more closely cropped than it's ever been before. He looks denuded, ridiculous.

His cheeks flush pinker.

'I was only obeying my orders,' Mr McDonagh says.

The customer in the next chair chuckles.

'Jesus,' he says. 'You look like something that walked in out of the camps. When is it you're off anyway?'

'In three days.'

'Bring us back some reading material,' says the other man. 'Will you do that?'

'A bit of culture,' Mr McDonagh tells Timmy. 'The Rhine maidens out of Wagner.'

'*Die grossen Frauen*, more like. Do you know what I'm getting at?'

Timmy shakes his head.

'Leave him be,' says Mr McDonagh, blowing quietly on Timmy's bent neck. 'The child's a holy innocent.'

Timmy peers up at Mr McDonagh's reflection in the mirror.

'The boy I'm going to,' he explains. 'His father was in the German army. He was in Russia. He got wounded there. It was the same year Mum and Dad got married. So while he was sheltering behind some tank during snowstorms, my parents were on honeymoon down in Parknasilla, except that the hotel was full of priests. Isn't that strange?'

'Not really,' says Mr McDonagh. 'Priests had a lot of money twenty years ago.'

'Do you remember the invasion of Russia, Mr McDonagh?'

'Do I remember the day I got engaged? Of course I do. I was in the army myself at the time.'

'Where? Whereabouts?'

'I was stationed in Limerick. I was in the Irish army.'

'Who did you want to win?'

'The Allies, of course. I wanted the Allies to win. But . . .'

'But what?'

Mr McDonagh cleans his glasses with the end of his navy-blue tie.

219

'I wanted the Allies to get a bloody good thrashing first. After what the British done to us.'

The boy looks down at his lap, around at the floor. Thick tufts of his own hair litter the lino. It was strange to think that your own bits and pieces, toenails, fingernails, follicles of skin, strands of hair, an assortment of your own bodily parts, could be sorted out and swept away, like dog-dirt or a broken salt-cellar. And it was still stranger to imagine the small, sodden mounds of human hair that the barbers of Belsen and Buchenwald had shaved from schoolchildren, from tots whose first teeth were still intact, from teenagers who cycled bikes without holding the handlebars.

'What about the Jews, Mr McDonagh? Did you know about the Jews?'

'Ah, the Jews,' he says, shaking the sheet he had taken from Timmy. 'The Jews. A very versatile people. Sure, every second actor is a Jew; and they're all over Hollywood. What happened to the Jews was such a pity.'

The other customer clears his throat. A soft ball of phlegm sits on his under-lip.

'There's some lovely Jewish women as well,' he says. 'Not so *grossen* now, but every bit as *frauen*. Now why the fuck wasn't I born in Munich?'

Frau Sterm shows Timmy round the house. She shows him the kitchen, the living-room, the study where Herr Sterm works on his legal cases, the narrow ground-floor bedroom for any visitors. He doesn't notice much at first, because the whole house has a strange smell he can't identify. Aerosol sprays are new to him; back home, the maid cleans the bookshelves and the tabletops and the brass canopy over the fireplace with sponge and spittle, the elbow-grease of ages. Here it's different, a bright, brittle world.

'You like it?'

Frau Sterm lets the bed down by pressing a catch. It emerges from the wall and folds away slowly to the floor. Timmy's never seen one like it before, or the double-glazed windows that overlook the front lawn, a lawn without a fence or a stone wall to protect it, a lawn that slopes unselfconsciously to the public pavement.

'Yes,' he says. 'It's very nice.'

She stretches out her hand to him.

'Come. I have more to show.'

The boy follows her back into the kitchen. There's a low whine, like the noise of a mosquito, from the overhead light. The skeleton of a fish sits on the draining-board. Across at the window there's a bowl piled with grapes and pale bananas, but when he looks more closely he finds they're made of glass. And beside him on the polished counter he can see a weighing scales with the brand name Krupps, loose flour in a circle round its stand. He has seen that name somewhere before; he can almost retrieve it, but not quite.

'I have a letter for you,' she tells him. 'A letter from your family. It was here two days.'

Timmy takes it, tears it open. It contains one sheet of paper, paper so thin it's almost transparent. The writing is his sister's.

Dear Timmy.

It is now about nine o'clock, and I am going to bed. You are already asleep upstairs, and Mummy is choosing your trousers for the journey. It is strange to think that when you read this, you will be in the land of Hansel and Gretel. That is why I am writing.

I will go to the shop each Wednesday, and collect your comics, so that when you come home again in ten weeks' time, you will not have missed anything. Isn't that typical of

Your Adorable Sister.

Frau Sterm is folding laundry at the other end of the kitchen. Timmy thinks that it's kind of her to have turned her back while he was reading his letter; it's the first thing she's done that has made him less panicked and petrified. If only the smells were not so different, if only there were one smell which reminded him of the hot-press or the scullery at home. He wants to sit down straightaway and write to his sister, telling her that he travelled on a jet plane without any propellers, that he saw strange magazines at the kiosks in the airport, magazines with sneering women sticking out their bottoms; that he lost his German phrase-book somewhere between Dublin and Dusseldorf, and he can't remember how to say that he's having a lovely time; that there's a weighing scales in the kitchen, made by Krupps, and weren't they the same factory that built the crematoria; and that he's tried, and tried, and tried, but he still can't go big ways.

Frau Sterm pounds the kitchen window very precisely with a twisted kitchen towel, and a bluebottle staggers for a moment around the juices of its stomach before dropping to the ledge. But the blow has activated the sensors on the ultra-modern burglar alarm system. The bell wails though the house like an old-style air-raid alarm. Timmy cannot hear her at first when Frau Sterm tries to explain, and anyhow she hasn't the words.

'I understand,' he says.

His father tucks him in, brushes a few shavings of wood from a pencil off the side of the bedspread. Timmy puts his sketch-pad down. They kiss. His father switches off the light.

'I can always talk more easily in the darkness. Why do you think that is? I often wonder.'

Timmy doesn't say. He works himself more comfortably into the sheets. And waits.

'About this trip. You mustn't be frightened. People are kind the world over. You'll see. That bloody Italian you have for Latin's been filling your head with all sorts of nonsense, just because his brother got a bayonet in the bottom somewhere in Sicily. And the comics you read are no better—Boche this, Boche that, Boche the other. Officers with monocles, infantry like wart-hogs. The Germans are no better and no worse than anyone else. Do you believe me?'

'Yes.'

'Most of the music I play is German. Don't you like Mozart and Mahler? Don't you like Beethoven?'

'Yes.'

'So you see. Herr Sterm's a lovely man. If he seems a bit . . . remote, well, that's the way Germans are. Until you get to know them, of course. Then it's party-time. You remember playing mushroom billiards with Herr Sterm last year, over in Connemara, and how he let you win all the time. Now I never let you win, not if I can help it.'

His father moves towards the door, a dark sculpture in the soft light from the landing.

'Remember this. To being with, the Germans didn't invent anti-semitism; they inherited it. And who did they inherit it from? I'll tell you. They inherited it from the different Christian churches. That's who. You couldn't say these things ten years ago, or people would think you were an out-and-out Communist. But now with the Vatican Council going on, folk are finding out that a mouth is for more than sucking spaghetti.'

'Yes.'

'If anyone annoys you, just tell them this: in the middle of 1944, the Allies precision-bombed a munitions factory outside Auschwitz. Precision-bombed it. Pulverised the whole complex. But they didn't bomb the train tracks leading to the camp. They knew perfectly well that the camp was there; they knew perfectly well what was happening inside it. Flame-throwers turned on pregnant women; newborn babies kicked like footballs. But they didn't bomb the train tracks. And now after twenty years, they talk about preserving the otter.'

The door swings open.

'I had a patient this morning. On the table. He was different.'

'Why?'

'He died. He died on me. I had to . . . rip open his ribcage. I had to hold his heart in my hand, and pump it with my fingers until it started to beat again. I worked his heart with my own hand, something I use to pick my nose with.'

He stretches out his hand.

'Want to touch it?'

'No.'

His father grins.

Timmy stands up, holding his shorts with one hand at his knees, and turns to stare into the toilet-bowl. He has finally managed to empty his bowels. It has never taken longer to do so, never been so distressing before. His bottom aches. He wipes it gently, inspects the paper before he discards it. It only partly covers the massive turd lying in the shallow bowl. The sheer size of it fascinates the boy. How can there be room for such a thing inside one's stomach?

But he mustn't delay. He's been inside the bathroom for almost fifteen minutes. Frau Sterm may come knocking. He presses the plunger firmly, and blue water gushes down the rim of the bowl. It swirls in a frothy fashion round the turd, spitting and bubbling; but then, slowly and silently, it ebbs away, it drains and disappears, it leaves the brown, bloated mass where it is. Timmy tugs the lever desperately. Nothing happens. The cistern is empty. It may take minutes to fill again. He hoists up his shorts, buttons the fly, washes his hands, runs them through the stubble on his scalp. Where is Frau Sterm? How long has he been now? How long? The room may be smelly. He opens the window, scatters toilet water on the cork floor. How long?

The cistern has filled again. It must have, because the noise of gurgling has stopped. Timmy forces the lever, more slowly this time, and again the blue water cascades in. He waits, he watches it settle. The waters clear.

The turd has not budged.

The boy runs out of the bathroom. There's a door to the left-hand side, but he hasn't been shown the rooms upstairs. Perhaps it's where the Sterms sleep; perhaps Frau Sterm is in there now. He stops, starts towards it again, reaches it, peers round the door. It's a child's room, a boy's room, Claus's room. There are Disney transfers on the walls, a beachball in the corner, a thin Toledo sword; and on the floor immediately in front of him, there's a model train-set, stacked train tracks, little level crossings, carriages, tenders, engines, miniature porters and stokers.

The boy listens. He can hear nothing. He leans forward, snatches a long length of train track, and rushes back to the bathroom. He locks the door, listens again. Then he drives the train track fiercely into the huge shit, working it this way and that, stabbing and slashing at it until the motion begins gradually to disintegrate. But he doesn't stop. He pounds and pummels, pounds and pummels again. At last, at long last, he's satisfied; he adds another mighty jab for good measure, and flushes. Piece by piece, fragment by fragment, the turd is swallowed up, swept down.

Timmy begins to cry; but he can't allow himself, not yet, not now. There's still the train track, the train track. How long has he been here now? He fumbles with the tap, turns it full on, holds the track beneath its blast of water, picks at the particles of shit with his fingernails; but it's no use. The thing is sodden, it stinks, he can't clean it. He stands for seconds, staring at the toy piece; then he rushes out of the bathroom, down the stairs to the ground floor, and stops, straining for a footfall, the least sound. Where is

Frau Sterm?

When he reaches the garden, he hurls the track with all his strength into the air and over the low wooden stockade behind the rhododendrons and the raspberry bushes. It lands among rosebeds in the neighbouring garden. Timmy has thrown it with such force that the muscle under his armpit hurts him. Now he can let himself cry.

'I won't hurt you.'

Timmy is standing in his pyjamas in front of his mother. It's late, the last night before he leaves for Germany. His bag is packed.

'I put a scapular inside the suitcase,' his mother says as she takes his penis out of his pyjamas. 'Do you know what a scapular is?'

'No.'

His mother pulls his foreskin up and down, up and down. She tries to be very gentle.

'A scapular will protect you,' she says. 'My mother gave me a scapular when I went on my honeymoon with Daddy.'

'Did it protect you?'

She laughs.

'What protection did I need?'

Timmy decides to tell her.

'I had a dream last night. A dream about you. I was sitting in a deckchair somewhere, and a whole herd of cows walked up to me. Their udders were dragging on the ground. They wanted to be milked.'

'And did you milk them?'

'Yes. I milked them with my bare hands, on to the grass. There was no end of milk.'

'And where did I come in?'

'You didn't. But I felt the way I always feel when I'm with you.'

His mother kisses the tip of his nose. She slips his penis back into his pyjamas.

'I want you to ask Frau Sterm to do that for you. Will you do that? It's very important. You'll understand when you're bigger.'

'Will you write to me?'

'Of course I'll write to you. Of course I will. And you must write back. But don't just write to me. Write to your daddy. Write to him at his hospital. He'd love that.'

'All right.'

The mother looks at her son, the son at his mother.

'Germany's not that bad. You remember how I told you I was there with Granny, just before the war.'

'You were getting better.'

'I was getting better. I was recovering. I'd been ill.'

'With pleurisy.'

'With pleurisy. That's right. And lots of people had it. It was rampant.'

'What's rampant?'

'Everywhere. All over. An epidemic. Many people died from it.'

'But you got better.'

'I got better. I got better in Germany. Or at least I finished getting better there. And I met some lovely people.'

'Who?'

'I met a woman. A girl, I mean. She owned her own café, a coffee-house. You could order the most beautiful cakes. And a cellist played there in the afternoons. She was a sweet person, but she wore too much make-up. She looked a little like a cake herself.'

'Did you ever meet a man you liked?'

'Yes, I did. He was very like Daddy, except smaller.'

'Was he a Nazi?'

'He was in the army. But his real ambition in life was to become a bee-keeper.'

'Did he?'

His mother gets off her knees, and brushes the wrinkles on her kneecaps.

'I don't know. Perhaps he died. Perhaps he died in the war. His name was Nikki.'

Timmy burrows down in the bed. He shifts his weight to one side, leaving enough room on the other, as he has always done and will always continue to do, for Bernard, his guardian angel.

Claus and Timmy have hit it off. Frau Sterm is certain of it. There may be a little diffidence on either side, but that sort of shyness is only to be expected. Dublin is not quite Dusseldorf, nor Krefeld Killarney. Frau Sterm rather likes the alliterative parallelism. She'll try it on her husband later.

Out in the garden, the two boys are smiling, circling each other. Claus opens his English phrase-book, picks sentences at random, reads them.

'This is not the room I asked for at reception.'

Timmy laughs, more loudly than he needs to.

'Is the museum open on Sundays as well?'

'*Jawohl*,' says Timmy, and salutes in the old style favoured by fascists. Claus looks at him closely. His face frowns. Timmy's unsettled, uneasy. He brings his arm down.

'I had a phrase-book too,' he tells him. 'Only I lost it. I don't know where. On the plane perhaps, or in the airport. But I'll get another. Then we can talk all the time. Can't we?'

Claus hasn't understood. He starts leafing through the Berlitz guidebook again. Thumbing the sections, looking up and over at his new acquaintance every so often. Eventually he finds what he's searching for.

'Can we reserve accommodation on this train?'

Timmy thinks of the train track under the rosebed, of the train-set scattered on the bright carpet upstairs. Is it remotely possible that Frau Sterm would collect the pieces into their box, counting them as she went along? Or that Claus would remember the exact number, the precise tally? Certainly the missing strip would never be found, but what if the whole Sterm family were to realise that, since the arrival of the stranger in their midst, things have been thieved? The word itself they might forgo, they might speak instead of disappearance, but thieving would be what they meant. He would be sent straight home, he might meet the same hostess on the Dublin flight. She might have to serve him breakfast, but she wouldn't look into his eyes. Instead she would look away.

'Is there a couchette available on this train?'

No one could have seen him do what he had done. The window in the bathroom was frosted, the door had been locked or at least he had tried to lock it. Frau Sterm had been nowhere to be found. The neighbouring house with the rosebed didn't overlook the garden. In fact, now that he saw it for the second time, he realised it was a bungalow. He could breathe easy.

'Or even standing room?'

Claus smiles at him. He's been saving the one bad English word he knows, learned from a mischievous scatterbrain in his *Mittelschule*.

'Shit,' he says.

Before Timmy can answer him, Claus bounds across the garden, and bends down at a forsythia tree. Moments later, he's back with a tortoise in his hands. Timmy steps forward a foot or two, and makes to touch the shell; but Claus throws the unfortunate creature high into the air, then catches it again. Timmy can't believe what he's seen, so Claus repeats the trick, then chucks the tortoise deftly to his new-found friend and pen-pal. Timmy returns it; it's tossed back. The tortoise has edged out of his shell. The boys can see its face and feet emerge. They go on throwing it, back and forth, one to the other, as if it were a rugby ball. But soon the inevitable happens. Claus fumbles a catch, drops the tortoise on the concrete walk, steps back, and stares in horror. Neither boy is sure whether the tortoise is still alive or, if alive, whether it's harmed. Neither speaks. A slight breeze darkens the lawn; sunflowers bob in their beds.

'Claus.'

But Claus doesn't answer. He walks the two steps to the tortoise, and nudges it with the toe of his sandal, nudges it in under the cover of a bush. No one will see it there. He'll come out later, after dinner, to examine it again. Timmy wonders if a tortoise has a spine. Perhaps a chip or even a hairline fracture in the shell won't matter.

'Shit,' says Claus again. 'Very shit.'

Father Eddy lines up his shot, and putts the ball briskly into the hole. Timmy claps.

'When I was a lad,' Father Eddy says as he moves to the next Latin numeral on the clockwork golf course at the bottom of Timmy's garden, 'Luther was another word for Lucifer. He was the Devil himself, every bit as bad as Hitler, and worse.'

'Really?'

'I kid you not. He divided Christendom against itself. He made war on the Church. You couldn't reason with him. And terrible things happened. Famine, assassinations, sacrilege. So, of course, when I was in the seminary, everybody looked on Luther as an utter blackguard. A bandit.'

The priest putts again, more cautiously this time.

'But now, with the Council and everything that Pope John tried to show us, we know different. We can see with the eyes of charity, the eyes of compassion. We can see that Luther wasn't all bad. He was just bonkers. Stark, raving mad.'

The ball wobbles on the edge of the hole, but it doesn't go in. Father Eddy's vexed.

'Even so, if the Sterms do ask you along to one of their services, say no. Say you're only allowed to attend the Catholic church. And if there isn't one in the area, don't fret. The obligation doesn't bind you when you're abroad. I was in Greece one time, a couple of years before I was ordained, and I went a month without mass. I was a spiritual skin-and-bones case by the time I got home.'

Timmy toes the golfball in, then takes it out again, and hands it back to Father Eddy. The priest crouches over his putter, practising.

'If anybody asks you, tell them you're Irish but that you learned English at school.'

'Yes.'

'Mind you, when you're away out of the country, your real nationality is Catholicism. The Faith. Think of the Irish monks who went out to convert Germany. Columbanus, Cillian. Holy men, whole men, men with a mission. You're following in their footsteps. You see what I'm saying?'

'Yes.'

Father Eddy looks around him at the twelve Latin numerals embedded in the lawn.

'Which is that?' he asks, pointing with his putter to the large metal 'V' under the plum-tree.

'Five,' Timmy says.

'And that?'

'Nine. I know them up to a hundred. A hundred is C.'

'Good man yourself.'

It's getting late. Only the upper windows of the glasshouse catch the sunlight. The priest and the boy walk back towards the house.

'Isn't it a strange thing all the same,' Father Eddy says. 'Those Latin numerals were used by Julius Caesar. Augustus used them. Housewives in Pompeii were counting them on their fingers the day Vesuvius burst. And that's not today, nor the day before it either. That's a long time ago.'

'How many popes ago?'

'Many, many, many. And yet, two thousand years later, you can come upon them laid out in a circle at the end of a private garden. Do you know who made that possible?'

'No.'

'Well, you should know. It was the Church. The Church preserved Latin, the language of the very soldiers who crucified Our Lord. That's called an irony.'

'What's that?'

'A wound that gives pleasure.'

The priest stoops to pick a bird's feather from the lawn.

'You could talk to Claus in the Latin you have,' he tells Timmy. 'I imagine he learns it in his school. You know the verb "to love" backwards. And that's enough to start with. It's enough for anyone. Or it should be. You're not nervous? There's no reason to be nervous. Sure, the two of you will be thick as thieves before the plane's refuelled.'

Behind them, out of the cypress-trees, magpies circle the clockwork golf course, land, and begin to pick at the glinting metal letters.

Herr Sterm leans back from the dining table, and tilts his chin towards the ceiling. Almost from the moment that he entered the house, his nose has been bleeding. Already the front of his shirt is stained, the green tie that he wore to honour Timmy is flecked with red. Yet Frau Sterm continues to tell the boy that this is no unusual occurrence. It happens all the time, it's a sign of health, not illness. It passes after a while, as all things pass. And she ladles more vegetables on to Timmy's plate, and sets the plate before him.

The food is unintelligible. There are strange, anonymous entities Timmy's never seen before. Shape, size, flavour and taste, are all new. He rummages with his knife and fork, sorts and separates the mess, but he can't bring himself to swallow the stuff. He can see fragments of his own reflection on the broad blade of the knife; his lower lip with the scrap of dead skin, his teeth in a white wobble, his eyebrows, eyelashes, eyes. His eyes stare back at him, confessing, concealing.

'Would you like to see a film tomorrow?'

He looks up at Frau Sterm. She seems distant, diminished.

'Yes. Thank you.'

'Would you like to see *The Sound of Music*?'

'Yes.'

Herr Sterm settles his chair back on its four legs again. He holds a large handkerchief to his nose as he speaks in a muffled way to his wife. He speaks first in German, then in English.

'*The Sound of Music* is not a good film. It is anti-German. The music is pretty, but the message, the message is propaganda. But there are other films. There are others; and these we will see.'

They eat in silence. Timmy forces a few mouthfuls of the green and purple rubbish into his mouth. Claus is in another world, playing soccer with the peas on his plate. Perhaps he's thinking about the tortoise; perhaps he's frightened. Herr Sterm begins to bleed again, over the napkin and the napkin ring. He swears in an undertone. His wife shushes him. Silence again for a spell...and then the bell rings.

The hall doorbell, its two tones, a little phrase.

The whole table tenses. Mother and father glance at each other. The husband rises, goes out. Frau Sterm peers out the window at the louvre doors into the kitchen.

'I think it is a neighbour,' she says.

And Timmy knows, knows in the pit of his stomach; deep in the boy's belly, there is certain knowledge. Why did the elderly passenger complain about the airhostess? Why had he said he wanted to be a Jew? What made him refuse to visit the cockpit? And how did Hardiman make his penis stand up straight? What was he thinking of when he did that? What was in his mind?

The door swings open. Herr Sterm walks back in. He says nothing. He's holding the train track. Why had he thrown his identification label into the toilet on the train? There must have been a reason. His father is always telling him there is a reason for everything. If so, why were the women sneering on the magazine covers? Herr Sterm begins to beat Claus around the shoulders and neck with the dirty train track. His wife screams. But Claus, Claus doesn't cry, doesn't cry out. He doesn't even try to cover his head. What did Mr McDonagh feel about Jews? What did he really feel? What did 'grossen Frauen' mean? Why was it funny?

Frau Sterm punches her husband in the side. She pleads with him; he doesn't answer. His nose has begun to bleed again. It drips on to Claus's T-shirt, runs down the back. The boy sobs and shudders. Herr Sterm raises the train track one last time, a soiled stretch, still filthy from the toilet and the garden; raises it, looks at it, lowers it. He runs his hand through his hair.

'I bought this . . . machinery for Claus yesterday. It is a new present. For him, but also for you. To play together.'

Why had he not touched his father's hand? And why had the Allied bombers not bombed the train tracks leading to Auschwitz? Why? And when would he know the answers? All the answers to everything, everything that made him feel scared and strange and examined. He looks at Herr Sterm, at Frau Sterm, at Claus. He feels sick in his stomach, sick and sore. The lenses of his glasses have begun to mist from the heat of his sweat. They start to slip forward down the bridge of his nose until the half of his field of vision is a blur, the other half is sharper than italics.

He says nothing. He says nothing at all.

THE THINGS THEY CARRIED

TIM O'BRIEN

First Lieutenant Jimmy Cross carried letters from a girl named Martha, a junior at Mount Sebastian College in New Jersey. They were not love letters, but Lieutenant Cross was hoping, so he kept them folded in plastic at the bottom of his rucksack. In the late afternoon, after a day's march, he would dig his foxhole, wash his hands under a canteen, unwrap the letters, hold them with the tips of his fingers, and spend the last hour of light pretending. He would imagine romantic camping trips into the White Mountains in New Hampshire. He would sometimes taste the envelope flaps, knowing her tongue had been there. More than anything, he wanted Martha to love him as he loved her, but the letters were mostly chatty, elusive on the matter of love. She was a virgin, he was almost sure. She was an English major at Mount Sebastian, and she wrote beautifully about her professors and roommates and mid-term exams, about her respect for Chaucer and her great affection for Virginia Woolf. She often quoted lines of poetry; she never mentioned the war, except to say, Jimmy, take care of yourself. The letters weighed 10 ounces. They were signed Love, Martha, but Lieutenant Cross understood that Love was only a way of signing and did not mean what he sometimes pretended it meant. At dusk, he would carefully return the letters to his rucksack. Slowly, a bit distracted, he would get up and move among his men, checking the perimeter, then at full dark he would return to his hole and watch the night and wonder if Martha was a virgin.

The things they carried were largely determined by necessity. Among the necessities or near-necessities were P-38 can openers,

TIM O'BRIEN

pocket knives, heat tabs, wristwatches, dog tags, mosquito
repellent, chewing gum, candy, cigarettes, salt tablets, packets of
Kool-Aid, lighters, matches, sewing kits, Military Payment
Certificates, C rations, and two or three canteens of water.
Together, these items weighed between 15 and 20 pounds,
depending upon a man's habits or rate of metabolism. Henry
Dobbins, who was a big man, carried extra rations; he was
especially fond of canned peaches in heavy syrup over pound
cake. Dave Jensen, who practiced field hygiene, carried a
toothbrush, dental floss, and several hotel-sized bars of soap he'd
stolen on R&R in Sydney, Australia. Ted Lavender, who was scared,
carried tranquilizers until he was shot in the head outside the
village of Than Khe in mid-April. By necessity, and because it was
SOP, they all carried steel helmets that weighed 5 pounds including
the liner and camouflage cover. They carried the standard fatigue
jackets and trousers. Very few carried underwear. On their feet
they carried jungle boots — 2.1 pounds — and Dave Jensen carried
three pairs of socks and a can of Dr Scholl's foot powder as a
precaution against trench foot. Until he was shot, Ted Lavender
carried six or seven ounces of premium dope, which for him was
a necessity. Mitchell Sanders, the RTO, carried condoms. Norman
Bowker carried a diary. Rat Kiley carried comic books. Kiowa, a
devout Baptist, carried an illustrated New Testament that had been
presented to him by his father, who taught school in Oklahoma
City, Oklahoma. As a hedge against bad times, however, Kiowa
also carried his grandmother's distrust of the white man, his
grandfather's old hunting hatchet. Necessity dictated. Because the
land was mined and booby-trapped, it was SOP for each man to
carry a steel-centered, nylon-covered flak jacket, which weighed
6.7 pounds, but which on hot days seemed much heavier. Because
you could die so quickly, each man carried at least one large
compress bandage, usually in the helmet band for easy access.
Because the nights were cold, and because the monsoons were

wet, each carried a green plastic poncho that could be used as a raincoat or groundsheet or makeshift tent. With its quilted liner, the poncho weighed almost two pounds, but it was worth every ounce. In April, for instance, when Ted Lavender was shot, they used his poncho to wrap him up, then to carry him across the paddy, then to lift him into the chopper that took him away.

They were called legs or grunts.

To carry something was to hump it, as when Lieutenant Jimmy Cross humped his love for Martha up the hills and through the swamps. In its intransitive form, to hump meant to walk, or to march, but it implied burdens far beyond the intransitive.

Almost everyone humped photographs. In his wallet, Lieutenant Cross carried two photographs of Martha. The first was a Kodacolor snapshot signed Love, though he knew better. She stood against a brick wall. Her eyes were gray and neutral, her lips slightly open as she stared straight-on at the camera. At night, sometimes, Lieutenant Cross wondered who had taken the picture, because he knew she had boyfriends, because he loved her so much, and because he could see the shadow of the picture-taker spreading out against the brick wall. The second photograph had been clipped from the 1968 Mount Sebastian yearbook. It was an action shot — women's volleyball — and Martha was bent horizontal to the floor, reaching, the palms of her hands in sharp focus, the tongue taut, the expression frank and competitive. There was no visible sweat. She wore white gym shorts. Her legs, he thought, were almost certainly the legs of a virgin, dry and without hair, the left knee cocked and carrying her entire weight, which was just over one hundred pounds. Lieutenant Cross remembered touching that left knee. A dark theater, he remembered, and the movie was *Bonnie and Clyde*, and Martha wore a tweed skirt, and during the final scene, when he touched her knee, she turned and looked at him in a sad, sober way that made him pull his hand back, but he would always remember the feel of the tweed skirt and the knee beneath it and the sound of the gunfire that killed Bonnie and Clyde, how embarrassing it was, how slow and oppressive. He remembered kissing her good night at the dorm door. Right then, he thought, he should've done something brave. He should've carried her up the stairs to her room and tied her to the bed and touched that left knee all night long. He should've risked it. Whenever he looked at the photographs, he thought of new things he should've done.

What they carried was partly a function of rank, partly of field speciality.

As a first lieutenant and platoon leader, Jimmy Cross carried a compass, maps, code books, binoculars, and a .45-caliber pistol that weighed 2.9 pounds fully loaded. He carried a strobe light and the responsibility for the lives of his men.

As an RTO, Mitchell Sanders carried the PRC-25 radio, a killer, 26 pounds with its battery.

As a medic, Rat Kiley carried a canvas satchel filled with morphine and plasma and malaria tablets and surgical tape and comic books and all the things a medic must carry, including M&Ms for especially bad wounds, for a total weight of nearly 20 pounds.

As a big man, therefore a machine gunner, Henry Dobbins carried the M-60, which weighed 23 pounds unloaded, but which was almost always loaded. In addition, Dobbins carried between 10 and 15 pounds of ammunition draped in belts across his chest and shoulders.

As PFCs or Spec 4s, most of them were common grunts and carried the standard M-16 gas-operated assault rifle. The weapon weighed 7.5 pounds unloaded, 8.2 pounds with its full 20-round magazine. Depending on numerous factors, such as topography and psychology, the riflemen carried anywhere from 12 to 20 magazines, usually in cloth bandoliers, adding on another 8.4

pounds at minimum, 14 pounds at maximum. When it was available, they also carried M-16 maintenance gear — rods and steel brushes and swabs and tubes of LSA oil — all of which weighed about a pound. Among the grunts, some carried the M-79 grenade launcher, 5.9 pounds unloaded, a reasonably light weapon except for the ammunition, which was heavy. A single round weighed 10 ounces. The typical load was 25 rounds. But Ted Lavender, who was scared, carried 34 rounds when he was shot and killed outside Than Khe, and he went down under an exceptional burden, more than 20 pounds of ammunition, plus the flak jacket and helmet and rations and water and toilet paper and tranquilizers and all the rest, plus the unweighed fear. He was dead weight. There was no twitching or flopping. Kiowa, who saw it happen, said it was like watching a rock fall, or a big sandbag or something — just boom, then down — not like the movies where the dead guy rolls around and does fancy spins and goes ass over teakettle — not like that, Kiowa said, the poor bastard just flat-fuck fell. Boom. Down. Nothing else. It was a bright morning in mid-April. Lieutenant Cross felt the pain. He blamed himself. They stripped off Lavender's canteens and ammo, all the heavy things, and Rat Kiley said the obvious, the guy's dead, and Mitchell Sanders used his radio to report one US KIA and to request a chopper. Then they wrapped Lavender in his poncho. They carried him out to a dry paddy, established security, and sat smoking the dead man's dope until the chopper came. Lieutenant Cross kept to himself. He pictured Martha's smooth young face, thinking he loved her more than anything, more than his men, and now Ted Lavender was dead because he loved her so much and could not stop thinking about her. When the dustoff arrived, they carried Lavender aboard. Afterward they burned Than Khe. They marched until dusk, then dug their holes, and that night Kiowa kept explaining how you had to be there, how fast it was, how the poor guy just dropped like so much concrete. Boom-down, he said. Like cement.

In addition to the three standard weapons — the M-60, M-16, and M-79 — they carried whatever presented itself, or whatever seemed appropriate as a means of killing or staying alive. They carried catch-as-catch-can. At various times, in various situations, they carried M-14s and CAR-15s and Swedish Ks and grease guns and captured AK-47s and Chi-Coms and RPGs and Simonov carbines and black market Uzis and .38 caliber Smith & Wesson handguns and 66 mm LAWs and shotguns and silencers and blackjacks and bayonets and C-4 plastic explosives. Lee Strunk carried a slingshot; a weapon of last resort, he called it. Mitchell Sanders carried brass knuckles. Kiowa carried his grandfather's feathered hatchet. Every third or fourth man carried a Claymore antipersonnel mine — 3.5 pounds with its firing device. They all carried fragmentation grenades — 14 ounces each. They all carried at least one M-18 colored smoke grenade — 24 ounces. Some carried CS or tear gas grenades. Some carried white phosphorus grenades. They carried all they could bear, and then some, including a silent awe for the terrible power of the things they carried.

In the first week of April, before Lavender died, Lieutenant Jimmy Cross received a good-luck charm from Martha. It was a simple pebble, an ounce at most. Smooth to the touch, it was a milky white color with flecks of orange and violet, oval shaped, like a miniature egg. In the accompanying letter, Martha wrote that she had found the pebble on the Jersey shoreline, precisely where the land touched water at high tide, where things came together but also separated. It was this separate-but-together quality, she wrote, that had inspired her to pick up the pebble and to carry it in her breast pocket for several days, where it seemed weightless, and then to send it through the mail, by air, as a token of her truest feelings for him. Lieutenant Cross found this romantic. But he wondered what her truest feelings were, exactly, and what she meant by separate-but-together. He wondered how the tides and waves had come into play on that afternoon along the Jersey shoreline when Martha saw the pebble and bent down to rescue it from geology. He imagined bare feet. Martha was a poet, with the poet's sensibilities, and her feet would be brown and bare, the toenails unpainted, the eyes chilly and somber like the ocean in March, and though it was painful, he wondered who had been with her that afternoon. He imagined a pair of shadows moving along the strip of sand where things came together but also separated. It was phantom jealousy, he knew, but he couldn't help himself. He loved her so much. On the march, through the hot days of early April, he carried the pebble in his mouth, turning it with his tongue, tasting sea salt and moisture. His mind wandered. He had difficulty keeping his attention on the war. On occasion he would yell at his men to spread out the column, to keep their eyes open, but then he would slip away into daydreams, just pretending, walking barefoot along the Jersey shore, with Martha, carrying nothing. He would feel himself rising. Sun and waves and gentle winds, all love and lightness.

What they carried varied by mission.

When a mission took them to the mountains, they carried mosquito netting, machetes, canvas tarps, and extra bug juice.

If a mission seemed especially hazardous, or if it involved a place they knew to be bad, they carried everything they could. In certain heavily mined AOs, where the land was dense with Toe Poppers and Bouncing Betties, they took turns humping a 28-pound mine detector. With its headphones and big sensing plate, the equipment was a stress on the lower back and shoulders, awkward to handle, often useless because of the shrapnel in the earth, but they carried it anyway, partly for safety, partly for the illusion of safety.

On ambush, or other night missions, they carried peculiar little odds and ends. Kiowa always took along his New Testament and a pair of moccasins for silence. Dave Jensen carried night-sight vitamins high in carotene. Lee Strunk carried his slingshot; ammo, he claimed, would never be a problem. Rat Kiley carried brandy and M&Ms candy. Until he was shot, Ted Lavender carried the starlight scope, which weighed 6.3 pounds with its aluminum carrying case. Henry Dobbins carried his girlfriend's pantyhose wrapped around his neck as a comforter. They all carried ghosts. When dark came, they would move out single file across the meadows and paddies to their ambush coordinates, where they would quietly set up the Claymores and lie down and spend the night waiting.

Other missions were more complicated and required special equipment. In mid-April, it was their mission to search out and destroy the elaborate tunnel complexes in the Than Khe area south of Chu Lai. To blow the tunnels, they carried one-pound blocks of pentrite high explosives, four blocks to a man, 68 pounds in all. They carried wiring, detonators, and battery-powered clackers. Dave Jensen carried earplugs. Most often, before blowing the tunnels, they were ordered by higher command to search them, which was considered bad news, but by and large they just shrugged and carried out orders. Because he was a big man, Henry Dobbins was excused from tunnel duty. The others would draw numbers. Before Lavender died there were 17 men in the platoon, and whoever drew the number 17 would strip off his gear and crawl in headfirst with a flashlight and Lieutenant Cross's .45-caliber pistol. The rest of them would fan out as security. They would sit down or kneel, not facing the hole, listening to the ground beneath them, imagining cobwebs and ghosts, whatever was down there — the tunnel walls squeezing in — how the flashlight seemed impossibly heavy in the hand and how it was tunnel vision in the very strictest sense, compression in all ways, even time, and how you had to wiggle in — ass and elbows — a swallowed-up feeling — and how you found yourself worrying about odd things: Will your flashlight go dead? Do rats carry rabies? If you screamed, how far would the sound carry? Would your buddies hear it? Would they have the courage to drag you out? In some respects, though not many, the waiting was worse than the tunnel itself. Imagination was a killer.

On April 16, when Lee Strunk drew the number 17, he laughed and muttered something and went down quickly. The morning was hot and very still. Not good, Kiowa said. He looked at the tunnel opening, then out across a dry paddy toward the village of Than Khe. Nothing moved. No clouds or birds or people. As they waited, the men smoked and drank Kool-Aid, not talking much, feeling sympathy for Lee Strunk but also feeling the luck of the draw. You win some, you lose some, said Mitchell Sanders, and sometimes you settle for a rain check. It was a tired line and no one laughed.

Henry Dobbins ate a tropical chocolate bar. Ted Lavender popped a tranquilizer and went off to pee.

After five minutes, Lieutenant Jimmy Cross moved to the tunnel, leaned down, and examined the darkness. Trouble, he thought — a cave-in maybe. And then suddenly, without willing it, he was thinking about Martha. The stresses and fractures, the quick collapse, the two of them buried alive under all that weight. Dense, crushing love. Kneeling, watching the hole, he tried to concentrate on Lee Strunk and the war, all the dangers, but his love was too much for him, he felt paralyzed, he wanted to sleep inside her lungs and breathe her blood and be smothered. He wanted her to be a virgin and not a virgin, all at once. He wanted to know her. Intimate secrets: Why poetry? Why so sad? Why that grayness in her eyes? Why so alone? Not lonely, just alone — riding her bike across campus or sitting off by herself in the cafeteria — even dancing, she danced alone — and it was the aloneness that filled him with love. He remembered telling her that one evening. How she nodded and looked away. And how, later, when he kissed her, she received the kiss without returning it, her eyes wide open, not afraid, not a virgin's eyes, just flat and uninvolved.

Lieutenant Cross gazed at the tunnel. But he was not there. He was buried with Martha under the white sand at the Jersey shore. They were pressed together, and the pebble in his mouth was her tongue. He was smiling. Vaguely, he was aware of how quiet the day was, the sullen paddies, yet he could not bring himself to worry about matters of security. He was beyond that. He was just a kid at war, in love. He was twenty-four years old. He couldn't help it.

A few moments later Lee Strunk crawled out of the tunnel. He came up grinning, filthy but alive. Lieutenant Cross nodded and closed his eyes while the others clapped Strunk on the back and made jokes about rising from the dead.

Worms, Rat Kiley said. Right out of the grave. Fuckin' zombie.

The men laughed. They all felt great relief.

Spook city, said Mitchell Sanders.

Lee Strunk made a funny ghost sound, a kind of moaning, yet very happy, and right then, when Strunk made that high happy moaning sound, when he went *Ahhooooo*, right then Ted Lavender was shot in the head on his way back from peeing. He lay with his mouth open. The teeth were broken. There was a swollen black bruise under his left eye. The cheekbone was gone. Oh shit, Rat Kiley said, the guy's dead. The guy's dead, he kept saying, which seemed profound — the guy's dead. I mean really.

The things they carried were determined to some extent by superstition. Lieutenant Cross carried his good-luck pebble. Dave Jensen carried a rabbit's foot. Norman Bowker, otherwise a very gentle person, carried a thumb that had been presented to him as a gift by Mitchell Sanders. The thumb was dark brown, rubbery to the touch, and weighed four ounces at most. It had been cut from a VC corpse, a boy of fifteen or sixteen. They'd found him at the bottom of an irrigation ditch, badly burned, flies in his mouth and eyes. The boy wore black shorts and sandals. At the time of his death he had been carrying a pouch of rice, a rifle, and three magazines of ammunition.

You want my opinion, Mitchell Sanders said, there's a definite moral here.

He put his hand on the dead boy's wrist. He was quiet for a time, as if counting a pulse, then he patted the stomach, almost affectionately, and used Kiowa's hunting hatchet to remove the thumb.

Henry Dobbins asked what the moral was.

Moral?

You know. *Moral*.

Sanders wrapped the thumb in toilet paper and handed it across to Norman Bowker. There was no blood. Smiling, he kicked the boy's head, watched the files scatter, and said, It's like with that old TV show — Paladin. Have gun, will travel.

Henry Dobbins thought about it.

Yeah, well, he finally said. I don't see no moral.

There it *is*, man.

Fuck off.

They carried USO stationery and pencils and pens. They carried Sterno, safety pins, trip flares, signal flares, spools of wire, razor blades, chewing tobacco, liberated joss sticks and statuettes of the smiling Buddha, candles, grease pencils, *The Stars and Stripes*, fingernail clippers, Psy Ops leaflets, bush hats, bolos, and much more. Twice a week, when the resupply choppers came in, they carried hot chow in green mermite cans and large canvas bags filled with iced beer and soda pop. They carried plastic water containers, each with a two-gallon capacity. Mitchell Sanders carried a set of starched tiger fatigues for special occasions. Henry Dobbins carried Black Flag insecticide. Dave Jensen carried empty sandbags that could be filled at night for added protection. Lee Strunk carried tanning lotion. Some things they carried in common. Taking turns, they carried the big PRC-77 scrambler radio, which weighed 30 pounds with its battery. They shared the weight of memory. They took up what others could no longer bear. Often, they carried each other, the wounded or weak. They carried infections. They carried chess sets, basketballs, Vietnamese-English dictionaries, insignias of rank, Bronze Stars and Purple Hearts, plastic cards imprinted with the Code of Conduct. They carried diseases, among them malaria and dysentery. They carried lice and ringworm and leeches and paddy algae and various rots and molds. They carried the land itself — Vietnam, the place, the soil — a powdery orange-red dust that covered their boots and fatigues and faces. They carried the sky. The whole atmosphere, they carried it, the humidity, the monsoons, the stink of fungus and decay, all of it, they carried gravity. They moved like mules. By daylight they took sniper fire, at night they were mortared, but it was not battle, it was just the endless march, village to village, without purpose, nothing won or lost. They marched for the sake of the march. They plodded along slowly, dumbly, leaning forward against the heat, unthinking, all blood and bone, simple grunts, soldiering with their legs, toiling up the hills and down into the paddies and across the rivers and up again and down, just humping, one step and then the next and then another, but no volition, no will, because it was automatic, it was anatomy, and the war was entirely a matter of posture and carriage, the hump was everything, a kind of inertia, a kind of emptiness, a dullness of desire and intellect and conscience and hope and human sensibility. Their principles were in their feet. Their calculations were biological. They had no sense of strategy or mission. They searched the villages without knowing what to look for, not caring, kicking over jars of rice, frisking children and old men, blowing tunnels, sometimes setting fires and sometimes not, then forming up and moving on to the next village, then other villages, where it would always be the same. They carried their own lives. The pressures were enormous. In the heat of early afternoon, they would remove their helmets and flak jackets, walking bare, which was dangerous but which helped ease the strain. They would often discard things along the route of march. Purely for comfort, they would throw away rations, blow their Claymores and grenades, no matter, because by nightfall the resupply choppers would arrive with more of the same, then a day or two later still more, fresh watermelons and crates of ammunition and sunglasses and woollen sweaters — the resources were stunning — sparklers for the Fourth of July, colored eggs for Easter — it was the great American war chest — the fruits of science, the smokestacks, the canneries, the arsenals at Hartford, the Minnesota forests, the machine shops, the vast fields of corn and wheat — they carried like freight trains; they carried it on their backs and shoulders — and for all the ambiguities of Vietnam, all the mysteries and unknowns, there was at least the single abiding certainty that they would never be at a loss for things to carry.

After the chopper took Lavender away, Lieutenant Jimmy Cross led his men into the village of Than Khe. They burned everything. They shot chickens and dogs, they trashed the village well, they called in artillery and watched the wreckage, then they marched for several hours through the hot afternoon, and then at dusk, while Kiowa explained how Lavender died, Lieutenant Cross found himself trembling.

He tried not to cry. With his entrenching tool, which weighed five pounds, he began digging a hole in the earth.

He felt shame. He hated himself. He had loved Martha more than his men, and as a consequence Lavender was now dead, and this was something he would have to carry like a stone in his stomach for the rest of the war.

All he could do was dig. He used his entrenching tool like an ax, slashing, feeling both love and hate, and then later, when it was full dark, he sat at the bottom of his foxhole and wept. It went on for a long while. In part, he was grieving for Ted Lavender, but mostly it was for Martha, and for himself, because she belonged to another world, which was not quite real, and because she was a junior at Mount Sebastian College in New Jersey, a poet and a virgin and uninvolved, and because he realised she did not love him and never would.

Like cement, Kiowa whispered in the dark. I swear to God — boom, down. Not a word.

I've heard this, said Norman Bowker.

A pisser, you know? Still zipping himself up. Zapped while zipping.

All right, fine. That's enough.

Yeah, but you had to see it, they guy just —

I *heard*, man. Cement. So why not shut the fuck *up*?

Kiowa shook his head sadly and glanced over at the hole where Lieutenant Jimmy Cross sat watching the night. The air was thick and wet. A warm dense fog had settled over the paddies and there was the stillness that precedes rain.

After a time Kiowa sighed.

One thing for sure, he said. The lieutenant's in some deep hurt. I mean that crying jag — the way he was carrying on — it wasn't fake or anything, it was real heavy-duty hurt. The man cares.

Sure, Norman Bowker said.

Say what you want, the man does care.

We all got problems.

Not Lavender.

No, I guess not, Bowker said. Do me a favor, though.

Shut up?

That's a smart Indian. Shut up.

Shrugging, Kiowa pulled off his boots. He wanted to say more, just to lighten up his sleep, but instead he opened his New Testament and arranged it beneath his head as a pillow. The fog made things seem hollow and unattached. He tried not to think about Ted Lavender, but then he was thinking how fast it was, no drama, down and dead, and how it was hard to feel anything except surprise. It seemed unchristian. He wished he could find some great sadness, or even anger, but the emotion wasn't there and he couldn't make it happen. Mostly he felt pleased to be alive. He liked the smell of the New Testament under his cheek, the leather and ink and paper and glue, whatever the chemicals were. He liked hearing the sounds of night. Even his fatigue, it felt fine, the stiff muscles and the prickly awareness of his own body, a floating feeling. He enjoyed not being dead. Lying there, Kiowa admired Lieutenant Jimmy Cross's capacity for grief. He wanted to share the man's pain, he wanted to care as Jimmy Cross cared. And yet when he closed his eyes all he could think was Boom-down, and all he could feel was the pleasure of having his boots off and the fog curling in around him and the damp soil and the Bible smells and the plush comfort of night.

After a moment Norman Bowker sat up in the dark.

What the hell, he said. You want to talk, *talk*. Tell it to me.

Forget it.

No, man, go on. One thing I hate, it's a silent Indian.

For the most part they carried themselves with poise, a kind of dignity. Now and then, however, they were times of panic, when they squealed or wanted to squeal but couldn't, when they twitched and made moaning sounds and covered their heads and said Dear Jesus and flopped around the earth and fired their weapons blindly and cringed and sobbed and begged for the noise to stop and went wild and made stupid promises to themselves and to God and to their mothers and fathers, hoping not to die. In different ways, it happened to all of them. Afterward, when the firing ended, they would blink and peek up. They would touch their bodies, feeling shame, then quickly hiding it. They would force themselves to stand. As if in slow motion, frame by frame, the world would take on the old logic — absolute silence, then the wind, then sunlight, then voices. It was the burden of being alive. Awkwardly, the men would reassemble themselves, first in private, then in groups, becoming soldiers again. They would repair the leaks in their eyes. They would check for casualties, call in dustoffs, light cigarettes, try to smile, clear their throats and spit and begin cleaning their weapons. After a time someone would shake his head and say, No lie, I almost shit my pants, and someone else would laugh, which meant it was bad, yes, but the guy had obviously not shit his pants, it wasn't that bad, and in any case nobody would ever do such a thing and then go ahead and talk about it. They would squint into the dense, oppressive sunlight. For a few moments, perhaps, they would fall silent, lighting a joint and tracking its passage from man to man, inhaling, holding in the humiliation. Scary stuff, one of them might say. But then someone else would grin or flick his eyebrows and say, Roger-dodger, almost cut me a new asshole, *almost*.

There were numerous such poses. Some carried themselves with a sort of wistful resignation, others with pride or stiff soldierly discipline or good humor or macho zeal. They were afraid of dying but they were even more afraid to show it.

They found jokes to tell.

They used a hard vocabulary to contain the terrible softness. *Greased* they'd say. *Offed, lit up, zapped while zipping*. It wasn't cruelty, just stage presence. They were actors. When someone died, it wasn't quite dying, because in a curious way it seemed scripted, and because they had their lines mostly memorised, irony mixed with tragedy, and because they called it by other names, as if to encyst and destroy the reality of death itself. They kicked corpses. They cut off thumbs. They talked grunt lingo. They told stories about Ted Lavender's supply of tranquilizers, how the poor guy didn't feel a thing, how incredibly tranquil he was.

There's a moral here, said Mitchell Sanders.

They were waiting for Lavender's chopper, smoking the dead man's dope. The moral's pretty obvious, Sanders said, and winked. Stay away from drugs. No joke, they'll ruin your day every time.

Cute, said Henry Dobbins.

Mind blower, get it? Talk about wiggy. Nothing left, just blood and brains.

They made themselves laugh.

There it is, they'd say. Over and over — there it is, my friend, there it is — as if the repetition itself were an act of poise, a balance between crazy and almost crazy, knowing without going, there it is, which meant be cool, let it ride, because Oh yeah, man, you can't change what can't be changed, there it is, there it absolutely and positively and fucking well *is*.

They were tough.

They carried all the emotional baggage of men who might die. Grief, terror, love, longing — these were intangibles, but the intangibles had their own mass and specific gravity, they had tangible weight. They carried shameful memories. They carried the common secret of cowardice barely restrained, the instinct to run or freeze or hide, and in many respects this was the heaviest burden of all, for it could never be put down, it required perfect balance and perfect posture. They carried their reputations. They carried the soldier's greatest fear, which was the fear of blushing. Men killed, and died, because they were embarrassed not to. It was what had brought them to the war in the first place, nothing positive, no dreams of glory or honor, just to avoid the blush of dishonor. They died so as not to die of embarrassment. They crawled into tunnels and walked point and advanced under fire. Each morning, despite the unknowns, they made their legs move. They endured. They kept humping. They did not submit to the obvious alternative, which was simply to close the eyes and fall. So easy, really. Go limp and tumble to the ground and let the muscles unwind and not speak and not budge until your buddies picked you up and lifted you into the chopper that would roar and dip its nose and carry you off to the world. A mere matter of falling, yet no one ever fell. It was not courage, exactly; the object was not valor. Rather, they were too frightened to be cowards.

By and large they carried these things inside, maintaining the masks of composure. They sneered at sick call. They spoke bitterly about guys who had found release by shooting off their own toes or fingers. Pussies, they'd say. Candy-asses. It was fierce, mocking talk, with only a trace of envy or awe, but even so the image played itself out behind their eyes.

They imagined the muzzle against flesh. So easy: squeeze the trigger and blow away a toe. They imagined it. They imagined the quick, sweet pain, then the evacuation to Japan, then a hospital with warm beds and cute geisha nurses.

And they dreamed of freedom birds.

At night, on guard, staring into the dark, they were carried away by jumbo jets. They felt the rush of takeoff. *Gone!* they yelled. And then velocity — wings and engines — a smiling stewardess — but it was more than a plane, it was a real bird, a big sleek silver bird with feathers and talons and high screeching. They were flying. The weights fell off; they was nothing to bear. They laughed and held on tight, feeling the cold slap of wind and altitude, soaring, thinking *It's over, I'm gone!* — they were naked, they were light and free — it was all lightness, bright and fast and buoyant, light as light, a helium buzz in the brain, a giddy bubbling in the lungs as they were taken up over the clouds and the war, beyond duty, beyond gravity and mortification and global entanglements — *Sin loi!* they yelled. *I'm sorry, motherfuckers, but I'm out of it, I'm goofed, I'm on a space cruise, I'm gone!* — and it was a restful, unencumbered sensation, just riding the light waves, sailing that big silver freedom bird over the mountains and oceans, over America, over the farms and great sleeping cities and cemeteries and highways and the golden arches of McDonald's, it was flight, a kind of fleeing, a kind of falling, falling higher and higher, spinning off the edge of the earth and beyond the sun and through the vast, silent vacuum where there were no burdens and where everything weighed exactly nothing — *Gone!* they screamed, *I'm sorry but I'm gone!* — and so at night, not quite dreaming, they gave themselves over to lightness, they were carried, they were purely borne.

On the morning after Ted Lavender died, First Lieutenant Jimmy Cross crouched at the bottom of his foxhole and burned Martha's letters. Then he burned the two photographs. There was a steady rain falling, which made it difficult, but he used heat tabs and Sterno to build a small fire, screening it with his body, holding the photographs over the tight blue flame with the tips of his finger.

He realised it was only a gesture. Stupid, he thought. Sentimental, too, but mostly just stupid.

Lavender was dead. You couldn't burn the blame.

Besides, the letters were in his head. And even now, without photographs, Lieutenant Cross could see Martha playing volleyball in her white gym shorts and yellow T-shirt. He could see her moving in the rain.

When the fire died out, Lieutenant Cross pulled his poncho over his shoulders and ate breakfast from a can.

There was no great mystery, he decided.

In those burned letters Martha had never mentioned the war, except to say, Jimmy, take care of yourself. She wasn't involved.

She signed the letters Love, but it wasn't love, and all the fine lines and technicalities did not matter. Virginity was no longer an issue. He hated her. Yes, he did. He hated her. Love, too, but it was a hard, hating kind of love.

The morning came up wet and blurry. Everything seemed part of everything else, the fog and Martha and the deepening rain.

He was a soldier, after all.

Half smiling, Lieutenant Jimmy Cross took out his maps. He shook his head hard, as if to clear it, then bent forward and began planning the day's march. In ten minutes, or maybe twenty, he would rouse the men and they would pack up and head west, where the maps showed the country to be green and inviting. They would do what they had always done. The rain might add some weight, but otherwise it would be one more day layered upon all the other days.

He was realistic about it. There was that new hardness in his stomach. He loved her but he hated her.

No more fantasies, he told himself.

Henceforth, when he thought about Martha, it would be only to think that she belonged elsewhere. He would shut down the daydreams. This was not Mount Sebastian, it was another world, where there were no pretty poems or mid-term exams, a place where men died because of carelessness and gross stupidity. Kiowa was right. Boom-down, you were dead, never partly dead.

Briefly, in the rain, Lieutenant Cross saw Martha's gray eyes gazing back at him.

He understood.

It was very sad, he thought. The things men carried inside. The things men did or felt they had to do.

He almost nodded at her, but didn't.

Instead he went back to his maps. He was now determined to perform his duties firmly and without negligence. It wouldn't help Lavender, he knew that, but from this point on he would comport himself as an officer. He would dispose of his good-luck pebble. Swallow it, maybe, or use Lee Strunk's slingshot, or just drop it along the trail. On the march he would impose strict field discipline. He would be careful to send out flank security, to prevent straggling or bunching up, to keep his troops moving at the proper pace and at the proper interval. He would insist on clean weapons. He would confiscate the remainder of Lavender's dope. Later in the day, perhaps, he would call the men together and speak to them plainly. He would accept the blame for what had happened to Ted Lavender. He would be a man about it. He would look them in the eyes, keeping his chin level, and he would issue the new SOPs in a calm, impersonal tone of voice, a lieutenant's voice, leaving no room for argument or discussion. Commencing immediately, he'd tell them, they would no longer abandon equipment along the route of the march. They would police up their acts. They would get their shit together, and keep it together, and maintain it neatly and in good working order.

He would not tolerate laxity. He would show strength, distancing himself.

Among the men there would be grumbling, of course, and maybe worse, because their days would seem longer and their loads heavier, but Lieutenant Jimmy Cross reminded himself that his obligation was not to be loved but to lead. He would dispense with love; it was not now a factor. And if anyone quarreled or complained, he would simply tighten his lips and arrange his shoulders in the correct command posture. He might give a curt little nod. Or he might not. He might just shrug and say, Carry on, then they would saddle up and form into a column and move out toward the villages west of Than Khe.

HO FOR HAPPINESS

STEPHEN LEACOCK

'Why is it,' said someone in conversation the other day, 'that all
the really good short stories seem to contain so much sadness
and suffering and to turn so much on crime and wickedness?
Why can't they be happy all the time?'

No one present was able to answer the question. But I thought
it over afterwards, and I think I see why it is so. A happy story,
after all, would make pretty dull reading. It may be all right in real
life to have everything come along just right, with happiness and
good luck all the time, but in fiction it would never do.

Stop, let me illustrate the idea. Let us make up a story which
is happy all the time and contrast it as it goes along with the way
things happen in the really good stories.

Harold Herald never forgot the bright October morning when
the mysterious letter, which was to alter his whole life, arrived at
his downtown office.

His stenographer brought it in to him and laid it on his desk.

'A letter for you,' she said. Then she kissed him and went out
again.

Harold sat for some time with the letter in front of him. Should
he open it? After all, why not?

He opened the letter. Then the idea occurred to him to read
it. 'I might as well,' he thought.

'Dear Mr Herald' (so ran the letter), 'if you will have the
kindness to call at this office, we shall be happy to tell you
something of great advantage.'

The letter was signed John Scribman. The paper on which it
was written bore the heading 'Scribman, Scribman & Company,
Barristers, Solicitors, etc, No. 13 Yonge St.'

A few moments later saw Harold on his way to the lawyers' office. Never had the streets looked brighter and more cheerful than in this perfect October sunshine. In fact, they never had been.

Nor did Harold's heart misgive him and a sudden suspicion enter his mind as Mr Scribman, the senior partner, rose from his chair to greet him. Not at all. Mr Scribman was a pleasant, middle-aged man whose countenance behind his gold spectacles beamed with good-will and good-nature.

'Ah, Mr Harold Herald,' he said, 'or perhaps you will let me call you simply Harold. I didn't like to give you too much news in one short letter. The fact is that our firm has been entrusted to deliver to you a legacy, or rather a gift . . . Stop, stop!' continued the lawyer, as Harold was about to interrupt with questions, ' . . . our client's one request was that his name would not be divulged. He thought it would be so much nicer for you just to have the money and not know who gave it to you.'

Harold murmured his assent.

Mr Scribman pushed a bell.

'Mr Harold Herald's money, if you please,' he said.

A beautiful stenographer wearing an American Beauty rose at her waist entered the room carrying a silken bag.

'There is half a million dollars here in five-hundred-dollar bills,' said the lawyer. 'At least, we didn't count them, but that is what our client said. Did you take any?' he asked the stenographer.

'I took out a few last night to go to the theatre with,' admitted the girl with a pretty blush.

'Monkey!' said Mr Scribman. 'But that's all right. Don't bother with a receipt, Harold. Come along with me: my daughter is waiting for us down below in the car to take us to lunch.'

Harold thought he had never seen a more beautiful girl than Alicia Scribman. In fact he hadn't. The luxurious motor, the faultless chauffeur, the presence of the girl beside him and the bag of currency under the seat, the sunlit streets filled with happy people with the bright feeling of just going back to work, full of lunch – the sight of all this made Harold feel as if life itself were indeed a pleasant thing.

'After all,' he mused, 'how little is needed for our happiness! Half a million dollars, a motor-car, a beautiful girl, youth, health surely one can be content with that . . .'

It was after lunch at the beautiful country home of the Scribmans that Harold found himself alone for a few minutes with Miss Scribman.

He rose, walked over to her and took her hand, kneeling on one knee and pulling up his pants so as not to make a crease in them.

'Alicia!' he said. 'Ever since I first saw you, I have loved you. I want to ask you if you will marry me?'

'Oh, Harold,' said Alicia, leaning forward and putting both her arms about his neck with one ear against the upper right hand end of his cheekbone. 'Oh, Harold!'

'I can, as you know,' continued Harold, 'easily support you.'

'Oh, that's all right,' said Alicia. 'As a matter of fact, I have much more than that of my own, to be paid over to me when I marry.'

'Then you will marry me?' said Harold rapturously.

'Yes, indeed,' said Alicia, 'and as it happens so fortunately just now, papa himself is engaged to marry again and so I shall be glad to have a new home of my own. Papa is marrying a charming girl, but she is so much younger than he is that perhaps she would not want a grown-up stepdaughter.'

Harold made his way back to the city in a tumult of happiness. Only for a moment was his delirium of joy brought to a temporary standstill.

As he returned to his own apartment, he suddenly remembered that he was engaged to be married to his cousin Winnie . . . The thing had been entirely washed out of his mind by the flood-tide of his joy.

He seized the telephone.

'Winnie,' he said, 'I am so terribly sorry I want to ask you to release me from our engagement. I want to marry someone else.'

'That's all right, Hal!' came back Winnie cheerfully. 'As a matter of fact, I want to do the same thing myself. I got engaged last week to the most charming man in the world, a little older, in fact quite a bit older than I am, but ever so nice. He is a wealthy lawyer and his name is Walter Scribman . . .'

The double wedding took place two weeks later, the church being smothered with chrysanthemums and the clergyman buried under Canadian currency. Harold and Alicia built a beautiful country home at the other side – the farthest-away side of the city from the Scribmans'. A year or so after their marriage, they had a beautiful boy and then another, then a couple of girls (twins), and then they lost count.

There. Pretty dull reading it makes. And yet, I don't know there's something about it, too. In the real stories Mr Scribman would have been a crook, and Harold would have either murdered Winnie or been accused of it, and the stenographer with the rose would have stolen the money instead of just taking it, and it wouldn't have happened in bright, clear October weather but in dirty old November – oh no, let us have romance and happiness, after all. It may not be true, but it's better.

BIOGRAPHICAL NOTES

Mary BECKETT was born in Belfast in 1926, where she worked as a primary school teacher. She moved to Dublin in 1956 and she lives in Templeogue. She wrote short stories and these were published in periodicals and newspapers during the 1950s. Her first collection of short stories, *A Belfast Woman*, was published in 1980. She has also published two novels for adults, *Give Them Stones* and *A Literary Woman*. *Orla was Six, Orla at School, A Family Tree* and *Hannah or Pink Balloons* are novels for children. 'The Cypress Trees' is taken from Mary Beckett's novel *A Literary Woman*, which is a series of ten separate yet interconnecting short stories.

Helen Lucy BURKE was born in Dublin and works as a journalist. In 1979 she published a novel, *Close Connections*. Her short story collection, *A Season For Mothers*, was published in 1980.

Ethan CANIN was born in Ann Arbor, Michigan in 1960, grew up in California and studied medicine at Harvard. He published his first book, a collection of short stories called *Emperor of the Air*, when he was twenty-seven and in 1991 he published a novel, *Blue River*. His most recent book is *The Palace Thief*, which consists of four novellas.

Anne ENRIGHT was born in Dublin in 1962. She studied at Trinity College Dublin and at the University of East Anglia. Her first book, *The Portable Virgin* (1991), is a collection of short stories. In 1995 she published a very clever, original novel called *The Wig My Father Wore*.

Ellen GILCHRIST was born in 1935 in Issaquena County,

Mississippi, and won the National Book Award in America for her second collection of short stories, *Victory over Japan*. To date she has published nine books, including *In the Land of Dreamy Dreams* (short stories), *The Land Surveyor's Daughter* (poems), *Falling Through Space* (journals) and *The Anna Papers*, *Net of Jewels* and *Starcarbon* (novels).

Stephen LEACOCK was born in Swanmore, Hampshire in 1869 but grew up in Canada. He published several collections of humorous essays and short stories. He was a professor of political economy at McGill University, Montreal. From 1910 he published on average one humorous book a year for the remainder of his life. He died in 1944.

David LEAVITT was born in 1961 in Pittsburg, Pennsylvania, grew up in California and went to Yale University. He published his first collection of short stories, *Family Dancing*, when he was twenty-three. 'Gravity' is from his 1990 collection, *A Place I've Never Been*. He has also published three novels – *The Lost Language of Cranes*, *Equal Affections* and *While England Sleeps*.

Colum McCANN was born in Dublin in 1966 and now lives in New York. His first book was a collection of short stories, *Fishing the Sloe-black River*. He has also published a novel, *Songdogs* (1995).

John McGAHERN was born in Dublin in 1934, grew up in Leitrim, and is now hailed as one of Ireland's finest writers. He has written novels (*The Dark*, *The Leavetaking*, *Amongst Women*) and short stories. He has published a *Collected Stories*.

John MacKENNA was born in Castledermot, County Kildare. He has written two collections of short stories, *The Fallen* and *A Year of Our Lives* and a novel, *Clare*. He is head of religious programmes in RTE radio.

Aidan MATHEWS was born in Dublin in 1956. He is poet (*Windfalls* and *Minding Ruth*), novelist (*Muesli at Midnight*), playwright (*Exit/Entrance*) and short story writer (*Adventures in a Bathyscope* and *Lipstick on the Host*). He is head of radio drama in RTE.

Lorrie MOORE was born in Glen Falls, New York, and now teaches English at the University of Wisconsin in Madison. She has published two novels, *Anagrams* and *Who Will Run the Frog Hospital* (this one is terrific), and two collections of short stories, *Self-Help* and *Like Life*.

Alice MUNRO was born in Canada in 1931 and is generally considered to be one of the best short story writers of the twentieth century. Her books include *Dance of the Happy Shades*, *Lives of Girls and Women*, *The Moons of Jupiter*, *The Progress of Love*, *Friend of my Youth* and *Open Secrets*.

Eilís Ní DHUIBHNE was born in Dublin in 1954. She studied folklore and is now a Keeper in the National Library of Ireland. She has published two collections of short stories, *Blood and Water* (1988) and *Eating Women is Not Recommended* (1991). She has also written a novel, *The Bray House*, and novels for children.

Tim O'BRIEN was born in Worthington, Minnesota in 1946 and was drafted to serve in Vietnam, where he was a foot soldier from 1969 to 1970. He was wounded near My Lai and later worked as a national affairs reporter for the *Washington Post*. In 1973 he published *If I Die in a Combat Zone*, an account of his time in Vietnam. He has published two novels, *Going After Cacciato* and *In the Lake of the Woods* and a short story collection, *The Things They Carried*.

Bridget O'CONNOR was born in London in 1961 of Irish parents. In 1990 her story 'Harp' won the *Time Out* London Writing Competition and she published her first collection of short stories, *Here Comes John*, in 1993.

Joseph O'CONNOR was born in Dublin in 1963 and has published two novels, *Cowboys and Indians* and *Desperadoes*, a collection of short stories, *True Believers*, and *The Secret World of the Irish Male*. He has also written a play, *Red Roses and Petrol*.

Mary O'DONNELL was born in Monaghan in 1954. She has published two poetry collections, a novel, *The Light-Makers*, and a collection of short stories, *Strong Pagans,* from which 'Come In – I've Hanged Myself' is taken.

Muriel SPARK was born in Edinburgh, lived in Africa and England and now lives in Italy. She is best-known for her 1961 novel *The Prime of Miss Jean Brodie,* which anyone who has ever been to school should read. She has written nineteen novels as well as poetry, criticism and biography.

William TREVOR was born in Mitchelstown, County Cork in 1928. He now lives in Devon in England. His *Collected Stories* contains eighty-five short stories and he has also written several novels, including *Felicia's Journey*.

ACKNOWLEDGEMENTS

Thanks to Jenny Agnew (whose photograph is on the cover), Kate Bateman, Patricia Byrne, Mary Clayton, Sandra Cooke, Annetta Kavanagh, Kate O'Carroll (Ho!) and Louise Tallan.

Grateful acknowledgement is made to the following authors, publishers and agents for permission to reproduce copyright material: Reed Consumer Books for 'Last of the Mohicans' from *True Believers* by Joseph O'Connor; Faber and Faber Ltd for 'Victory Over Japan' from *Victory Over Japan* by Ellen Gilchrist; Poolbeg Press for 'Come In – I've Hanged Myself' by Mary O'Donnell; David Higham Associates for 'You Should Have Seen the Mess' by Muriel Spark; the Blackstaff Press for 'Absent Children' from *The Fallen* by John MacKenna; Random House and Jonathan Cape as publisher for 'I'm Running Late' from *Here Comes John* by Bridget O'Connor; Attic Press for 'Midwife to the Fairies' from *Blood and Water* by Eilís Ní Dhuibhne; Sheil Land Associates Ltd for 'Places to Look For Your Mind' from *Like Life* by Lorrie Moore and 'Along the Riverwall' from *Fishing the Sloe-Black River* by Colum McCann, copyright © Colum McCann 1994; Reed Consumer Books for 'The Brat' from *The Portable Virgin* by Anne Enright, published by Martin Secker and Warburg Ltd; Penguin Books for 'Gravity' from *A Place I've Never Been* by David Leavitt, copyright © David Leavitt 1990 and 'The Turkey Season' from *The Moons of Jupiter* by Alice Munro, Allen Lane, 1983, copyright © Alice Munro 1980; Helen Lucy Burke for 'All Fall Down'; William Trevor for 'Nice Day at School'; Bloomsbury Publishing PLC for 'Cypress Trees' from *A Literary Woman* by Mary Beckett, copyright © Mary Beckett 1990; Macmillan Publishers for 'Star Food' from *Emperor of the Air* by Ethan Canin; John McGahern for 'Like All Other Men'; A. P. Watt Ltd, literary agents, for 'Train Tracks' from *Lipstick on the Host* by Aidan Mathews; HarperCollins Publishers Ltd for 'The Things They Carried' from *The Things They Carried* by Tim O'Brien.

AND YET THE BOOKS

I imagine the earth when I am no more:
Nothing happens, no loss, it's still a strange pageant,
Women's dresses, dewey lilacs, a song in the valley.
Yet the books will be there on the shelves, well born,
Derived from people, but also from radiance, heights.

Czeslaw Milosz

The books are out there. If you hate the idea of my suggesting a list of titles which I think you'd enjoy then ignore this page. If not, here are a few books (all in paperback and easily available) which you can check out for yourself. Naturally, there are more and more. Don't waste your energies thinking, 'But he's forgotten . . .' Just add them to the list!

Cat's Eye, Margaret Atwood
The Grapes of Wrath, John Steinbeck
Cal, Bernard McLaverty
Who Will Run the Frog Hospital? Lorrie Moore
The Grass is Singing, Doris Lessing
Catcher in the Rye, J. D. Salinger
The Last Shot, Hugo Hamilton
The Bell Jar, Sylvia Plath
To Kill a Mockingbird, Harper Lee
The Go Between, L. P. Hartley
Less than Zero, Bret Easton Ellis
The Well, Elizabeth Jolley
Felicia's Journey, William Trevor
On the Road, Jack Kerouac
The Lives of Girls and Women, Alice Munro
Paddy Clarke, Ha Ha Ha, Roddy Doyle

Good Behaviour, Molly Keane
The Collector, John Fowles
Tess of the D'Urbervilles, Thomas Hardy
Night Shift, Dermot Bolger
Dr Fischer of Geneva, Graham Greene
Jazz, Toni Morrison
Victory over Japan, Ellen Gilchrist
Tarry Flynn, Patrick Kavanagh
The Great Gatsby, F Scott Fitzgerald
Nice Work, David Lodge
Brightness Falls, Jay McInerney
Sacred Country, Rose Tremain
Lipstick on The Host, Aidan Mathews
Utz, Bruce Chatwin
Lord of the Flies, William Golding
A Summons to Memphis, Peter Taylor
Providence, Anita Brookner
The Palace Thief, Ethan Canin
A Farewell to Arms, Ernest Hemingway
Jerusalem the Golden, Margaret Drabble
The English Patient, Michael Ondaatje
The Prime of Miss Jean Brodie, Muriel Spark
An Answer from Limbo, Brian Moore
Amongst Women, John McGahern
The Good Soldier, Ford Madox Ford
A Portrait of the Artist as a Young Man, James Joyce
The Sea, The Sea, Iris Murdoch
The Book of Evidence, John Banville
The Heather Blazing, Colm Tóibín
Where Angels Fear to Tread, E M Forster
Decline and Fall, Evelyn Waugh
The Remains of the Day, Kazuo Ishiguro
The Shipping News, E. Annie Proulx

All Fall Down, Ita Daly
Great Expectations, Charles Dickens
All the Pretty Horses, Cormac McCarthy
Black Baby, Clare Boylan
First Love, Last Rites, Ian McEwan
Empire of the Sun, J. G. Ballard
The Matisse Stories, A. S. Byatt
Independence Day, Richard Ford
Herzog, Saul Bellow
Emma, Jane Austen
Wuthering Heights, Emily Bronte
The Portrait of a Lady, Henry James
Middlemarch, George Eliot
Love in the Time of Cholera, Gabriel Garcia Marquez
Anna Karenina, Leo Tolstoy

REAL COOL, POEMS TO GROW UP WITH

EDITED BY NIALL MacMONAGLE

'For young and new readers certainly; for poetry lovers an absolute must.'

RTE Guide

'It's a lovely anthology – it really is – and MacMonagle should be admired for his firm conviction that poems such as these speak directly to young people.'

Cork Examiner